THE
LAST
WORD

ALSO BY TAYLOR ADAMS

Hairpin Bridge
No Exit
Our Last Night
Eyeshot

TAYLOR ADAMS

WILLIAM MORROW

An Imprint of HarperCollins*Publishers*

THE
LAST
WORD

A Novel

HarperCollins books may be purchased for educational, business, or sales promotional use. For information, please email the Special Markets Department at SPsales@harpercollins.com.

FIRST EDITION

Art © brickrenna/Shutterstock, Inc.

Library of Congress Cataloging-in-Publication Data has been applied for.

ISBN 978-0-06-322289-2

23 24 25 26 27 LBC 5 4 3 2 1

For Nolan

THE
LAST
WORD

PROLOGUE

THE END.

Emma Carpenter drops her e-reader. Like surfacing from a deep dive with aching lungs, she has never been so grateful to see those two words on her paper-white screen.

"Thank God." She rubs her eyes.

She downloaded this bizarre e-book for ninety-nine cents on her neighbor's recommendation. The novel's cover art was featureless black with a white Comic Sans title: *Murder Mountain.* Sinister but in a lo-fi way, like a VHS snuff tape. For less than the cost of a candy bar, how can you go wrong?

Post-purchase, she'd noticed the subtitle: *The Scariest Book You'll Ever Read.*

Uh-oh.

The raving blurb was in quotation marks, to appear quoted from a review or notable person, but there was no attributed source. It was the author's personal boast.

Uh-oh.

Emma persevered and read on anyway, as the horror novel followed two college coeds backpacking alone in the Appalachian foothills. One is a psych major and the other is a prelaw student studying for the LSAT. They're more ornaments than people: vain, shrill, stupid, and perhaps the least-convincing lesbians ever written. It's telling that the most authentic character in the entire book is the serial killer.

Beyond Emma's usual gripes with the trapped-in-a-remote-place-with-a-scary-person formula (*Why is there never a cell signal? Why does no one ever carry a gun? For the love of God, why do they keep splitting up?*), the only thing that kept her reading this hundred-thousand-word death march was an interesting artistic choice: from the first page, the novel is narrated entirely from the villain's first-person point of view. The two women—the characters readers are meant to sympathize with—are only ever described through the killer's eyes.

Written in the *past* tense.

One more time: uh-oh.

No surprise, then, that after hours of tedious stalking, the narrator/killer catches Psych alone in her tent and starts to strangle her. Prelaw intervenes to save her, but—instead of picking up the killer's night vision rifle, which he has carelessly set aside—she chooses to fight him hand to hand like a dumbass. She's promptly disemboweled and Psych is promoted to Final Girl. Psych also misses the memo to pick up the goddamn gun and instead flees screaming through the forest, stumbling across an abandoned cabin that's within walking distance but never mentioned until now. Of course the parked truck fails to start. Of course she traps herself in the only room without an exit. Of course he drives home with her head in a duffel bag.

The End.

Thank God for that, at least.

Amazon has the audacity to ask her to rate the book. Out of five stars? One. She makes sure zero isn't an option. Then she types a brief review—likely better written than all of *Murder Mountain*—but before clicking Submit, she hesitates.

Why?

She's unsure. Her finger hovers in a hair-trigger pause. She imagines her own future self desperately warning of something terrible on the horizon, that she's about to sign her own death warrant and this is her last chance to change course. The e-book is still unrated, so her one-star review will be its first and only. Will the author personally read it?

Something bangs against the window behind her. It's a strange and fleshy sound, sickening in its heaviness. Her heart jolts in her chest.

She turns but sees only watery sky outside. Acres of yellow beach grass, dewed with rain and rippling in low wind. The rolling whitecaps of the ocean beyond.

A bird.

She's alone.

A bird flew into the window.

Still, she stands, slips on a raincoat, and checks the backyard. Sure enough, she finds the bird motionless in the sandy flower-bed just below the floor-to-ceiling windows. A frail brown and reddish thing. Eyelids shut, as if asleep.

With cupped hands, Emma sets the bird in a lawn chair on a rumpled blue beach towel. Sometimes, she knows, they'll stir back to life. Their little brains just have to reboot.

She returns inside.

On her e-reader, she discovers her review of *Murder Mountain* has already posted. Her index finger must have twitched in surprise. There it is. Her words. One star. Too late now.

So she deletes the novel and tries to forget about the two fictional college students and their lovingly detailed murders. She has countless more e-books to read. The internet is a vast ocean of stories, and troublingly, she's realizing lately that the book's quality doesn't even matter. Superb, mediocre—whatever. It must only be a world sufficiently different from Emma's, here on this sandy gray coast.

She studies her own words for a moment longer. Was she too harsh on this stranger? For all she knows, this author could be twelve. In fact, that would explain a lot.

Who cares?

Stop looking at it.

She decides she'll walk her golden retriever, Laika, on the beach before the next rainstorm blows in. On her way out, she passes the bird on the lawn chair, still motionless, and she hopes that when she returns, she'll find the towel empty, the stunned animal alive and free.

She'll never think about *Murder Mountain* ever again.

UNTIL TWO HOURS LATER, WHEN SHE RETURNS INSIDE WITH salt in her hair and sand in her sneakers, and a red icon in the corner of her web browser informs her that her user review has received a comment.

She feels a faint tug in her stomach. Opinions are like assholes, the saying goes, and the internet has millions of both. But somehow she already knows exactly who commented.

She clicks.

The satellite Wi-Fi chugs briefly before displaying:

Hello Emma86,

Nice to meet you! I'm the author of the acclaimed thriller MURDER MOUNTAIN. Thank you very much for reading my novel. It's readers like you who make it all possible!

However, I see you didn't like my book. And that's OK! But let me ask you: why review it, then? Readers should only post their positive reviews. And you may have nothing at stake here—but I do. Other potential readers will see your 1-star review, and that might discourage them from buying my books, which hurts me financially!

I work hard so someday I can quit my day job and write full time. It's been my lifelong dream ever since I was a kid. I'm sure you're a wonderful person in real life, and you wouldn't wish to attack my financial security, so I was wondering if you could please kindly remove your review?
Best wishes,
H. G. Kane

She reads it twice.

She's never seen an author comment on an online review of their own book, let alone ask for its removal. This breaks some unwritten rule, right? She reaches to shut her laptop—pulling the screen half down—but something here demands to be answered.

Don't do it.

Maybe it's the manufactured cheer, coming from a writer who described the tendons in a woman's neck "snapping like pale spaghetti strings." Or maybe it's the excessive exclamation points, like baby talk.

Don't respond.

Or maybe it's the victimhood, the cringy implication that this "author" is entitled to a full-time living from a job without actually being competent at it.

Don't-don't-don't—

She reopens her laptop. Quickly she types:

Hi. Thank you for taking the time to comment on my review. I'm sorry that your book wasn't for me. But I will respectfully choose to keep my review posted, because this is a forum for readers to share their honest views, positive and negative alike.

She almost adds her own initials but doesn't. She clicks Submit, this time without pause. Her comment blinks into existence below his.

Done.

The author's name snags in her mind. *H. G. Kane.*

It does ring vaguely familiar. Maybe this person engineered their pen persona to sound that way, like a sexy transmutation of H. G. Wells and Stephen King? He or she can't actually be famous, if Emma herself just posted *Murder Mountain*'s first and only—

She's received another comment. Already.

Seriously?

A chill runs down her spine as she reads:

Emma86, with all due respect, I spent 6 months writing MURDER MOUNTAIN. It took you just a few seconds to type that hateful review and tarnish all my hard work. Little sapsuckers like you don't understand what's really at stake for me.

I implore you, please take your review down.

Best,

HGK

This one, she can read only once.

I implore you. Does anyone in this century still say that? And *little sapsuckers like you*—is that an insult? It's all so brazenly weird. Keys crunch under her fingers.

Sorry, but my answer is still no. Good luck with your future books.

She considers, before adding:

Also, FYI for your future books, no woman would EVER hike in high heels.

This is getting excruciating. She wonders if other users will read this chain and jump in. What will they think? Whose side will they take?

There are no sides, she reminds herself. Readers should have opinions. Authors shouldn't comment on them. And the more she rereads this stranger's words, the more her pulse spikes in her neck. Why should Emma care that this self-proclaimed "writer" spent six months of his or her life producing that literary bowel movement? She spent four hours of hers reading it. They both lost.

She needs air. Again.

She realizes she's forgotten about the stunned bird outside.

The first raindrops are falling when she returns to check the lawn chair. To her disappointment, the feathered body is still there in the towel. Exactly as she left it. Wiry legs stiffening. Eyes shut. And now, under a crackle of approaching thunder, Emma notices something she missed earlier.

A bead of dried blood between wincing avian eyelids, like a tiny red teardrop.

She returns inside.

On her screen, another message from the author—now tinged with menace.

I won't ask you again.

Without sitting, she answers.

Good.

Then she shuts her laptop.

PART ONE

Never rewrite.

—H. G. Kane, "Writing Tips from a Professional Author," 2015,
  hgkaneofficial.com

SOMETIME AFTER THREE A.M., EMMA AWAKENS TO SEE A MAN standing in the darkened corner of her bedroom. He's mostly obscured by the door's angular black shadow.

She blinks, expecting the figure to vanish like a fading dream. He's still there.

She focuses her eyes and the room sharpens. A ray of moonlight catches a rumple of coat fabric on the apparition's shoulder. A fold of flabby neck flesh. And the rim of a hat. Like something a gangster might wear in an old-timey film.

Staring at her.

Watching her sleep.

She doesn't dare move. Not even a toe. If he sees that she's awake, the fragile moment will shatter. He'll spring forward and slice her throat or gouge out her eyes or worse. She blinks again, trying to find more detail in the darkness, trying not to open her eyes too noticeably wide.

The figure doesn't move, either.

She realizes she's holding her breath. Her lungs burn. She draws in a mouthful of air as quietly as she can, a gentle hiss between her teeth. She wonders if he can hear it.

How long has he been standing there, watching me?

The room teeters on a knife-edge.

Emma lives alone. This bedroom is on the second floor. Her phone is charging downstairs. There are no guns in the house. And no neighbors close enough to hear her scream. She considers hurling off the blankets now, jumping to her feet and bolting past the stranger and down the stairs. But it's still too dark to be certain. He might still be just a hanging coat, she tells herself. An illusion.

To her left, there's a bedside lamp with a pull chain. She slides her hand toward it, inching her fingers under the bedsheets like a serpent underwater.

Silence.

The figure hasn't moved. And he hasn't seen her hand move— not yet, at least. Emma shuts her eyes and focuses on the ambient sounds. The low roar of the waves. The rattle of raindrops on roof shingle. She tries to locate the stranger's breathing or the flex of his coat, but he's eerily quiet. She braces for the creak of a floorboard announcing his first step toward her bed. It never comes.

One, she counts. Her hand slides free of the blanket now, her fingers spider-crawling up the cold porcelain. Feeling for the chain.

Two.

She finds it. A dry click between her fingers. Did he hear that? If so, he still hasn't attacked. No motion.

Three?

She's afraid to break the stillness. But she swallows her fear. She's fully awake now, her muscles tense under the sheets, and she must be ready. No excuses.

Three.

She tugs the chain. A nuclear flash. She winces in a blaze of light and throws the blankets left while heaving her body right, landing hard on bare feet. She spins—elbows up for defense—

and kicks into a sprint for the bedroom door. As she hurtles toward it, she glimpses the spot where the hat-wearing stranger had been standing, now a bare wall.

He's gone.

She's alone in the bright bedroom.

Was he even there?

EMMA TRIES TO FALL BACK ASLEEP BUT CAN'T.

She decides to clear the house room by room.

First, the upper floor—a master bedroom, a bathroom with dual vanities, and a walk-in closet. She checks every corner, every shadow, every gap where an intruder might lurk.

Upper floor: clear.

Then downstairs. The main floor is daunting—a cavernous family space plus an open kitchen and dining area exposed to the outside by three walls of floor-to-ceiling glass. Part beach house, part aquarium. Then two bedrooms, a bathroom, and a laundry room with a chute to the upstairs. Long sight lines, yet honeycombed with dangerous hiding places. She opens every door and scans every square inch. She methodically flicks on lights as she goes, creating a growing safe zone of light. It's satisfying, like claiming territory.

First floor: clear.

One level left.

"Fuck this basement."

A staircase leads down into a mouth of darkness. She stops in the doorway, inhaling the cave-like odor. A few steps down, the stairs take a ninety-degree turn under a low copper pipe, noticeably rust-eaten. Even at five-foot-three, Emma has to stoop. Then ten steps deeper, whiffing mildew and mouse scat, like entering the house's stomach. At the bottom her bare feet touch cement foundation, slick with moisture.

It's always damp down here. Basements are rare near beaches for this very reason. Even with a sump pump, as in this house, it's impossible to keep a coastal basement dry. The only light downstairs is controlled by a plastic outlet on the concrete wall to her left—too dark to see. She's feeling for it with outstretched fingertips when something moves behind her. A current of air touches her exposed lower back. She recognizes it immediately, the warmth of it. It's an exhaled breath.

She recoils with surprise and her elbow bumps a shelf. Some heavy object drops to the cement, a sound as earsplitting as a gunshot.

She's lost the light switch. Total darkness.

The next breath is just inches behind her. It's deeper, almost snotty. A cold nose presses wetly against her bare skin.

"Laika," Emma whispers, "you are the worst guard dog on earth."

She finds the switch. Let there be light.

Laika is a golden retriever, but she isn't quite golden. She's an English cream breed with a near-white coat, because of which onlookers often mistake her for a white Lab or a Great Pyrenees. Emma crouches now to ruffle the silky fur under Laika's ears. "You would have barked if Ted Bundy was inside the house. Right?"

Black eyes answer her. Flat, dumb, and eager.

"Right?"

Nothing.

"Right?"

Behold the void.

Maybe not a bark, Emma decides. But friendly-to-a-fault Laika would have followed an intruder upstairs, eagerly nudging his thigh for attention. She's feeling better now. The figure in her bedroom was just a leftover fragment of a nightmare.

Basement: clear.

Emma is perfectly alone. The way she likes it. This solitary house—ten feet above sea level, three hundred from high tide—is her safe vessel, a tiny pinprick of light on a vast shore. Sometimes she looks out the windows and imagines she's the last survivor on earth. Only voided sky, miles of dune grass, and the dull crash of the breakers beyond.

On the main floor, she verifies that the front and back doors are locked (they are) and that every window is untouched (they are, impeccably). After that, what can you do? An intruder couldn't have escaped without tripping the perimeter of motion-sensor lights outside. Still, she keeps the interior lights on while the Pacific sky grays with dawn. Even with every room searched and her golden retriever's keen senses on her side, she still has to remind herself that the stranger can't possibly be locked *inside* the house with her.

Back upstairs, she'd hoped the bedroom lamp would reveal her own clothes draped carelessly over a chair where the figure had stood, or a raincoat hanging scarecrow-like. But there is just a bare wall. And she *knows* she saw the rim of a hat.

Right?

She brews ginger tea and studies the windows, trying to focus her eyes on both the foggy coast outside and the room's interior reflection, half expecting to notice the figure standing behind her in a violin-screeching jolt. She's seen that movie before.

She pours Laika a bowl of food. The retriever sniffs at it indifferently.

"I know," Emma says. "I'm not hungry, either."

BY THE AFTERNOON, SHE HAS READ TWO MORE E-BOOKS from start to finish. One decent, one quite good. They're quick hits, four hours apiece, comfortable little dioramas with flawed detectives and quirky suspects and bloodless murders. Red herrings. Tragic backstories. She already has another down-loaded for the evening. It's nice to submerge yourself in someone else's world, to luxuriate in the handcrafted details and admire the false ceilings. In happier times Emma liked to read Tolstoy and Dostoevsky, and she knows she's slumming on Amazon's bargain and free listings. She's not reading for pleasure, exactly, or enrichment—but then again, there's nothing wrong with reading to escape, is there?

At the end of each, Amazon prompts her to write a review.

She declines.

She's forgotten the name of that weird author, but the experience still needles her. She rarely engages with strangers, even online. Since she arrived on this beach three months ago, she's taken great efforts to cut all social threads and cocoon herself from human contact. Her books teleport in from cyberspace. Her groceries coalesce magically at her door. Whenever she hears a delivery van coming down the quarter-mile driveway, she hides. Time slows to a strange and turgid crawl when you're a grown-ass adult hiding under a window.

She's lost twelve pounds since arriving here. Not on purpose. Maybe something is wrong with her body, but eating has become a dull and unrewarding process, as joyless as sitting on the toilet. Some days she forgets entirely. Others, she wishes only to sleep and must drag herself down the halls like a zombie. The house seems to be miles wide. Boiling a kettle of ginger tea is insurmountable. Nothing is worth the immense labor it will take.

She's not sure when she last heard a human voice. Four weeks ago?

Or five?

She's been told introverted personalities recharge with alone time, something like managing a social battery. And while that's accurate—because most people tend to exhaust the ever-loving shit out of Emma—she's always pictured herself more like clay, a shapeless form that reluctantly morphs to meet the daily needs of her surroundings. Smile at the neighbor's kids. Pay the car insurance. Make a dental appointment. And here on this desolate coast, she's discovered a worse truth—that without a job, tasks, friends, family, Emma Carpenter will happily float apart. Every molecule of herself will take the path of least resistance. Sometimes she glimpses herself in mirrors or reflective glass, a gray and unformed face she doesn't recognize. Eyeless, mouthless, nose flattened to soggy mush. Her own ghost.

Very little frightens her—the worst thing that can happen to any human already happened to her months ago—but she fears what she becomes when she's alone, where her mind will go if she lets it wander.

Her steady diet of digital fast food—ninety-nine-cent distractions good, bad, and everything in between—is enough to keep her occupied.

For now.

A STORM IS COMING.

Emma first sees it from the laundry room while she climbs up onto the dryer, opens a tiny window, twists her spine into a scorpion-arch, and smokes a cigarette. She cranks a plastic Dollar Tree fan with each puff, making certain every ash grain flutters outside while she watches thunderheads loom over the ocean. Then she squishes her cigarette with licked fingertips and tucks it into a ziplock bag with the others.

Sure enough, raindrops tap the windows while she starts reading her third e-book on the sofa. The wind growls and she wonders if she's really hearing a forgotten closet door click open in the next room. Or stealthy footsteps downstairs? Gloved fingers gripping a machete?

Periodically she stops reading and listens.

This house is full of sounds. Even after living here three months, she still discovers new oddities. Doors refuse to shut. Gutters drip a steady heartbeat. The guest toilet sometimes flushes itself. The first time she heard this happen from across the house was bone-chilling, but now it's something of a charming quirk, like a ghost occasionally stopping by to take a shit. This is Emma's first time house-sitting, and it feels so much more invasive than merely renting. Maybe it comes down to whether it's your silverware in the kitchen drawer or theirs, but she feels like a burglar at nights, padding guiltily through a stranger's family room.

The house's owner? A nice lady from Portland named Jules Phelps.

At least Emma *thinks* it's a lady.

They've never physically met.

And part of why it feels so invasive is that Emma can't help but draw conclusions about Jules's private life. It's unavoidable. You can't *not* do it. There's blood pressure medication and stool softener in the bathroom closet—Jules must be middle-aged or older? There's an antique Polaroid camera on the shelf—Jules must dabble in photography? One bedroom has been recently cleaned, but a teenage musk still clings thickly—Jules must have raised a son? On a poster there, a stoic samurai warrior kneels under a thicket of moonlit bamboo and sharpens his sword. Maybe the boy went off to college. Maybe he moved. Maybe Jules murdered him and his hacked limbs are rotting in the walls right now.

Maybe Emma has just been reading too many crime novels.

But something about that room has always disturbed her. She finds herself avoiding the teenager's bedroom and keeping the door shut, lest its ill energy seep out in a cloudy funk of Axe body spray, Mtn Dew, and socks. And something else—something sour. Stale. Yeasty.

Keep reading.

It's none of Emma's business. She's here to run the heaters, watch for roof leaks, and bring in Jules's mail. Everything else is like the waves: white noise.

The ropelike eleven-mile island of Strand Beach (known by locals as *the Strand*) joins the mainland with one single-lane causeway. It's a flat and grassy landmass dotted with remote houses like this one, all separated by acres of negative space and mostly served by one road called Wave Drive. There's spotty cell service, weak water pressure, and when the weather cooperates, just enough satellite internet bandwidth for Netflix in 480p. No surprise that ninety-nine percent of these homes are dark October through April—summer retreats owned by well-to-do urbanites like Jules, locked down and mothballed for the miserable rainy season. In annual precipitation, Strand Beach is second only to a certain Washington town a short drive north, famous for its sparkling vampires.

Out here, Emma doesn't have neighbors in the plural—she has *a* neighbor. This lone confirmed human occupies the next house up Wave Drive, a quarter mile north. From her reading spot on the sofa, the distant structure resembles a tombstone set against watery sky. She can see a faint interior glow. And in the living room window, a whiteboard.

With a handwritten message.

"Finally."

She lowers her e-reader. She steps over Laika, snoring on the bearskin rug, and approaches the nautical telescope by the window. She leans into the eyepiece, adjusting focus until her neighbor's faraway message sharpens into clarity.

It's . . . a stick figure. Hanging from a hand-drawn gallows.

"Damn."

Another loss. Her guess—*oxygen*—wasn't even close.

She doesn't know her elderly neighbor's full name, only how he spontaneously introduced himself via whiteboard one afternoon (HELLO. I'M DEEK). For a week or two prior, his board had contained a friendly invitation (WANT TO PLAY HANGMAN?), which sounds like something Jigsaw might say if you've never heard of the popular whiteboard game Hangman. Emma hadn't.

In short: One player tries to guess the letters of a mystery word while the other draws a stick figure in a noose, adding a limb for each incorrect guess. A complete stick figure means the poor guy hangs. Deek, as it turns out, is an absolute beast at Hangman. His guesses are surgical, his words impenetrable. Emma hasn't won once.

It's impossible to know someone through a telescope, but as is true of house-sitting for a stranger, you find yourself logging observations anyway. Emma knows the old man lives alone amid heaps of junk—an entire Ikea sales floor of crowded furniture, bulging file cabinets, towers of stacked books, and a (presumably) uninstalled toilet on the back porch. She knows he keeps an antique revolver framed over his fireplace. She knows he drinks only coffee before three and only whiskey afterward—and that on his most shit-faced evenings, he sometimes lights off aerial fireworks directly from his balcony.

Usually Emma lets hours pass between Hangman guesses—the pleasantly glacial pace to life on the Strand—but she glimpses motion. The old hermit is in his kitchen. So she uncaps her dry-erase marker, draws a gallows on her own whiteboard, and picks a word.

He guesses it in four turns flat.

ZEPHYR?

"Asshole."

She's not sure how he does it.

Sometimes she likes to study her neighbor's rainy windows for clues and speculate on the exotic past career of a man who lives alone with a cowboy gun and five tons of hoarded crap. She's been guessing for weeks. Antiques dealer? Archivist? Retired movie star? He does look a bit like George Clooney, if you stuck *Michael Clayton* in a dehydrator. Whatever his past, the man who calls himself Deek is a fascinating mystery.

Now her neighbor stands up from his telescope, as if startled by a sharp noise. He picks up his blue marker and writes on his board: WHO IS THAT?

Emma pauses mid-sip.

She sets her tea mug on the table—a bony click—and raises her hands in an exaggerated shrug: *What?*

He's writing more. But the storm intensifies, battering the windows and blurring his words with running droplets. She squints into her telescope.

MAN IN YOUR LIVING ROOM

BEHIND YOU

She leans back from the eyepiece. She senses a faint chill in the room behind her, like a breeze of displaced air. But she ignores it and raises her marker.

NICE TRY, she writes.

He's kidding, she knows. And she won't fall for it.

A quarter mile away, the old man shakes his head. He waves behind watery glass. Then he turns back to his whiteboard.

I'M SERIOUS, he scrawls. WHO IS THAT?

He points at her.

No. *Behind* her. Into the adjacent living room. Ten feet away. She refuses to look behind herself. "Nope."

HE'S RIGHT THERE

"Yawn."

HAS KNIFE

"A knife? Be more imaginative."

She holds rock-hard eye contact with her neighbor through windows streaked with rainwater, holding it, holding it, long past the point when any self-respecting serial killer would have grabbed her scalp, twisted her head back, and cut her throat. Finally the old man gives up and shrugs. Begrudging defeat.

I win, she thinks.

Deek is an incessant practical joker, and this only deepens the old man's mystery. Maybe the boredom out here maddens everyone a little differently, but this is the third murderer to stalk Emma's house. He's also told her that the structure is haunted, that Jules previously ran a burlesque show out of the basement, and that the prior house-sitter was a serial killer. There are only so many pranks you can pull from a quarter mile, so last week (presumably after observing she was a reader), Deek recommended the single worst e-book she's ever read: *Murder Mountain* by H. G. Kane.

For that, she writes: YOU OWE ME 99 CENTS

WAIT. Deek pauses. YOU ACTUALLY BOUGHT IT?

She nods.

SERIOUSLY?

She nods harder.

WOW. SORRY. The old man pauses and shakes his head, genuinely baffled. AND YOU READ THE ENTIRE THING?

She smiles guiltily. Deek vastly underestimates her spare time.

OKAY, he writes. LET ME POSE YOU A QUESTION

"Sure."

YOU OPEN THE FRIDGE

She nods.

YOU TAKE A SIP OF MILK

"Okay."

IT TASTES SPOILED

She sighs. "I know where this is going."

DO YOU:
A. THROW THE MILK OUT?
B. DRINK THE ENTIRE GODDAMN CARTON, TO MAKE SURE
IT'S SPOILED?

She pretends to laugh for Deek's telescope, but it's soundless, airless. She appreciates the old man's eccentric sense of humor—at least she thinks she does, the same way she's pretty sure she appreciates tiny, expensive oysters served raw—but Deek can't possibly understand her situation. He's still just an onlooker. Since arriving here Emma downloads her e-books by the cartload, picking Amazon's free and bargain lists clean every week. It's not about the story's quality. It's about distracting herself, putting her mind on a treadmill.

Anything is better than being alone with her thoughts.

Even *Murder Mountain*.

Still grinning, Deek writes: EVER HEARD OF THE CLASSIC FILM "PLAN 9 FROM OUTER SPACE"? I THINK IT'S QUITE SKILLFULLY MADE

She rolls her eyes.

AN INTELLIGENT AND SCARY FILM

"Dick."

KILLER STILL BEHIND YOU, BTW

"Maybe he'll murder you next."

I CAN LIP-READ

She's almost certain he can't. It's too far.

Among hundreds of vacant summer homes, it's something of a statistical miracle that two occupied ones should happen to be adjacent like this. Emma visualizes herself and Deek as the pilots of two spacecraft on differing vectors, briefly passing within eyeshot of each other. Able to transmit and receive written messages for as long as the window lasts.

His grin fades. He writes: YOU DOING OK?

She tries not to overthink her answer. YEAH

YOU SURE?

Oh, come on. Now for the real stuff, the parts of human relationships that Emma has always been deficient at. Suddenly even a quarter mile feels too close. She draws another Hangman scaffolding—but he's still writing, leaning crookedly against his whiteboard before stepping back and revealing: I SAW YOU

She freezes. *What?*

ON THE BEACH
YESTERDAY

A faint chill crawls up her spine as Deek adds a question mark with an emphatic dot: WHAT WERE YOU DOING?

Then he leans back into his own telescope.

Watching her.

Waiting.

Emma twirls her dry-erase marker between her fingers. She smiles weakly, guiltily, unsure if the old man really can read lips. If his magnification is powerful enough to detect a lie.

Say something, Emma.

He's waiting for her answer.

Say anything.

Finally she does.

JUST OUT WALKING. I'M FINE

Then she caps her marker and returns to the sofa. This time she nearly trips over Laika, who wakes with a surprised snort. She hates feeling studied in her neighbor's lens. Deek's spaceship has veered alarmingly close to hers. She lifts her e-reader and pretends to read her current book—a police procedural about a serial killer who attends his victims' funerals—knowing the old man is still watching her. She pretends not to see him. She waits until she's certain he's lost interest and moved on.

For the rest of the day, she avoids her telescope—even approaching it might invite another long-distance exchange—but if she squints, she can still read Deek's message.

EMMA—IF YOU EVER NEED TO TALK, I'M HERE

She reminds herself that these telescopes magnify both ways. She's being watched, too. And strangely, over several months, dozens of hanged stick figures, and countless whiteboard conversations, she can't remember ever giving her name.

Deek has always been superhumanly good at guessing, right?

_____

WHEN EMMA WALKS THE BEACH, SHE LIKES TO CLOSE HER eyes and let her mind go perfectly, painlessly blank.

If you could have one superpower, what would it be?

In a past life, she was twenty-two, sharing a seven-dollar bottle of wine with her boyfriend over a chessboard in her studio apartment. Trying to focus on blurry pieces. Laika was just a pup back then, a white roly-poly pawing at their ankles.

One superpower, Em. Go.

She didn't know.

Flying? Telepathy? Super-reflexes?

She shrugged.

Why is it so easy for some people to talk on and on? She feels broken sometimes. She tries to self-edit in her brain, and by the time she knows what she means to say, it's too late to say it. She has dashed first dates single-handedly with her inability to maintain a conversation. But Shawn was different, and somehow even back then, she already knew she loved him. He talked enough for the both of them (which took some of the pressure off Emma), but to gently nudge her along, he also liked to tee up bafflingly random questions. What's your favorite musical? Your favorite vacation? Apparently superheroes were on his mind that night, as Shawn explained his own ideal superpower: to live forever. Immortality.

That's a fucking terrible superpower, Emma said, sipping directly from the bottle.

He laughed. One of the first times she heard what she would know as a Shawn-laugh: an abrupt, genuine bark of surprise.

Okay, he said. *Please explain.*

She took a deep breath. No self-editing.

One.

Two.

Three.

Okay, she said. *First, if you're immortal, you won't age, right? But everyone around you will. Your friends, your family*—she tapped her chest—*me, hopefully. You'll watch everyone you care about grow old and fall sick and die, and at first you'll grieve and move on and form new connections with new people. But you'll keep using them up. Watching them wilt like spinach.*

He nodded. Still listening.

And if you're immortal, your perception of time will change, too. Ever notice how as you get older, time seems to accelerate? Picture that on warp speed. You'll be on, like, your eighty-sixth wife and kids, with more descendants than you can possibly care about, and every birthday and graduation will race by in a heartbeat. You'll start to wonder—what's the point if they keep turning to dust, anyway?

And that's not even the worst part.

Somewhere around here, she remembered to breathe.

Eventually, humanity will end. She lifted the bottle and took a long swig. *You know it. I know it. Could be an asteroid. Nuclear war. Supernova. Or, in a few billion years, the sun will just swell up into a red giant and incinerate the earth anyway. Right? It'll happen. And where does that leave Immortal Shawn? You can't burn up or die. But the earth will be gone. No people, no cities, no ground to stand on. You'll drift helplessly in the frictionless void of space for eternity. Unable to move and unable to die, no matter how desperately you'll wish to. And I promise, you will.*

Her voice lowered to a whisper.

Floating.

Forever alone.

Wishing you'd picked a different superpower.

She'd set the empty bottle between them like a mic drop. Silence again. Shawn had only stared at her over the forgotten chessboard, staring, staring, until she was certain she'd lost him, or worse, scared him, that the rest of the evening would go fine, but he would politely break up with her sometime next week in search of a less complicated model.

Instead, her future husband smiled.

You should talk more, he said.

Something about this gave Emma a chill.

It still does, six years later and three states west, at the snarling edge of the ocean. Cold seawater laps at her ankles now. Her sneakers are soaked.

There's a violence to the storm swells on Strand Beach that entrances Emma. You can't know it from the safety of the shore. You have to be there, with the salty vapor in your eyes, or better yet, *inside* it, as ten-foot breakers crash at your feet, pushing and pulling with a million rolling tons. Like standing at the edge of a meat grinder—a few steps farther and it'll rip you away. Even the sound is deep enough to get lost in.

She whispers, "I miss you, Shawn."

She listens to the roar for a moment longer.

And another.

Another.

Until the hairs on the back of her neck tingle and she imagines a lensed, veiny eyeball crawling up her back. All these weeks and it's never occurred to her—despite the old man owning a damn telescope—that Deek might watch her at the beach. He obviously was yesterday. Now he's worried about her, the poor decent guy.

She'd turn and wave cheerily to his house if she could. Nothing to see here.

Everything is fine.

Then she turns away from the ocean, as if it were all a normal afternoon walk, and heads home in wet, squelching shoes.

Everything is fine.

On the way, she notices a second trail of footprints in the dark sand alongside her own. Joggers do sometimes pass through here, although she can't recall seeing a soul on the Strand today. She looks back, making sure the beach is still empty, and then she walks a little faster.

Everything is perfectly fine.

THE WALK BACK ALWAYS FEELS LONGER.

Laika greets her at the trail's sandy edge, happy and oblivious as always, and Emma falls into a crouch. The dog leans against her, and for a moment, the sturdy love of a golden retriever is all she needs. She grips fistfuls of cream-white fur.

"Space Dog," she whispers.

That's me, those black eyes seem to say.

"I love you."

I love you, too.

Laika can't comprehend this, but she's named after history's very first dog in space. In 1957, Soviet Union scientists fired off the original Laika (an adopted stray mongrel) into low-earth orbit inside the six-foot cone of the Sputnik 2 satellite. What's it like, to hurtle so far from every soul on the marble? Emma can only wonder.

Laika twists her neck to look up at her, now eerily direct, and Emma wonders how well golden retrievers can intuit human emotion. Reading faces is one thing—after the funeral, Emma mastered the wincing *I'll be okay* smile. But does it fool Laika? Has it ever?

I know, those black eyes say.

I know everything.

She notices Laika's fangs are red. "What's wrong with your mouth?"

It's blood.

She catches the dog's muzzle, knuckles her jaws open, and sweeps her fingers behind her teeth. She recovers a knot of slimy gristle.

"Laika?"

Warm breath in her face. Goatish, rancid. Emma struggles to hold her.

"Laika—"

As the retriever nuzzles back down to something in the grass. A hand-sized slab of pale flesh, dusted with sand, pawed around. Sour with decay.

Laika glances up proudly.

I've found a treasure.

Emma studies it. Carrion? A chunk of sea lion, picked by gulls? Turning it over with her foot, she sees the tissue is too naked, too perfectly cut. Like something plastic-wrapped in a grocer's meat department. Another possibility nips at her thoughts, but she knows there's a mundane explanation, that she reads too many crime novels and it can't possibly be human flesh.

Still.

She digs a trench in the sand with her shoe and buries it. Laika watches with disappointment, another bead of blood-drool hanging from her lip. She's cut her mouth, probably on a shard of sharp bone.

Emma wipes it away. "You dumbass."

Then she tugs her back to the house without looking back. "Let's get your mouth fixed."

NIGHT FALLS AS EMMA CLEANS THE GASH WITH HYDROGEN peroxide. It's an inch long, cutting along Laika's outer gum. Painful but not serious. No sutures needed. Laika lies still on the kitchen tile, those black pupils locked on Emma's, whining only occasionally from the Q-tip's antiseptic sting. Such trust breaks her heart. No creature should trust another so entirely.

I love you, Mother.

"Yeah? Stop eating stupid shit."

Yes. I ate a bad thing.

Since arriving on the Strand, Laika has happily devoured rotten crabs, jellyfish, and kelp. Every low tide reveals a fresh banquet of chipped teeth and gastrointestinal hell. She licks her gums, watching Emma stash the peroxide under the sink.

It was a bad thing.

But I do not regret it.

Lastly, Emma reties Laika's *Don't Stop Retrievin'* bandanna over the collar around her neck. For some reason, Laika genuinely loves this stupid piece of fabric. When it's off, she mopes. When it's in the laundry, she searches the house for it. Emma remembers when Shawn bought it at a pet store years ago—no reason, just because he liked her dog—one of those jokey little gestures that, over time, hardens into part of your life. She thinks of him every time she sees it.

The edges are fraying. It'll come apart soon.

Emma showers. She indulges in a single cigarette at her tiny smoking window in the laundry room, making sure to blow every last molecule outside with her handheld fan. She finishes her cold cheese pizza and returns to her e-book about the serial killer who frequents his victims' funerals—a stupid premise, honestly. Every few chapters, she takes a turn at Hangman.

In silence, her mind returns to troubling things.

The man in her bedroom the other night was only a dream. He couldn't have evaporated through locked doors like a phantom. *Unless* . . .

No. Not possible.

He can't still be *inside* the giant house. Emma has already searched every inch. She even checked illogical places, like inside the cobwebbed laundry chute. But now her mind returns to ground zero: the master bedroom. In the bathroom, a long and luxurious vanity with dual sinks—Jules must have been married at least once—leads to a walk-in shower with heated tile and a cast-iron claw-foot tub she's never used. Cutely, the hot and cold valves are starfish. But back to that long vanity . . . it's so long, in fact, that the bathroom has *two* entrances.

Her stomach flutters.

Because a cunning intruder could have silently circled the upper rooms while she searched. He could still be upstairs, right now—

She stops herself. *I'm being paranoid.*

If she had been a spiritual person, she might have been tempted to believe the house is haunted. The structure is alive with suspicious creaks and groans, and Laika often reacts to noises too subtle for Emma's ears to detect. The gutters drip. The wiring crackles. Moisture sweats from the walls and pools in the basement. One of the most frequent semi-paranormal events is also the oddest. A few times a week, Emma is struck by the scent of butter, sickening in its oily richness. The odor seems to move around the house, sometimes lingering in doorways, sometimes wafting from the closets. It seems especially fond of the teenager's room. But she's not spiritual—not remotely—and it's just a house. Just timber and nails and concrete. And glass walls facing the sea.

Whatever bad shit she senses here, she knows: *I brought it with me.*

And I'll take it wherever I go.

In the distance, Deek has already guessed her word.

AUSTRALIA?

She flips him off.

It shouldn't be possible. Lately she's been cheating by googling words that are statistically harder to guess. It hasn't helped. Deek bulldozes her every time, like his telescope can see into the open cavity of her brain. It's upsetting. Emma doesn't like to be *seen*. Being seen burdens you with an image you have to maintain.

Even out here, miles from cell signals and traffic lights, Emma must be conscious of her clothing. Her hygiene. Her daily routines have an observer, as benevolent and presumably nonjudgmental as Deek is (a man with a spare toilet on his deck). She still must wear a shirt. People—no matter how kind—still mean *work* to Emma. She often wishes Deek's spaceship would veer off, or that this minor miracle never happened at all.

TALK SOMETIME? her neighbor writes hopefully. IN PERSON?

She responds in a perfectly noncommittal way, editing it in her brain first to find the correct blend of cordial and aloof. No promises, but no excuses. She's danced this dance for years and knows every step.

She's not antisocial.

She thinks.

As a child she remembers feeling paranoid that she was being watched, that every reflective surface was actually a secret camera a la *The Truman Show*. A world full of eyes studying her, judging her, narrating her actions. No room was safe. At no point was she ever alone. Later as a teenager, she experienced episodes of sudden and overwhelming dread, a wave of strange fear that hit without warning and halted her in her tracks. There was no cause, no explanation. All tension. No release. She remembers hiding in a school restroom stall because only the ceramic walls felt safely opaque, with her arms crossed over her chest and gasping shallow breaths and later telling her mother: *I don't understand what's wrong with me. My heart races sometimes and I feel like I'm afraid of something.*

But there's nothing there.

That's called hormones, her mother had laughed, slurping box wine on the couch.

Neither of them knew that her mother's liver would fail that year. Or that she'd be granted a lifesaving transplant the following October. Or that she'd continue to drink her shitty box wines, kill her new liver, and die of complications three hours before Emma's senior prom. She was putting on her dress at a friend's house when she got the call.

Things got better in college, when Emma focused all of her energy on her physics degree. And Shawn was a uniquely good person, perhaps lifesaving in his goodness. For a few years she was happy in Salt Lake City—even with her unfulfilling job— with Shawn's love and a small house in Wasatch Hollow, praying every month for a baby to fill the guest room.

Now, here on the Strand, it's all caught up to her again. But it's not paranoia anymore. It's aged into something worse: an alarming numbness. She's aware of her senses, but she can't really feel them. Cheese pizza is tasteless. Ocean air is odorless. Flannel bedsheets feel like nothing at all against her skin. Sometimes she experiences a sickening jolt, like realizing the parking brake is off and the car is moving without your permission.

She never chooses to walk to the ocean's edge.

She just *finds* herself there.

And now, as she dances this dance for the millionth time in her life, she knows it's not about reading time or self-care anymore—she's keeping Deek at a distance to protect him.

He's written a final message, illuminated by a faraway desk lamp.

JUST KNOW YOU'RE NOT ALONE

His house is dark. He's asleep.

It's suddenly past ten, as if time has skipped, and the recessed lightbulb above Emma's reading sofa is the only other illumination for miles. No cars. No passing ships or planes.

She notices Laika is standing rigidly.

"What is it?"

Those black canine eyes stare out into the night. Her normally floppy ears move forward with attention.

Emma rises. "Did you hear something?"

She joins her golden retriever at the floor-to-ceiling windows and looks out into the vast panorama of dark beach. The stars are choked by rain clouds. This makes her strangely heartsick—December's new moon was always her favorite time to view the spiral of Messier 31 with Shawn. The Andromeda Galaxy, dense with stars.

Laika whines with concern.

"Don't worry, Space Dog. We're—"

Alone, she's about to say, when something triggers the motion-sensor light outside.

THE LED FLOODLIGHT IS STERILE AND BLUE-TINGED, LIKE the illumination for a surgery wing, highlighting every blade of grass outside. The gravel driveway is drawn in harsh detail.

Emma squints through the windows and scans the sea of waist-high grass for a deer's ass, for a human face, for anything. She knows Jules has four motion-activated lights installed to deter intruders, one guarding each direction. She's tripped the lights before herself, and she knows the activation range is extremely short. About thirty feet from the house.

Meaning whatever moved, just now, is close.

Closer than the driveway.

The front windows are narrow. Her view is hemmed in. The house's inland side is mostly wall, while the other three are mostly glass. She considers unlocking the front door and stepping outside onto the porch for a clear look.

It was probably a deer.

She stands at the front door. She tightens her fingers around the doorknob, one by one. With her other hand, she finds the lock latch.

Laika whimpers again. *Don't open the door.*

"It's fine," she whispers.

But something isn't. She can't explain it. So she holds her face to the wood and checks the peephole first. The fish-eye lens shows a bright empty porch, but Emma isn't fooled. She knows the aperture's view is limited. A stranger can stand just beside the door, inches away, and remain unseen. She recalls Jules once mentioning that there's a camera installed in the doorbell, but Emma doesn't have the app to view it.

She realizes her fingers are already unlocking the door automatically, out of muscle memory. She stops herself.

Laika watches nervously. *Please, Mom.*

Don't.

Her thumb and index finger hold the latch exactly on its edge. Another millimeter and it will release. This will make a distinct sound, a dead-bolt *click-clack,* audible to someone standing outside. He'll know the door is unlocked.

Outside, the floodlight silently flicks off. Darkness again.

This also means nothing, she knows. It's just a motion sensor. You can trick it by standing still. An intruder could be hiding on the porch, just inches away from her. Right beside this thin door. Waiting with a chest full of tense breath for her fingertips to nudge the latch the final millimeter, to make the error that costs everything.

Instead, Emma locks it back into place. *Click.*

She steps back. "It was probably a deer," she tells Laika. "You wuss."

In the kitchen, she gulps the rest of her ginger tea, now disgustingly cold. Printed on Jules's coffee mug, a photograph of a bug-eyed Chihuahua that looks about ninety: *Stewie 2008–2020.* She keeps an eye on the motion lights, though.

Before going to bed, she checks every window and both doors—all locked and secure. There's no way an intruder could get inside without breaking something. But she keeps turning it over in her mind, and by the time she's finally asleep, her thoughts are a toxic swirl. The slimy carrion in Laika's teeth, the second set of footprints in the sand, the accidental prophecy to Deek's words: *Just know you're not alone.*

That night, she sees the apparition in her bedroom again.

"GETTING SICK OF THIS SHIT."

The next morning, Emma paces room to room and spreads a fine layer of sand under every door and windowsill. Just a dusting, too faint to draw the eye, but enough to imprint an intruder's shoe treads. So next time—if there is a next time—she'll have evidence.

She rechecks the doors. Still locked.

The ghost's appearance was fuzzier this time. The night was stormy and the bedroom was near pitch-black. She sensed a humanoid shadow by the closet door, but she couldn't make out any features at all. No hat. No coat. Through the haze of sleep, she couldn't even be sure if he was really there at all, were it not for the small noise he made this time.

Scritch-scratch.

Just audible over the rainfall. Dry and papery.

Scritch-scratch.

It might have been this sound that woke her, subtle but alarmingly close. She can't be certain what it was, exactly. It could have been as innocent as scratching an itch.

Scritch-scratch.

By the time she snapped fully awake, the bedroom was empty. Again.

Emma is still mostly convinced that she's dreamt this figure. It's the most logical explanation. The *only* logical explanation.

She's been haunted by nightmares ever since she arrived here. And up until now it's always been the same dream: that she's trapped underwater. Far below and still plunging into frigid blackness, watching the watery stars fade above. Her mouth is open. She's already inhaled. It's already done and she has drowned, her lungs and throat and sinuses full of chilled seawater. But somehow, like Immortal Shawn, she's not dead. She's only awake and alone in darkness, at the end of the world.

She always tries to think about Shawn as she falls asleep—sometimes she even hears her own half-asleep voice slur his name—but it never works.

The same nightmare. Every night.

She was due a refresh, right?

Still, she checks the sand throughout the day. If her unknown friend enters—or exits—he'll leave a shoeprint. And Emma will know.

"I'm not crazy." She sips her tea.

Not crazy, Laika agrees.

She's surprised by her own calmness. This can't be how hauntings or home invasions usually go. But in truth, it's another valuable distraction. With the cartloads of e-books slowly losing her interest, she finds it a relief to have a new project to focus her energy and intelligence upon. She knows that in the Hollywood version of this, she's supposed to gasp and cower and wring her hands, but she truly hopes this stranger is real, because a serial killer would still only be Emma's second-biggest problem.

Her biggest, she sees every day.

So often she forgets it's there.

Next to the house's back door, just beside her sandy sneakers, rests a frayed green Osprey backpack. She's owned it since college. She's taken it caving, mountain climbing, and hiking through the Grand Canyon on a six-day honeymoon trip with Shawn. It smells like sweat and trail dust, blisters and laughter, early morning granola bars and sex under the stars. But right now it weighs sixty pounds, its zippers bulging and fabric stuffed taut with rocks she can't remember gathering.

SEE ANYONE SUSPICIOUS LAST NIGHT? SHE ASKS.

Deek frowns and shakes his head.

Then he writes: WHY?

She's not sure how to answer this without sounding paranoid. Will the old prankster laugh at her? Will he even believe her? She almost tells him about the ghost in her bedroom, but decides she should leave out everything she can't prove—which is basically everything. She tries to focus on Hangman, which she's losing.

Another stick figure swings.

Today's word? Deek fills in the letters. EMBOLISM

"Bastard."

He smiles coyly in her telescope. But this also gives Emma an idea—because his first word, in their very first Hangman game over a month ago, was also medical: *propofol* (a powerful anesthetic, according to Google). Now *embolism*. Maybe Deek's vocabulary is a tell. Maybe this will crack his mysterious past wide open.

She writes: YOU WERE A DOCTOR!

She underlines it twice.

Deek checks his telescope and then shakes his head. *No.*

NURSE?

No.

SOMETHING MEDICAL?

Still no.
"You know what? I don't care."
He grins and writes: YOU'LL NEVER GUESS
To Emma, this reads like a dark promise. "Yeah? Give me time, old man."
Sometimes she examines the sum total of what she knows about her neighbor—his antique firearm on display, his penchant for "made you look" practical jokes, his isolated and alcohol-assisted life amid hoarded junk and memories—and wonders: *Exactly who the hell are you?*
And . . . *can I trust you?*
She isn't naive.
Even her husband had secrets.
Years back, they were moving into their first apartment when one of Shawn's Rubbermaid bins tipped in his truck. He'd been mortified when she saw inside it, like it contained human body parts instead of N Gauge sectional track. He was terrified of what she'd think of his hobby, and this broke Emma's heart. She thought his model trains were fascinating. And even if she hadn't, she would've lied.
That Christmas, she'd wanted to buy him a new locomotive, but the options were dizzying (and shockingly expensive), so she settled on a striped blue train conductor's hat.
He'd laughed. *Even I think this hat is fucking terrible.*
It's an atrocity, Emma agreed.
I love it.
I knew you would.

Afterward, he always wore that hat in his train basement. The year they married, he began construction of his largest layout yet—four feet by eight, a double-track masterpiece of rolling plaster hills and lichen shrubbery. An epic trestle. Two tunnels. A small town that gradually accumulated plastic buildings and cars. Emma was usually afraid to touch it, but sometimes she sat and watched her husband paint tiny boxcars or soak strips of plaster, as he explained every small step in building his miniature world.

In return, she taught him about the stars.

On clear nights they'd slide out the second-floor window onto the roof, after midnight when the city lights were dimmest. In the summer, she'd show him Aquila, Corona Borealis, and Cygnus. In the winter, Orion, Gemini, and the Bull's Eye. Sometimes she named the constellations in Russian, the way her grandfather first taught her when she was five.

You never told me about your grandpa, Shawn said once as a shooting star traced overhead. Courtesy of the Perseids, a spectacular August meteor shower.

I don't have many memories of him, Emma answered. This was true. And her family has always embarrassed her—her selfish and alcoholic mother, her Houdini-escape-act of a father, her uncertain family tree. She is the sole survivor of her own lineage, and only her grandfather truly lives in her heart. The rich, smoky scent to his clothes she always liked, that she associated with love and safety. The cigarettes that would later kill him.

Why do you like space so much? Shawn asked her.

She deflected. *Why do you like model trains?*

I'm serious.

She considered for a long moment.

Her husband was patient. He waited in silence, watching the sky for the next meteor.

It's . . . it's like being inside the oldest, greatest clock, she said finally. *I don't believe in God. But sometimes when I look out at the universe, I want to. There's so much wonder out there. Planets made entirely of diamonds or ice, worlds where it rains molten glass whipped into knives by hurricane-force winds. Deep, dark places where the laws of physics as we understand them simply cease to be. Swirls of red and violet nebulae hundreds of light-years across. A human lifetime, traveling at the speed of light, couldn't even cross a tiny fraction.* She smiled. *I guess I'm in love with the beauty and terror of it.*

Shawn never interrupted her. But this time he came close.

I hope I have more time with you, he said abruptly. *Like, I know statistically we probably have forty or fifty years together, give or take. Assuming you stop smoking.*

I'll quit, she promised.

But I hope there's something after death, too. Because I know you're right, that being immortal would be agony. But I guess . . . I guess I just want to know *you for longer than forty years. It's not enough time.*

She stared down at the driveway. Tears prickled in her eyes.

I hope so, too, she said.

Shawn vowed he'd haunt her if he died first. She laughed and told him she expected nothing less. Wrapped in his arms, feeling warm and safe and small, she realized they weren't even paying attention to the best meteor shower of the year.

He kissed the top of her head. *I love you, Em.*

I love you, too.

These nights were the exception, though.

More often, their comfortable evenings at home were spent apart. Rather than joining each other in their respective worlds, she would read alone with Laika curled at her feet while Shawn quietly toiled on his model trains downstairs.

She regrets this now.

You never know how finite your time together really is until it's up.

AROUND NOON, EMMA'S FLIP PHONE VIBRATES ON THE DINING
table. An abrupt and shattering intrusion, as harsh as a buzz saw.

Nope, she thinks, raising her e-reader to ignore it.

HER PHONE RINGS AGAIN.

Still nope.

BUZZ. A TEXT MESSAGE NOW.

Oh, come on.

Weeks ago, she unplugged the house's landline phone and
stuffed it in the pantry. This cell phone is a burner she bought
in Idaho; a prepaid Cricket briquette that cost forty bucks at a
Love's truck stop. There's only one person alive who knows this
number.

"Jules."

Which means it must be important.

Reluctantly Emma opens her phone and finds an image still
loading, squeezing pixel by pixel through the sluggish Wi-Fi.
She reads the text message first.

Emma LOOK what the doorbell camera saw last night

Strand Beach Police Department

Incident No. 000671-12C-2023
12:35 PST

Operator: Strand Beach Police.

Caller: Hi. I, uh, need to make an incident report for last night.

Operator: What's your name?

Caller: Jules Phelps.

Operator: And what happened?

Caller: I'm in Portland for the winter, but my doorbell camera caught a weird man standing in front of my beach cabin last night. Really weird. I have a house-sitter there. Her name is Emma. She was home at the time. I'll, uh, email you the photo—

Operator: What did this man look like?

Caller: I . . . don't even know how to describe it.

Operator: Can you try?

Caller: Just have someone look at the photo, please.

Operator: And your house-sitter—

Caller: Her name is Emma.

Operator: She didn't see this man?

Caller: No. She says she'd noticed something set off the motion lights, but she didn't open the front door. I'm so glad she didn't.

It's just . . . I don't know. Emma is just a young woman living alone with her dog, defenseless, all the way up the Strand, with no help for miles.

She must be absolutely *terrified*.

"THERE YOU ARE," EMMA WHISPERS.

Jules's doorbell camera photo has finally loaded in black-and-white night vision. In the grainy foreground stands a figure, big-bellied and broad-shouldered.

Its face isn't human.

It has no mouth. Its lips seem to have grown together and fused with ropy flesh. Its skin is rubbery, its eyes sunken and unreadable. Two tall black horns protrude from its brow, curved and goatlike. The image is time-stamped for last night.

She remembers being so close to opening the door. The latch just a free-floating millimeter from unlocking, her fingers wrapped around the doorknob. Just a twist.

So close.

It's difficult to tell in low resolution, but based on the orientation of the porch railing, the stranger in a Halloween demon mask seems to be standing just off-center. To the left of the door, just outside the peephole's view. Exactly as she suspected. Waiting for Emma to open the door.

Laika chuffs. *I told you.*

This is vindicating. Her ghost is real. She's not crazy. And it's not lost on Emma that as deviously as this stranger avoided her view through the peephole, he overlooked the doorbell camera. He allowed himself to be photographed in close-up. The cops can practically read the Walmart barcode on his rubber mask.

"Dumbass."

Jules has already called the police. And via text she confesses—with an apology—that her prior house-sitters have reported similarly unsettling nighttime incidents. Most notably: Jules's son stayed here last winter, and one night in January he'd heard loud barking echo up from the beach. This wasn't unusual—just a stray dog or coyote—until he realized it wasn't an animal at all. It was a human voice *pretending,* yipping, snarling, howling. It seemed to subside after a few minutes. Then, after midnight, he awoke to hear a stranger circling the house, quietly testing the locked doors and windows with timid clicks and gentle exploratory taps. A dry run for a burglary, perhaps.

This is why Jules has motion lights.

And a doorbell camera.

You could've mentioned that in the Craigslist ad, lady.

With just under seven hundred permanent residents, Strand Beach is remote but hardly crime-free. Transients sometimes make camp by the rocky seawall at the island's northernmost edge. Every summer, a few returning families find their cabins ransacked by squatters. Darker things have happened here, too. In 2011 a local high schooler famously went missing, and only the girl's purse was found washed ashore, waterlogged and empty. Speculation still abounds on her true fate. This explains a mournful signboard Emma remembers reading in front of a local church: HAPPY 26TH BIRTHDAY, LAURA B. WE MISS U

According to Jules, local police will monitor the house and check in regularly. The island's unique geography means all traffic must first pass through town before reaching Emma's house, creating a secure bottleneck. What else can you do? Emma can't leave. Without this lease she's homeless again, and she doesn't know a single person within a thousand miles. And technically, no crime has been committed.

Yet.

Unless Emma can prove she wasn't dreaming, that the figure wasn't just at her door but physically inside the house. Which she plans to do.

Tonight.

She has a plan.

In the meantime, she's getting annoyed by Jules's incessant texts. Every time she manages to focus on her book (which is already difficult, as the novel's detective duo has an embarrassingly hard time catching a killer who repeatedly puts himself on a damn guest list), a grating electric buzz jolts her back out.

Emma THANKS AGAIN for watching my house

She's welcome.

I SO appreciate it

Yep.

Sorry about the weirdo

It's fine.

My son said the isolation REALLY got to him some nights out there. He always felt like someone was watching him through the windows. Crouched in the tall grass. Waiting. And he's a man, so he didn't even have to worry about being raped.

Jesus Christ, lady.

Want me to order you a Taser? I found a good one

Emma starts to type: *Oh, wow. That's nice of you to offer, but that sounds too expensi—*
Buzz! Another text.

Too late, bought you a stun gun

Buzz!

Five stars on Amazon

Buzz!

Wait, not sure if batteries are included

Buzz!

Yes they are

Emma silences her phone. Then she sets down her e-reader—still unable to focus—and goes to smoke her daily cigarette through the tiny laundry room window. As she cranks her plastic fan, she can't help but scan the tall grass outside for a crouched figure. His motives still unknown.

Jules has no idea who the stranger is.

Nor do the police.

But as Emma pinches and bags her cigarette, she realizes: *I might.*

THAT MASK.

He wore it while photographed by Jules's doorbell camera—and not while he was inside Emma's bedroom.

It aligns with something half-remembered. That shitty e-book. In *Murder Mountain,* the narrator/killer took great care to wear a rubber Halloween mask whenever he suspected he might be captured on film. But when he was close to his victims, the young coeds Prelaw and Psych, he didn't bother with disguises because dead people can't describe their killer.

Maybe being seen by the doorbell wasn't an error.

Maybe it was a message.

She remembers typing her one-star review. Her baffling exchange with the book's author. His vanity, his victimhood, his bizarre use of *sapsucker* as an insult. *I won't ask you again,* he'd finally threatened. Her answer? *Good.*

Easy to say online.

In person, it's different. Especially for Emma.

But she reminds herself that such a scenario is impossible. There's no way an online stranger—even a psychotic one—could glean her address from a single online book review and appear, literally, on her doorstep in Strand Beach, Washington.

He could live anywhere in the country. He'd need either god-like omniscience or an NSA security clearance. Right?

H. G. Kane. What a dumb name.

He has no author photo. No Facebook. No Instagram or Twitter. The domain of his website—hgkaneofficial.com—seems to have expired, too. The only evidence that this digital ghost exists at all is right back where she started, on Amazon.

His self-written author bio.

Who is H. G. Kane?
He's like you, perhaps. He grew up in small-town Americana,
and from an early age he learned from the literary greats:
Faulkner, Twain, Shakespeare, Dickens. By age ten, he had
famously read every book in his local library.
So . . . perhaps he's not like you.

Gag, Emma thinks. But she keeps reading.

Oddly, a career in writing never occurred to this precocious
young boy. It wasn't until a world-renowned author recognized
the young boy's talents and committed to mentoring him. Over
many years through his adolescence, H. G. honed his skills
under the expert tutelage of one of our generation's finest.
The rest, as they say, is history.
H. G. Kane's horror fiction is RAW, POWERFUL, and above
all, AUTHENTIC. His novels have been described as "deeply
disturbing" (reviewer Ellie_McCoy), "scary as hell" (reviewer
Paul48), and "a tour de force of nerve-shredding dread and
finely-tuned suspense" (reviewer 420Blaze_It). Some say
H. G. Kane is among the finest horror scribes of the new
century. But he doesn't buy into that. He's not in it for the
attention or the fame.
So, who is H. G. Kane?

Let's be honest. You'll never find him.

But if you could, you'd find him living the lone-wolf life of
a sigma male, tending to his sword collection, enjoying
quality vape, and dutifully typing away at his next opus.
To preserve the secrecy of his identity, H. G. Kane avoids
speaking engagements and public signings, but he can always
be troubled for a (reasonably priced) signed paperback at
HGKANEofficialauthor1@gmail.com.

Emma is fairly sure it's a joke.

Seventy percent.

It's also strangely conflicted. H. G. Kane wants to be a tantalizing enigma, but he also wants you to know how amazing he is. And there's an uncomfortable desperation to quoting online reviewers' profile names, likely without permission.

Okay, sixty-five percent.

According to Amazon, he's self-published sixteen horror novels, all sporting the same minimalist black covers as *Murder Mountain*. Same Comic Sans font. Same unattributed boasts—each one declares itself the most gripping novel you will ever read, or the creepiest or the goriest. Each seems to be a similarly cold-blooded tale of stalking, torture, and eventual murder, and interestingly, all are written entirely from the killer's point of view.

H. G. Kane's gimmick, apparently.

His most popular book is *Murder Lake*, with fifty-eight user reviews and an aggregated rating of two and a half stars. Per the summary, something about a husband and wife violently attacked on their houseboat. Along with their white Lab. Lovely.

Then *Murder Glacier*, with a two-star average, depicting the home invasion and torture of two sisters in rural Alaska. Especially cruel and graphic, according to user reviews.

Murder Valley. One and a half stars. An idyllic family camping trip becomes a bloodbath.

Murder River. Same thing, on a river.

Murder Rock. Same thing, near a rock formation.

Murder Falls. A waterfall, apparently?

Murder Marsh. Yep.

Murder Prairie. Okay.

Murder Fjord. That one is a bit of a stretch.

Whatever the setting, the victims never seem to win. Emma figures *Murder Mountain* to be H. G. Kane's newest, published just weeks ago. It now has eleven reviews, including her familiar one-star. The other ten are positive. They all loved or at least liked it, praising the graphic violence and vivid detail.

Stomach-turning and scary, says SluttyGodzilla51.

Well-written, says OodleMcPoodle.

His best novel to date, says HowieGK'sTopFan.

These reviews baffle Emma. They must be fake accounts, sock puppets controlled by the author himself. She studies one user—HowieGK'sTopFan, which has no profile pic and has reviewed only H. G. Kane books. Five stars all around.

Probably his mother.

She tries to see this from the author's perspective, to labor for years writing a deeply personal creative work, to finally summon the courage to share it with the world—only to be mocked by a critic you'll never meet. She tries to feel sympathy but can't. Far worse things can happen to you than some stranger hurting your feelings on the internet. Emma knows this.

She reminds herself that H. G. Kane couldn't possibly have found her here.

No one has.

But out of curiosity, she googles her own name and immediately finds her past addresses in Salt Lake City, accurate to the apartment number. Her phone number. Her age. Her parents' and grandparents' names. Shawn's data is equally transparent. It's all out there, her old life laid out for autopsy. It wasn't even difficult to find. So it's not unreasonable to suspect that her for-warding address here at Strand Beach is somewhere out there, too, within reach of someone savvy enough to find it.

Or *vengeful* enough.

Still, she has the guy's email address now.

She types her email without thinking it through. She's sick of the uncertainty, of waiting in a stranger's house like a caged bird, unable to assert herself.

HG Kane: You don't scare me. I'm keeping my 1-star review up.

She hits Send.

It's done.

WAS I TOO HARD ON HIM?

Maybe.

But then she remembers moments of reading *Murder Mountain* when she'd felt a visceral need to hurl her e-reader to the floor, to stomp on it like it was a hairy tarantula until the screen cracked. It was the written equivalent of a snuff tape. H. G. Kane didn't care who Prelaw and Psych were, and he didn't seem to expect the reader to care, either—all that mattered was the lovingly imag-ined violence they were destined for. Bodily destruction.

Machetes to fingers.

Bullets to bone.

Thumbnails into eye sockets.

The last two hundred pages read like something a psychopath might masturbate to. At times, she swore she could feel the au-thor's unwelcome presence materialize in the room. His weight sagging the sofa cushion beside her, peering over her shoulder with his moist breath on her neck, perhaps adjusting himself with his free hand.

Scritch-scratch.

She shivers.

She's alone, of course. She circles the main floor and rechecks the locks, just to be certain. Her scattered sand is untouched. Laika naps peacefully.

Rain clicks against the windows, thick and oily. She stands still in the living room, rubbing goose bumps on her arms. From here she can see north, west, and south for literally miles—an endless expanse of sandy coast and flatlands flocked with waist-high grass. The house should feel as secure as a sniper's nest. She knows, rationally, that this is the safest place to be. The island's geography is its own protection, the police are closely monitoring the road, and from here she'll see any intruder coming fifteen minutes out. But to the irrational part of Emma's mind the glass walls feel distinctly smothering. Like being inside an aquarium.

She watches her own breath fog the glass.

My son said the isolation really got to him some nights out there. He always felt like someone was watching him through the windows. Crouched in the tall grass. Waiting.

Minute by minute, the sky is darkening.

Night is falling.

Her gut tells her—he'll be back again tonight.

EMMA SITS CROSS-LEGGED INSIDE THE BEDROOM CLOSET with her phone in one hand and Jules's sharpest kitchen knife in the other.

Through the closet door's thin slats, she can see her own bed from roughly the same angle as last night's guest. She has carefully arranged pillows under the covers to form a human shape (surprisingly difficult with Jules's selection of stupid square pillows). Now, in full darkness, it's eerily convincing. Like there's a corpse in her bed.

Since noon today, she's switched from ginger tea to espresso. Five of them.

In retrospect, three would have been enough. Her nerves fizz with caffeine. Her heart slams in her chest. She figures she can set something on fire with her mind if she thinks about it hard enough. And now that she's shut the closet door, she hopes her bladder lasts the night. She's committed. This is a wild adventure, perhaps the most exciting thing she's done in months. When the apparition silently returns to her bedroom tonight to watch her sleep—or worse—his back will be turned to the closet. If things get violent, as they surely might, she'll have 911 in one hand and a serrated knife in another.

The night is long. The house groans and rain pelts the roof. She reads another book on her e-reader in low-light mode. Periodically, she rests her eyelids.

She flirts with sleep—nothing serious, just drowsy little whirls of imagination—and Shawn sits beside her inside the dark closet. *I miss you,* he tells her.

I miss you, too.

What's that?

Oh, this? She lifts the knife. *In case I have to disembowel some motherfucker.*

Cool, Shawn says.

He's a welcome presence. When her husband is around, Emma knows she's not fully asleep. She's asleep only when the nightmares take hold, when she's trapped under a surface of watery stars with her chest aching, her mouth and nose full of icy seawater.

Don't let him disembowel you first, Em.

I won't.

NOTHING HAPPENS.

The figure never appears. All night.

As sunlight breaks through rain-dewed windows, Emma carries her knife downstairs and clears the house room by room, eliminating every hiding place. Then she checks the sand under each entry point—all untouched. Zero evidence.

Until the final window in the teenager's bedroom. There, her heart pounds with excitement at a disturbance in the sand—before she recognizes a pawprint.

"Damn it, Laika."

Sorry, Mom.

Maybe this figure is only imagined. Or maybe the police have already scared him off—after all, Jules's son survived last winter just fine, didn't he?

Somehow, it doesn't matter. This is Emma's project, something she can't leave unfinished. Anything to make it to the next night, because the nights don't scare her. It's the gray and endless days, as mushy as cold oatmeal, when the Strand's maddening isolation is most acutely felt. The house feels like an organism that's slowly rejecting her, an alienating hodgepodge of stainless-steel appliances and sleek glass built around ancient pipework and spiderwebbed laundry chutes. It's both warm and cold, cozy and smothering, luxurious and fetid with rot. It's a home—and it's very much *not*. At night, you can pretend it's full of ghosts and serial killers to give you purpose.

But the days are long.

Without purpose.

Beyond the e-books and whiteboard games, all that's left is the green Osprey backpack loaded with rocks by the back door, like a trip she's already packed for.

"I'M NOT CRAZY," SHE TELLS HER GOLDEN RETRIEVER.

Laika ignores her, licking her food bowl as the sun traces its slow path behind a soup of thick clouds. *You already said that, Mom.*

Yes. She remembers.

Definitely not crazy.

But she did solve one mystery last night: her neighbor's former life. This explains the old man's conspicuous vocabulary, his heaped books and documents, his reclusive lifestyle. Even why he might recommend a shitty novel as a joke.

The clue was *propofol*—Deek's very first Hangman word. On a hunch, Emma was cross-checking the full name "Deacon" with "propofol" on Google's fifth or sixth page when an article came up on the Stockyard Slayer, a Fort Worth–area serial killer who preyed on women during the late eighties and early nineties. He was ostensibly a well-respected anesthesiologist, but his mug shot showed a chinless little bald man with vacant bovine eyes. The kind of man you'd barely notice as you passed him on the sidewalk—but you might hear the *plop* in your drink or maybe feel the prick of a needle. Then comes slushy, wide-eyed terror as his custom anesthetic cocktail melts the muscles, leaving his victims near-paralyzed but still horribly cognizant. It's nightmare fuel. In their final hours, some of these women assuredly experienced hell on earth.

To clarify: no, Deek is *not* the Stockyard Slayer.

The state of Texas barbecued his ass in 2008.

But the bestselling 1996 true crime novel *Silent Screams*—a vividly written and exhaustively researched account of the Stockyard Slayer's thirteen confirmed kills, which was widely acclaimed for exposing shoddy police work, catapulting the missing women into the national eye, and even aiding detectives in finally pinpointing the killer—was authored by a Dallas-based journalist named . . . Deacon Cowl.

She has it now.

YOU WERE A WRITER!

She underlines it.

A quarter mile away, Deek checks his telescope. A hold-your-breath moment as he reads—then he looks up, smirks, and guiltily spreads his arms. *You got me.*

"Hell, yes."

Honestly, she's a bit relieved. She'd half expected to learn he was a retired assassin or a child molester or a mob informant in hiding. Something disgusting or dangerous. You never know who your neighbors are, after all. But at least he's on the right team. And famous, even.

Deek shakes his head modestly: LONG TIME AGO. RETIRED

YEAH, Emma writes. RETIRED IN A BIG-ASS BEACH HOUSE

He laughs soundlessly.

She's pretty sure she's seen yellowed paperbacks of *Silent Screams* on shelves before, in thrift stores and garage sales. She might have even picked it up once or twice.

Somehow it saddens her to know Deek was once famous. She's seen how much he drinks now, some afternoons tripping over his own slippers. He'll pace restlessly around his house like a caged animal, appearing and reappearing behind stacks of heaped furniture while gulping from a generously poured glass. He's not enjoying himself. There's desperation to it.

Alcohol has always secretly scared Emma. Back in September, Jules left a pricey Cabernet on the kitchen counter as a housewarming gift, and it's still there now. The only person she's ever felt truly safe to drink around was Shawn. Losing control—even a little—is terrifying. She remembers the way her mother would belch loudly on the sofa while clutching her giant box of Walmart wine—these terrible gaseous watery belches that shook the house. No embarrassment or self-awareness. Like a dog. As a child, Emma used to giggle at her mother's burps. As a teenager, she was saddened by them.

Deek writes: SEE YOUR STALKER LAST NIGHT?

She shakes her head.

For a time, she'd suspected the figure in Jules's doorbell camera was just her neighbor in a Halloween mask, given his penchant for dark jokes. But she's ruled him out. The figure in the photo is too tall, and as barrel-chested as Jason Voorhees. It's not Deek.

He erases and writes: DID JULIE MENTION ME?

It takes her a moment to realize who he's talking about.

Julie. Jules.

Figures he'd know her.

And Emma doesn't have the heart to tell him the truth. Amid yesterday's hectic firehouse of text messages, of Tasers and incident reports and accounts of unknown men barking like dogs in the night, she'd offered to warn Deek of the strange visitor. Jules's answer had been swift and unsparing, almost as if it were pretyped.

Don't bother talking to the neighbor. He's a drunk + liar +
all-around 100-karat asshole. He's the reason I took my son to
Portland. If there's any justice in the world, Demon Face will
show up at his door next time.

Damn, lady.

Maybe she hated Deek's fireworks. Maybe his weird sense of humor offended her. Maybe they were past lovers and he still carries a torch for her. He does look vaguely hopeful right now, still staring. Awaiting her reply.

Say something, Emma.

After a long pause, she uncaps her marker.

NOPE, she writes.

DIDN'T MENTION YOU

SCRITCH-SCRATCH.

She hears it from the next room. Her heart heaves, a sickening plunge.

Scritch-scratch.

It's . . . just Laika, pawing at the back door.

Emma lets her retriever outside but stands in the doorway to watch. Although the backyard is fenced, she doesn't trust the sagging chain link. She's thinking more and more about that strange meat that cut Laika's gums, and yesterday, on a worried hunch, she'd even returned to the beach for a closer look at it. She dug three holes but found only wet sand. Maybe she was just misremembering where she buried it—or maybe someone took care to retrieve it.

"Recall," she orders.

Laika obeys, and Emma locks the door.

Back in the living room, she texts Jules a final time to ask if there's any other way into the house. Any crawl spaces or secret passages to the basement.

The answer is immediate.

Nope, just the two locking doors + main floor windows. Don't worry, Emma. The police are on it. And this house can play tricks on you.

Maybe.

Maybe it's just in her head. The rubber-masked stranger at the door is one of the Strand's transients searching for an unguarded house to steal from, already come and gone. The figure in her bedroom is just a dream. The real H. G. Kane is a harmless sweater-wearing forty-something living in his mother's basement in Michigan and utterly baffled by her email. Maybe she truly is alone with her thoughts in this maddening place.

Maybe. But Emma doesn't think so.

Buzz.

By the way—MERRY CHRISTMAS!

Today's date surprises her.

Honestly, she forgot.

6

WELL, THAT HAPPENED.

Hgkaneofficialauthor1@gmail emailed her back. With dread fluttering inside her stomach, she opens the message and sees a dense block of text.

She braces for it.

> Hi, you must be talking about Murder Mountain? I presume you're Emma86?

This means nothing. He might just be maintaining deniability.

> I don't know who you are, and I don't harbor any ill will toward you. As you know I'm a prolific author and very busy with all of my deadlines. I barely have time to write this email.

Uh-huh, she thinks.

> My issue with this review is that you're only a critic. Not even that—you're a consumer. You don't create things. You don't understand how hard it is to write a book, a hundred thousand words all chosen and typed by hand. It's easy for you to nitpick another's creation because you have no skin in the game. You're just a cold, negative woman with no friends.

So much for no ill will.

What you don't understand is, it's basically impossible to get published traditionally because the Big Five publishers only agree to publish mainstream books. And by slandering me and limiting my readers, you are attacking not only my daily income but also my chances of ever getting noticed by an agent or editor. This is the very definition of marginalization.

And no offense, but you're a female. I'm a nice guy, but I just have to shoot straight here on this—females generally don't like action or horror. It's just biology. Why are you even reviewing it? That's like me reviewing a bra. And some women always fancy themselves experts on whether a horror book is "realistic" or "unrealistic"—like YOU personally know how a .223-caliber Colt AR-15 rifle works? Can you load and fire one? Or how to tie a tourniquet? Or what a tension pneumothorax ("sucking chest wound") is? Please. That's what you don't understand. You're small-time and I shouldn't let your uninformed "opinion" bother me, but as I like to say, sometimes it's the small knife that cuts deepest.

That's why I'm now ordering you: take your 1-star review down.

Sincerely,
HGK

She almost hopes she gets a chance to stab this guy.

And, worryingly, she can sense the rage building under his words. Like a geothermal force pushing to the surface, scalding, uncontrollable. Pressure rising. All from an online book review, of all things.

She needs a cigarette. "Fuckin' *writers,* man."

Wait.

There's . . . more. She scrolls down further.

PS: If you'd CAREFULLY READ Murder Mountain, you would know that they didn't go hiking in high heels, they just HAD heels in their backpack.
Your wrong!

Nice typo.

Maybe it really is him after all. This is the man who haunted Jules's doorbell camera with a mouthless demon mask and dared her to open the door. Who watched her sleep.

But she still can't prove it. Not yet.

She answers with one word.

*You're

Sent.

The small knife cuts deepest, as an asshole on the internet once said.

THAT EVENING DEEK WRITES: THINK HE'LL BE BACK TONIGHT?

"I kind of hope so." Emma sips her espresso and watches the clock.

The police are "looking into it." Whatever that means. Every few hours she sees the glint of a Dodge Charger creep up Wave Drive, diligently guarding a deserted landmass. She had considered spending a few nights elsewhere, but the only motel in town still open for the winter doesn't allow dogs. She could jump in her beat-up Corolla and leave outright, she supposes. Break her agreement with Jules, hit the road with Laika, and be penniless and homeless again.

If the man following her is real, that's arguably more dangerous.

Still, she's considering it.

The sun lowers behind darkening clouds to the west. *On Strand Beach, there's always a next storm* (a local saying she saw printed on a T-shirt in a shop window), but this one is the biggest yet. The anvil thunderheads look solid enough to touch, like the skyline of a distant city rolling in over the waves. It'll be here sometime after dark.

WANT ME TO STAY UP? Deek asks. KEEP AN EYE OUT?

She hates involving him.

Every time she focuses her telescope on Deek's window, she half expects to see a figure with a mouthless rubber face standing there instead. The old man's body on the floor with an axe in his skull. And on the whiteboard, written by a bloody fingertip: *I warned you.*

Just paranoia.

I'LL KEEP WATCH, he insists. JUST IN CASE

"Thanks."

He shrugs. I'M NOT EXACTLY BUSY

She has asked Deacon Cowl about his family only once and immediately felt guilty—when you get drunk and watch fireworks with an Ikea's worth of crap in your house and a toilet on your deck, your life can't be going great. Deek's answer had been delicate. *Twin daughters,* he wrote after almost a minute of hesitation. *I lost them both.*

Emma never asked how they died. As a fellow lost soul on the Strand, she knows it doesn't really matter. If Deek wanted pity, he wouldn't be out here alone.

He writes more: YOU'RE MY FAVORITE NEIGHBOR

"I'm sure."

GOTTA LOOK OUT FOR EACH OTHER

"That's very sweet."

PLUS CATCHING ANOTHER SERIAL KILLER COULD REALLY RESTART MY CAREER

She laughs. It seems to rattle out of her, a surprised bark, and she barely recognizes her own voice. She's missed the feeling.

But . . . it was the sort of laugh only her husband could elicit from her. Her heart sinks like an anchor. Moments like this, she wishes she could cry instead.

She hasn't cried since July.

Not once. The memorial service was full of eyes—sympathetic eyes, but eyes all the same. You're expected to dress up and cover your face and sob in the front pew, and when you sit there like a tranced zombie in a baggy sweatshirt instead, people notice. People whisper. And she knows they aren't wrong to worry. Whatever healthy grieving looks like, this can't be it.

Maybe her brain has refused to accept what happened, like a laptop's frozen blue screen, and if it's a coping mechanism, it fucking sucks—because all she has then is the split second itself when two vehicles collided with a bony crunch. Five months. Zero progress. She's still right there. Inside it. She can still smell the scorched brake pads, the gritty highway dust, the coppery blood in her teeth. She can't taste pizza, but she can taste that.

Deek frowns. SERIOUS, EMMA. ARE YOU OKAY?

She exhales. What can she say? A psychopath may or may not be stalking her, and that's still somehow the best thing to happen to her in months because it's something to focus on other than the ocean outside. And the backpack by the door.

He's waiting.

His question stands. And this time, she senses a finality to it. She's lied to Deek several times now. She knows if she repeats her denial, he probably won't ask again. This will be it. Not everyone is as patient as Shawn was.

I'm not okay, she wants to say. *I haven't been okay for months.*

She twirls her dry-erase marker absently and forces a smile. It's all metastasized inside her chest, a swollen mass of scar tissue.

I'm afraid of myself, she wants to write.

I'm afraid of what I'll do when I'm alone, when no one is looking.

I'm so afraid.

This isn't about solving the mystery of the figure in her bedroom. Maybe it never was. There's a small secret part of Emma, a faulty sequence of genes somewhere, or a *thing* in her brain as real as a tumor. Maybe it's the same silent defect that made her mother choose to keep binge-drinking box wines even after a teenage stranger died for her lifesaving transplant, to pickle two livers in one lifetime.

This part of Emma hopes the stranger murders her.

So she won't have to do it herself.

For weeks the ocean has called to her with the promise of vanishing cleanly, completely. No body. No note. To be a mysterious and beautiful bird you'll only later realize was endangered, like leaving a stuffy college party where the music is too loud and she doesn't know anyone, the sly Irish goodbye—*Where's that Emma girl? I just saw her. Did she leave?* Meanwhile, she's halfway home. The girl who had once wanted to be an astronomer, who dreamed of naming new stars but settled for being a junior high math teacher, who now lives alone in a stranger's house and smokes through a tiny window. And not for much longer. Blink and you'll miss her.

Finally Deek shrugs in his distant spaceship. OK. TALK LATER I GUESS.

She feels a small stab of guilt. She guesses Deacon Cowl is a fascinating human being with a remarkable career. He could be a lifesaving ally or even a genuine friend. You'll never know if you don't *let people in.*

She almost didn't let Shawn in.

She met her husband by accident seven years ago. One of the college clubs had organized a day hike to the overlook at Turnkey Peak, and she'd signed up expecting a large turnout. Instead, it was only her and a skinny electrical engineering major named Shawn. The eight-mile hike they took together was excruciatingly awkward. At the trailhead, passing through a rusty (and vaguely sinister-looking) metal gate, she remembers apologizing for not talking.

He'd shrugged politely, as if he didn't mind one bit, looked up the hill, and said with a friendly smile: *I'll meet you there.*

For some reason, this is imprinted in her mind.

I'll meet you there.

She remembers walking fast. Trying to keep ahead of him, to avoid the skin-crawling discomfort of semi-introduced strangers walking side by side in silence. As it turned out, twenty-one-year-old Shawn was a hell of hiker. She nearly exhausted herself keeping ahead of his pace. But she pretended.

I'll meet you there.

According to the state website, the view from Turnkey Peak is akin to a religious experience, a stunning panorama of jutting granite, mile-high scree slopes, and distant rivers of ice wreathing the Rockies beyond. Emma remembers only sitting at the edge of the cliff, chewing her peanut butter sandwich and laughing at Shawn's jokes, because he'd finally caught her there and there was no escape short of the fatal drop. Shawn had a way about him. He was gentle, maybe a bit gawky, but quietly witty. Later, she would tell him that he reminded her of Schmendrick, the virtuous but slightly inept wizard from her favorite book, Peter Beagle's *The Last Unicorn.*

She liked him. Even then.

But even then, on that drizzly mountaintop, she held him at arm's length. She rationed her laughter. On the hike down she could feel herself sabotaging things, always a half step ahead, half listening, forcing him to chase her. She'd always known how to scupper a good thing.

At the day's end they waved a polite but aloof goodbye at the trailhead gate, and Emma sat alone in her car with the engine running and the doors locked. She hadn't given him her number or even her last name. They might never see each other on campus. She felt stupid, weak, and cold. Then, motion in her sideview mirror—it was Shawn again, speed walking toward her car. He held something in his hand. He looked nervous. Emma remembers rolling down her window and smiling at him, her heart fluttering with gratitude for another chance.

Until she saw what he was carrying.

A bloody severed finger.

She can't remember if she screamed—she probably did—but what sticks in her memory is how deeply apologetic Shawn was the entire time. He needed a ride to the hospital because the rust-eaten trailhead gate had slid shut under a gust of wind at the exact moment he rested his palm on the hinge. Amputating the top knuckle of his pinkie finger.

I'm so sorry, he kept saying.

With shaking hands, Emma found the only container she had—a ziplock sandwich bag she'd packed her lunch in. She remembers the sickening little *plop* as he dropped his fingertip in. There was no ice. No cell service. Seconds counted.

Oh, my God, I'm bleeding all over your car. I'm so sorry.

She tried to reassure him as she stomped the gas: *It's totally fine. Don't even think about that. Just keep pressure on it, okay?*

I didn't mean for this to— Shawn made a sudden, surprised grunt as she skidded down the road's first switchback: *Oh.*

What?

He said nothing.

What is it? She couldn't dare take her eyes off the road. *What happened?*

It's fine. He was leaning forward in his seat, doubled over with his head between his knees, sounding almost embarrassed. *I just . . . I dropped it.*

You what?

I'm so, so sorry—

Like, under the seat?

Um, yeah. A brittle creak as he reclined the passenger seat, reaching under with his unhurt hand. As Emma's little car bounced wildly over mud-splashed potholes, still barreling down the mountain. Her phone in her palm—no signal yet.

Find it?

No. It's somewhere down there. I just can't reach it. His breaths were shallow, his face pale and shiny with sweat. On the verge of tears, not from pain but humiliation. *I'm . . . I can't believe this happened—*

She reached over and squeezed his knee. *No biggie. We'll find it when we park, okay? It's always easier to find stuff under the seat when the car's parked.*

Okay, he sniffled.

For some reason, in all the blood and horror and lunacy of the moment as they hurtled down a steep mountain road, it's touching Shawn's knee that she remembers clearest. She met him just hours ago. She didn't know his last name. And she was touching his leg.

It's so strange, but losing a finger barely hurts at all. I feel completely fine, he said before vomiting on the floor of her car.

Five miles downhill, Emma parked at a run-down Shell station and ran inside for help. The clerk called 911 but insisted they pay full price for a bag of ice. When the ambulance arrived in a blaze of red and blue, gray-faced Shawn thanked her one last time and said he hoped to see her around on campus. This was almost it, their second goodbye—but instead Emma stepped forward and asked the paramedics which hospital they were taking him to. They gave her an address, and now it was Emma's turn to say it.

I'll meet you there, she told her future husband just as the ambulance door swung shut.

Before it did, he smiled.

Four words.

In her mind, they became a mantra for years. During a grueling day at work. During one of Shawn's achingly long business trips to Phoenix. Their individual paths might differ, but they always ended up in the same place together.

I'll meet you there.

Wherever *there* may be.

Ultimately, surgeons failed to reattach the tip of Shawn's pinkie finger. His left hand remained forever stunted and he relearned a few guitar chords, but he often joked that it was a fair trade for meeting his wife. He meant it wholeheartedly, but this had always secretly shamed Emma—because in truth he'd already met her on that mountaintop, and she was a cold bitch to him. It took a severed fingertip in a sandwich bag to break down her walls.

She's *hard to know.*

Now she uncaps her dry-erase marker and wipes away her last message to Deek. No more hiding. No more self-sabotage. No more *waiting,* because waiting on this beach is only a comfortable death glide. A warm seat and a good book on a stalled airplane.

Do it.

Do it.

Do it, Em. Be brave.

She exhales and writes: YES

YES, LET'S CHAT IN PERSON. DO YOU LIKE GINGER TEA?

But Deek is already gone. She's too late. His living room is dark, and one final message remains on his whiteboard. She squints through glass blurred with running droplets.

GOOD NIGHT, GOOD LUCK

Lights out, his spaceship now cruising on autopilot.

So *close.*

Thunder rumbles over the rising tide. The house seems to shiver atop its foundation and she wonders if the figure who has haunted her—H. G. Kane, Demon Face, whoever or whatever he is—is close enough to hear it, too.

She's made up her mind.

Not one more night here. She'll pack her toothbrush and spend tonight in a motel. She'll smuggle Laika in a suitcase if she has to. Then tomorrow morning, she'll apologize to Jules and leave the island forever. She'll roll the dice somewhere else, maybe somewhere dryer, somewhere warmer. Maybe inland, far from the ocean. Somewhere with witnesses. Anything to break the cycle, to stand up from her comfortable seat and storm the cockpit and grab the stick in a lucid moment when she's herself, really *herself,* and fight the stall.

Before it's too late.

If I don't, she knows, *I'll die on this beach.*

One way or another.

7

"HURRY UP."

From the doorway she watches Laika circle the backyard in the bright glare of the motion light, sniffing the grass. Emma's clothes are packed. Just one last bathroom break for Laika before they leave.

"Do it."

More hesitant circles. More sniffing.

"Just *pee*. It's not that hard." Squinting into the rain, Emma scans the dark grass for more suspicious cuts of meat. The wind growls over breaking waves. She knows her retriever is vulnerable—and so is she, standing in the open doorway.

Laika is still circling. Pacing. Sniffing.

"Come on."

More circling.

"Please."

Finally Laika finds a suitable spot. She doubles back, stops, and squats.

"Yes. There—"

Her ears perk. Then she stands up again, rigidly alert.

"Seriously?"

Then Emma notices Laika is staring farther inland, toward

the house's opposite side. A new glow illuminates the dune grass. The east motion-sensor light—the one that faces the driveway—has been silently triggered.

Someone is here.

From the front door, Emma hears a violent, hinge-rattling knock.

SHE CARRIES A KITCHEN KNIFE UNDERHAND. HER BARE feet pad on cold tile.

"Who is it?"

Silence.

She stops at the foyer's edge. From here she can see the paneled front door, reassuringly solid. The brass latch is still locked.

She raises her voice. "Identify yourself."

Seconds pass. Rain drums the roof. The gutters drip. The house's old bones settle around her with a low, bass creak.

No one answers.

For just long enough to get her hopes up.

"It's me. Deek."

She's never heard her neighbor's voice before. It's soft, surprisingly smooth for an elderly alcoholic. Nonthreatening as it is, it still makes Emma's heart explode inside her chest like a fragmentation grenade. She's gone weeks without hearing a human voice. Here, now, it's shattering. Just ten feet away, on the other side of a door.

She says nothing.

"Sorry if I scared you." He sounds winded.

She should feel relieved—it's not her stalker, after all—but she's still on edge. *Say something,* she urges herself.

Say anything—

"I was . . ." Deek is still catching his breath. Porch boards creak as he paces, as if he is making sure he wasn't followed. "This is going to sound crazy, Emma, but I think there's someone inside my house. Right now."

Fear quivers in his voice. She turns sharply and looks out the kitchen window. Far to the north, Deek's house stands dark and silent.

"I called the police," he pants. "They're coming."

She studies those distant windows for light. Motion. Anything.

Then back to the door.

"I was in bed when I heard it," Deek says. "A male voice downstairs, humming. Just softly humming. I ignored it for a while. I thought I'd just left the radio on. But then I heard movement. Stomping around my living room, searching for something. Opening cabinets, rifling through my old books."

Emma's heart flutters.

His *old books*.

Deacon Cowl isn't famous—at least, not anymore—but he's still summited every aspiring writer's dream. He's been published. He's hit bestseller lists. He's guest-starred on *The Tonight Show* and met Jay Leno, back when broadcast television was the apex of fame. Narcissists feel threatened by the achievements of others—what might H. G. Kane do now that he knows the real deal lives next door to Emma, alone and unprotected?

"From the top of the stairs, I could only see the guy's shadow on the floor. And his shoes." Deek swallows. "I saw . . . combat boots. Military-style."

Her skin prickles with goose bumps.

She remembers the exposed nerves, the raw pain in the author's words: *By slandering me and limiting my readers, you are attacking not only my daily income but also my chances of ever getting noticed by an agent or editor.*

Whatever his intentions with Emma, they pale beside what he might to do Deacon Cowl in the flesh. She imagines H. G. Kane begging Deek for an endorsement. Thrusting his latest literary excretion—*Murder Whatever*—into the old man's hands.

"I panicked." Deek's voice wavers. "I snuck down the stairs and ran outside through the back, as fast as I could. My keys were in the living room with him. I just ran through the grass and called 911. And I kept running until I got here. To you."

The rain intensifies, a sheet-metal rattle.

"I'm . . . I'm almost positive he's still in my house."

Almost positive.

She keeps her eyes locked on the faraway structure. Studying the windows. Somehow she doesn't believe this. The unhinged creature she's tangled with wouldn't allow a witness to escape. He's followed Deek here to her door. No question.

"Sorry. I . . ." He forces a laugh. "I haven't been this scared in years."

She says nothing.

"And I'm so sorry to bother you, Emma. I couldn't just stand around in the rain. I figured I'd take you up on that whiteboard offer. You know? Talk in person, finally. We could maybe have some ginger tea while we wait for the cops to—"

"No," Emma says. "I don't think so."

She won't dare approach the locked door.

"You're not Deek."

"THAT'S FINE," THE VOICE SAYS. "I'LL GET IN ANOTHER WAY."

Emma feels insects crawling on her skin.

It adds: "I can get inside whenever I want."

She grips her knife and watches the door with her breath held tight, bracing for a splintering crash. But nothing happens.

Yet.

Emma's thoughts are thick, sluggish. Her muscles slushy. It all feels like a dream. She forces herself to speak. "Who are you?"

No response.

"How did you find me?"

Nothing.

"Answer me." She takes a step forward. "How did you get my *address*?"

"In a story," the voice answers, "the author is God."

Now that it's no longer imitating her neighbor, the voice seems to have relaxed to a growl. Low, breathy, dispassionate. Emma feels a bead of cold sweat on her eyebrow.

"You already know who I am," it says. "Is there anything you'd like to change about your one-star review?"

Silence.

She should have expected this, but it's jolting all the same. The voice outside is waiting for an answer, and she's deeply unsure. Is this a trick question?

Say something, she thinks.

It's unfair. She was *so* close to leaving tonight. Her Seaview Inn reservations are made. Her toothbrush and clothes are bagged on the table. It's as if the stranger *knew*, somehow, and now he's standing in her way—literally—between her and her car.

He's still waiting for her response, but Emma's thoughts are water. She can't even remember what the hell she wrote, exactly.

Say anything—

"Okay, then," the voice continues, low and measured in its cadence. She can hear a strained smile. "Want to say it again, now that we're here in person? It's too easy to type hateful criticism in the anonymity of the internet. Go ahead. I invite you to open the door and say it to my face."

Nope.

"Please?"

Not a chance.

The door creaks in its frame, startling her. He must be leaning against it. "I always welcome feedback from my readers. Positive and negative alike."

Your book sucked, she wishes she could say. But she can't. She knows better. Maybe there's an invisible trigger somewhere; a razor-fine trip wire that will end the conversation and ignite violence. Like navigating a minefield.

With her thumb, she dials 911 on the phone in her pocket. It will quietly listen in. Emergency operators are trained to stay on the line, right?

A huff outside. "Well?"

She steps forward.

She needs to see the creature's face. To make it real. She approaches the door on her tiptoes. Carefully, with a swollen breath, she presses her face to the peephole and her cheekbone touches clammy wood. Her eyelashes flutter against the lens.

Blackness.

He's holding his finger over the aperture.

She backs away. She speaks clearly for the emergency operator listening in her pocket: "I don't know you. What are you doing at 937 Wave Drive?"

The voice outside says nothing.

Immediately, she worries. Was that too obvious?

"You're a shy girl, aren't you?" After a stomach-clenching silence, the voice softens. "As a sigma male, I've always been drawn to loners. And I liked that about you. Your solitude. Your independence. But you're grieving, too. I can tell. No offense, but you love that golden retriever too much. It's unhealthy."

Leave Laika out of this.

She hates him. She loathes him, this uninvited organism at her door who wears a rubber face and calls himself a sigma male. Whatever the hell that is.

"And now . . . now I'll ask you one last time. Do you stand by your review?"

She says nothing. Maybe there's no correct answer? She hears a sharp crackle outside the door, like paper unfolding.

Of course, she thinks.

Of course he printed my review—

The voice clears its throat, like a stern parent reviewing a report card. *"This was the worst book I have ever read."*

Yes. Now she remembers.

"It's not just crap," he reads. *"It's a giant, fifty-gallon cauldron brimming with ice-cold diarrhea. To any potential readers, I'll save you ninety-nine cents: the hikers both die at the end. I'm not sure if the author has ever encountered a human female before, but at one point he likens their breasts to 'sumo citruses,' a mental image I find viscerally terrifying."*

She had forgotten about that. Still true, though.

"And if you've ever seen a slasher movie, you'll predict every unrealistic trope. Of course the victims have no weapons. Of course there's no cell signal to call police. When one woman finds a truck, of course the engine won't start. When she takes refuge from the magically indestructible killer inside a cabin, of course she stupidly corners herself in a room with no exit. What are the odds of it all? Coincidences happen in real life—but in fiction, they're bad writing."

He pauses.

There's more, she knows. But the voice outside has stopped himself, gathering his composure before continuing. She hears a shaky breath.

"I would rather die than read Murder Mountain *ever again."*
Silence.

When she typed that sentence days ago, she never expected to hear it spoken aloud at her front door. Then a draft of cold air strokes the back of Emma's neck and she remembers with a growing pit in her stomach—the back door is still open. Just a few inches.

Laika is still outside.

"IN ADDITION TO BEING NASTY, YOUR REVIEW ISN'T HELPING anyone." She hears him lean closer to the door. "You know that, right? None of this is valid criticism of *Murder Mountain*. You call these 'unrealistic tropes,' but that's how it really happens. It's true to *real life*, Emma. How can it be unrealistic? You realize how stupid you sound, right?"

She says nothing.

"And the rest is just insults. You're cherry-picking pieces without any context to set up your little jokey-jokes. To invite people to laugh at me."

To laugh at me.

It's subtle, but she heard his voice quiver there. An exposed nerve.

"I mean, obviously I know breasts aren't like sumo citruses. I have a lot of experience with breasts. That was a metaphor. Don't you know what a metaphor is? And it's . . . it's so *grotesquely unfair* that some people will now be discouraged from reading my hundred-thousand-word novel because of your hundred-word review. With two minutes, you get to cancel out a year of my hard work."

From here, Emma can't see the backyard. Her stomach twists into anxious ropes. She hopes Laika is still safely enclosed in the fenced area, not circling the house right now to greet this new stranger.

"So to make it up to me, can you please describe what *things,* specifically, you didn't like about my novel?" The voice is bristling, rising. He's working himself toward a jagged edge.

She steps back.

"Specifically, Emma. What can I do better next time?"

Silence.

The knife is growing slippery in her hand. Her fingers are sweating.

"Answer the question."

She can't. It's too hard to remember.

"Emma?"

"I thought it was . . ." She strains for details. "I thought it was . . . convenient that the two hikers kept splitting up, so they'd be more vulnerable to—"

"People split up in real life."

"And they just die anticlimactically at the end."

"Like real life."

"And one of them even has a chance to grab the villain's gun," Emma remembers. "The serial killer sets his rifle down so he can strangle one, and the other comes up behind him and *doesn't pick it up.* Instead, she fights him hand to hand. The killer should've gotten his head blown off. The only reason the story doesn't end there is because the heroine is a dumbass—"

"*Just. Like. Real. Life.* What part of that is hard to understand?" The voice outside heaves with exasperation. "Emma, it's time to take the red pill. My books are realistic. You can't think clearly in a life-or-death situation because adrenaline overrides logic, okay? It's hormones. It's science. Readers expect characters to always make perfect decisions, one hundred percent of the time. Most average people won't survive an encounter with a killer. Most females, especially. You can't fault me, the author, for being authentic to—"

"I guess it just felt amateur."

He stops, his sentence severed as cleanly as a lopped limb.

She didn't meant to interrupt. She had been grasping for the word in the past few seconds and it finally came. She backs away from the door, keeping her eyes on the brass lock latch.

"I'm sorry," he whispers. "Could you . . . could you repeat that?"

"Repeat what?"

"Just now. What did you call me?"

"I was talking about the—"

"You called me an *amateur*." He forces a laugh, a ragged bark. "Really? That's your insult of choice? Amateur? Can an . . . can an amateur write sixteen novels, tens of thousands of words each? Does an amateur get five-star reviews describing his work as 'terrifying' and 'brilliant'? Do I sound like a fucking amateur, Emma?"

He's trying to laugh, like it's all a misunderstanding. But his words are strained and volatile, shivering with rage. She pats her phone in her pocket to make sure it's still there, still listening—somewhere, an emergency operator must be baffled.

"You thought . . . you thought the characters in *Murder Mountain* were stupid? Well, lucky you. The internet is full of unproven opinions, but tonight you get to prove yours. Let's see if you can do better."

Her spine chills. A slow climb, one vertebra at a time.

On the other side of the door, a long breath. "For what it's worth, I think you'll like this one better."

"What?"

"My next one," he says. "Tonight."

Wind howls over the waves outside. The downpour changes pitch—whipped sideways—and taps the house's sea-facing windows.

"It's all about you," he adds.

A new gritty sound makes her stomach turn. At first it's subtle, like a dentist's pick scraping gently. Then it digs in, hard, rising to a nerve-shredding peak. Alarmingly close. Just outside the door, something plastic snaps free.

Jules's doorbell camera, she realizes.

He's pried it open.

"Emma." His voice curdles with venom. "Welcome to *Murder Beach.*"

PART
TWO

My fans often ask me: "H.G., where do you get your story ideas?"
Easy! Real life.

My horror tales are 100% authentic to reality. All fiction is anchored in truth, after all. And the truth is: the unthinkable can happen to anyone. So I always like to start with a character. A character haunted by her past, let's say, reeling from a personal tragedy. And she can't quite grasp it yet, but she's caught the attention of a monstrous evil.

She knows it's coming. She's already locked her doors, she's called the police, she's taken every step a reasonable person should take as the sun sets.

But the night is long. And dark.

Full of terrors.

And away we go . . .

—H. G. Kane, "Where Do His Spine-Tingling Tales Come From?"
2017, hgkaneofficial.com

8

Excerpt from *Murder Beach*
(Draft 1)

He came to Strand Beach with a singular mission: to murder Emma Carpenter.

He drove a gray Honda CR-V and ate six Wendy's Jr. Bacon Cheeseburgers from the Drive-Thru Value Menu. He listened to a Spotify playlist of Ed Sheeran, Death Cab for Cutie, and Coldplay while driving exactly the speed limit with his fedora on the dashboard, hooked atop a plastic hat rack he'd purchased for $9.99 on Amazon.

His drive had been long and exhausting, the final hour a tedious meander around tidal bays and brackish mudflats. Finally the titular island ghosted into view through a bank of drizzly fog. At the end of a single-lane bridge, a grand concrete arch beckoned: W_LCOME TO STRAND BEACH. Hopefully they'd get that E replaced.

Whenever he visited a new locale for a book—city or town, forest or desert—he always preferred to walk a few miles on foot to get his bearings. Taste the air, read the signs, feed the birds, absorb the local twang. He'd always said that driving through a new place was akin to skimming its Wikipedia article. An author can't know a setting until he's put boots to ground.

Strand Beach was different, though.

He knew the area already. Intimately.

He parked his CR-V in a half-flooded lot near the boardwalk with public restrooms and beach access. If he studied the tide charts carefully, his all-wheel drive would navigate the entire eleven-mile landmass without passing a single traffic camera. Fully independent of the roads. Most vehicles couldn't manage it—which meant the police wouldn't expect it.

While he waited for the rain to subside, he vaped his favorite e-juice flavor—synthetic butter—and he allowed his mind to wander through curls of creamy fumes.

He had been only nine years old when he published his very first book.

Technically.

He often boasted that he'd been writing ever since he could hold a pen, and this was true. His mother still kept all of his stories from as far back as first grade, scribbled on wide-ruled paper in pen, pencil, and crayon. She had even purchased a publishing service for her young son. The company was a sort of vanity press for parents: the kid writes and illustrates a story on a few dozen blueprint sheets, which are then mailed off to some printing press in Hoboken, bound and covered with lushly textured hardcover jackets, and mailed back.

Thus his literary debut was *Propeller Head*. It was twenty-four pages long, including a brief author bio page written by his mother. Only six copies extant.

The story follows a young boy named Harry who faces a slew of problems. On pages 1 through 6, poor Harry is beaten up by playground bullies, mocked by his teacher Ms. Bristol for an unspecified speech impediment, and mugged by a knife-wielding high schooler on his way home. Worst of all, both Harry and his mother are implicitly abused by the boy's unnamed stepfather.

Then on page 7, the tale veers into the surreal. Harry wakes up the next morning with a boat propeller attached to his head. Or rather, in place of his head. His face is wholly gone (the transformation is never explained, nor how exactly he can see without eyes). In his bedroom mirror Harry studies his new biomechanical form, touching his veins of hydraulic fluid, his cranial dome, his curved blades.

The next dozen pages detail Harry's revenge.

First, he scares the playground bullies away with a single meat-grinder twirl. When Ms. Bristol calls him up to answer a difficult question, he lowers his head and saws her desk in half (this illustration is particularly detailed as the teacher's desk explodes into splinters and Harry's classmates duck in terror). On his way home, he encounters his mugger again and shears the high schooler's knife hand off at the wrist (pictured: a screaming teenager clutching a fresh stump spurting Technicolor blood). Interestingly, the text on this page mistakenly names Harry as Howard.

Returning home, he confronts his abusive stepfather once and for all. In a thrilling climax, Harry plows his propeller blades into the man's rib cage and spins as hard as his new form allows, and the gory moment is drawn out over three detailed pages. In the end, Harry's mother hugs him and bakes his favorite cheeseburger casserole in gratitude, while his stepfather remains evenly distributed on the walls and ceiling. A happy ending for all.

Until, in a shocking final-page twist, Harry realizes he can't take the blood-drenched propeller off. Whatever fickle magic engineered this change, it's irreversible.

He is forever Propeller Head.

The end.

Viewed today, *Propeller Head* remains startling in its intelligence. It's bluntly told, certainly, and hampered by a fourth-grader's stilted logic. Still, it's shocking that a child could tell a revenge story with such poise and power. Even the illustrations are evocative and smartly composed (a lesser-known talent of his).

Then and now, it heralds the voice of H. G. Kane in its infancy, a promise of dark and frightening things to come.

To take Emma's life, he'd made preparations.

The downpour finally eased at dusk, so he left

his weaponry in his CR-V and walked the town's main drag to take in the (admittedly lackluster) sights.

. . . A motel with a flooded parking lot.

. . . A DVD rental store.

. . . The tarped-over bones of a burnt-down Thai restaurant.

. . . A family fun center with a rust-eaten Ferris wheel.

Strand Beach is a charming summer destination but a ghost town during the off-season. He crossed the wide street to check in on one of the few businesses that operated year-round: a local free-admission museum called Grundy's. Grundy's specializes in marine artifacts—shark bones, nautical balls, nails from ancient shipwrecks. Washington's coast is often called the "graveyard of the Pacific," and Strand Beach is particularly notorious—flypaper for vessels of all eras. Under the dark tide, modern-day trawlers rest beside the bones of eighteenth-century whaling ships. Something about the shifting sandbars fuels a deadly and unpredictable current, "stranding" the living and dead alike against rock-studded shores. Hence, locals claim, the name. Maybe this is true, but *strand* is also an Irish term for beach—so it's literally named Beach-Beach.

He didn't yet understand why Emma Carpenter chose to isolate herself here, of all places. Nor was he particularly interested. He'd readily admit that nuanced character development has never been a particular strength in his writing.

Throughout Grundy's, he allowed himself to

be recorded on several security cameras as he browsed the new exhibits, studied the kitschy gemstones and dead-eyed marionettes, and fed a few quarters to test his sexiness atop the Love Chair. "Hot stuff," the chair cooed.

On his way out he purchased two items with cash. He smiled chivalrously at the cashier, who wouldn't remember him (his gift: invisibility to attractive women).

He took his paper bag and left.

As the sky darkened, he stopped at the local watering hole, a dive named Rip's with two-dollar beers and a topless mermaid above the bar. He sat alone near the back and ate a four-piece crispy cod and oyster platter with fries, extra tartar sauce, and a calamari appetizer. He washed it down with two twenty-ounce IPAs and a second calamari appetizer for a deep-fried dessert. He loved it here. He was well aware of the security camera on the wall, and even took care to look at it directly while he chewed. A little Easter egg for the cops later.

Downtown was just a short stop. He would set up his true base of operations eleven miles out, by the boulder jetty on the Strand's northernmost edge. He would park his CR-V just under the berm of slick rocks, where his campsite would be near invisible to onlookers from land and sea alike.

Licking fryer grease from his fingers, he opened his brown paper Grundy's bag and studied its contents.

First: a bag of Swedish fish (his favorite candy).

Second: a seashell (every purchase at Grundy's comes with a free seashell).

Third: a pack of barbed fishhooks.

AS EMMA DRAWS HER PHONE FROM HER POCKET, SHE RE- members that lump of suspicious flesh on the beach. The way it seemed to disappear in the days after, the slash it left on Laika's gums as she tugged it away. Not a shard of bone. And—she's now certain—not a coincidence.

This man was trying to kill Laika. With razor-laced meat.

"You *fucker.*"

Her phone screen is idle. Did her 911 call fail? She redials and scans the windows. The blue-tinged LED floodlights have triggered and now cast pin-sharp shadows in the tall grass. But the voice at her front door is gone.

He's vanished.

The man who enthusiastically detailed how the bones fractured inside Psych Major's neck when he took her head as a trophy, who had the audacity to compare breasts to sumo citruses; the self-proclaimed master of horror is here in Strand Beach. He's driven hours or days to get here from an unknown origin. All for her.

She feels a spreading coldness inside herself. As another thunderclap echoes over the ocean, the author's words ring in her mind.

The internet is full of unproven opinions, but tonight you get to prove yours.

That breathy snarl muffled by wood.

Let's see if you can do better.

He didn't expect much of a fight from Emma.

Prior to the night's attack, he'd already spent

days observing his victim, creeping through the vast house at night and sniffing her hair while she slept. He'd mapped the area, drawn his careful plans, and made his own conclusions about the woman herself.

Emma Carpenter's estranged friends and family would certainly describe her more kindly, but in his determination she was damaged goods. Easy prey. A human feeder fish. A lost and tormented shut-in living alone on a deserted coast. He could see how her grief had broken her. He'd noted the crippling social anxiety that pinned her indoors, subsisting on e-books and cold leftovers. She avoided speaking to people at all costs—whether it was whiteboard word games with her neighbor or ordering groceries online. She didn't even dare open the front door for deliveries. She always waited for the driver to leave the drive-way before creeping out to retrieve the parcel like a guilty mouse.

Clearly this woman had suffered an immense loss. Something unimaginable. She still wore her wedding ring, he'd observed, and a ster-ling silver locket around her neck. That locket never left her body. She slept with it. Even when she showered, she kept it within reach. He'd never seen the photo inside, but he was certain he already knew exactly who it was. And after his many evenings of silent surveillance, he'd logged another interesting behavior of Emma's.

Sometimes she filled the upstairs bathtub with water, left a bag of dog food open on the floor, and walked alone to the beach. Right up to the ocean's edge, at least once a day. She'd go ankle-deep. Then knee-deep. Waist-deep. A few feet, maybe a few inches from the undertow's snarling grasp. The Strand Beach current is famously mercurial, a wild animal that's as likely to hurl you back ashore as it is to swallow you forever.

She never quite made it.

Not yet.

He couldn't even fathom what was going on inside her mind. Maybe she'd made a dark game of testing her own limits? Self-preservation is a powerful instinct. Maybe she felt like a passenger inside her own body, fighting to grab the steering wheel and veer the car into oncoming traffic? Maybe that's why she'd packed a green Osprey backpack full of rocks and kept it by the door. A final resort.

Mentioning this now is not to dwell on a poor woman's struggle, nor to speak ill of the dead. Emma Carpenter deserves to rest in peace.

But it told him two critical things in plotting her murder.

First: If left alone, she would likely take her own life soon. Eventually the final string inside her would snap and she would carry that backpack under the rolling waves. It could be a month or a week or sooner. So he could comfortably justify his actions here: in a way, he was only giving Emma what she seemed to wish for. And what exactly was her futureless life worth, by his estimation? She was on the verge of discarding herself into the sea like a paper cup, but he could give her life purpose. Through his talents, he could honor her with the opportunity to play a part in H. G. Kane's legacy, something that would outlive her heartbeat and touch thousands more people than she ever could (or would) in life.

And second?

Well, this one is a little less grand, but no less important: It meant there were no firearms inside the house.

THE MOTION LIGHTS FLICK OFF.

The front yard and driveway go pitch-black. The sudden silent plunge into darkness pulls the air from Emma's lungs.

Beep-beep.

She checks her phone. Her 911 call has failed again.

"Impossible."

The Wi-Fi signal is gone. Keeping her eyes on the darkness outside, she speed walks to the living room and checks Jules's satellite cable modem. The gadget is still plugged in, still powered. A happy green light indicates all is well.

But her phone is disconnected from the Wi-Fi. She retries Jules's password, still clamped to the fridge on a Post-it Note (STEWIE7). Nothing.

What the hell?

Her e-reader is disconnected, too.

And her laptop.

And—presumably—Jules's doorbell camera.

All were connected just minutes ago. What changed? The storm? Internet outage? Like the strained logic of *Murder Mountain,* when Prelaw and Psych, exhausted and afraid, climbed a precarious granite ledge in a doomed attempt to catch cell signal and call for help—

It doesn't matter.

He's just a man. He has no supernatural power.

Emma swipes her car keys from the countertop. Same plan as before: she's not sticking around. She'll stuff Laika in her dented Toyota Corolla and drive like hell straight for downtown, straight for Strand Beach's shoebox-sized police station. She stops at the back door, still ajar, stepping in pooled rainwater leaking inside. "Laika. We're leaving."

The backyard is empty.

Laika is gone.

Her heart drops fifty floors.

A chain link post wobbles in the storm, pushed askew. The retriever must have escaped into the dark grass beyond the sensor's range—"Of *course*"—so Emma hurries down the half-rotten steps into the lawn and whistles a sharp note into the night. "Laika. Recall."

She waits in icy rain. No sign of Space Dog.

"Recall."

Nothing.

She tells herself to stay calm, that she will mentally count to five and then call out again with her preprogrammed command from puppy school, but makes it only to two before gritting her teeth and shouting: "Laika, get your *fucking white ass* back here!"

An abrasive snap of wind answers her. No panting, no scuttling paws in the sand. In the pit of Emma's stomach, centipedes coil. She shimmies through the gap in the fencing and into waist-high grass. She twists her ankle on uneven sand. Raising both hands to her mouth, she screams her dog's name again.

She circles the property, squinting into driving rain. A motion sensor triggers, blasting the dunes with a cone of brightness. Her night vision is instantly scorched away. But she glimpses something—a pale shape—through the wet reeds. Just over the next rise.

She recognizes Laika's white fur. It's always had a shine to it, even in darkness. She blinks, rubbing rainwater from her eyes, blocking the floodlight's glare with her other hand, trying to see more detail.

Her voice stings her throat. "Laika."

The shape is motionless. Head down. Low in the grass.

No, she thinks helplessly.

No, no, no—

He'd been working on Emma's English cream golden retriever for days. It was a slow and halting process, as tedious as zeroing a rifle's scope.

The animal had proven to be an unexpectedly finicky eater, which had kept her alive up to that night. Milk-Bones were too crumbly, and the finest cuts of meat the local grocer had to offer were still somehow no match for rotten crabs, dead jellyfish, and kelp. But then, on the fourth day, her dog had finally succumbed to the siren song of raw chicken breast (although Emma ripped it out of her mouth before the concealed fishhooks did any damage).

Boneless chicken breast.

Four ninety-nine per pound at Strand Beach Grocery.

He'd dialed the animal in. And in truth, those wicked-looking fishhooks from Grundy's were simply too large to be swallowed whole anyway. So he changed his tactics.

He'd pinpointed the delivery mechanism.

He just needed a payload that was smaller, deadlier.

IT FEELS LIKE RUNNING IN QUICKSAND. SHE CAN'T *GET*
there fast enough. Time smears as she screams her dog's name
again. This can't be happening.

Please, God. She can't remember praying since she was a child.

Laika's pale form draws closer through wet blades. Another
motion light triggers—the north now—blinding her again. She
doesn't even bother checking over her shoulder to make sure it's
not the stranger racing up behind her in ambush.

She's nearing Laika.

Ten feet.

Five.

Please-please-please—

She finds her retriever resting on her stomach in the dune
grass, upright and (*oh, thank God*) alive. Emma grasps wet fur,
hitting her knees in the sand. She nearly bowls the animal over,
collapsing into a bracing hug.

"Laika—"

She feels the animal resist, turning rigid in her arms—she's
focused on something in the sand. Licking, chewing with gut-
tural snaps. She's *eating something*—

With fresh terror, Emma wrenches the dog's head backward,
swats aside her *Don't Stop Retrievin'* bandanna, and plunges her
fingers into her mouth—sweeping past Laika's molars—but she's
already swallowing it. Emma clenches her hand into a fist and
plunges it down the animal's throat, grasping inside warm wet-
ness, hoping to God she's not too late—

Her fingers close around something solid.

She rips it out.

Laika coughs again and retches, shrinking away as Emma

holds the cold lump in her palm. She raises it to the house's floodlights, revealing a chunk of slimy flesh. Gray-pink. Raw chicken breast, just like last time.

But this time, it's speckled with bright red dots. Like chicken pox.

With her thumbnail, Emma peels one of the dots out and inspects it, trembling, in the LED glare. It's a pellet. The size of a pill. There are no markings, but somehow she already knows exactly what it is. Years ago, when she worked at a grocery store as a teenager, she'd laid out dozens of black canisters containing these very pellets.

Rodent poison.

9

JUST ONE PELLET CAN BE FATAL.

She remembers the store manager explaining once: *Those little sons of bitches like to eat just one tiny bite of unknown food, then head home for the day. If they feel the slightest bit sick, they'll know it's poison and never touch it again.*

The solution? A nicotine grin, clear in her memory.

Kill 'em with that one tiny bite.

Meanwhile, Laika just tried to inhale the whole goddamn thing like cotton candy. Emma knows the author must be close. H. G. Kane would want to watch and listen, to experience every detail so he can recount it all in his next shitty book. Just like Prelaw and Psych. He's toying with her as he did them, salting his kill with fear.

She hugs Laika. She loves this big innocent creature. Those black eyes regard her with confusion. *I love you, too, Mom.*

But why'd you take my food?

She kisses the top of Laika's head and hopes to God, to whoever's out there, that no poison pellets have made it into her stomach. She'll need to induce vomiting to be certain.

First, she has to escape.

Right now.

She hurls the laced meat out toward the ocean. Gripping Laika's collar, she races back to the driveway where her Corolla is parked. She scans all sides on her way past the garage. Every unknown space she passes, she braces for a waiting figure to lunge out with gloved fingers to her throat, and in the final few steps her heart clenches into a leaden ball inside her chest. But he never appears. She's alone. All tension. No release.

She reaches her car. East-facing floodlights kick on and spotlight her. Before unlocking the doors, she checks the Corolla's shadowed back seats for a crouched killer waiting to slice her throat from behind—she's seen enough movies to know *that* trick.

Empty.

She opens the door. Laika crashes inside with her usual enthusiasm (*I love car rides, Mom!*) as Emma leaps into the driver's seat and jams her key into the ignition.

He'd already disabled her Toyota.

Last night he'd silently popped the hood and snipped both battery cables.

He wasn't a car guy. In daily life, he never even dared to change the oil of his own Honda CR-V. But this is the dirty little secret of the modern fiction author: you're only a Google search away from knowing anything. You needn't be a mechanic to write a scene involving vehicular sabotage or a physicist to write an escape from a supernova. All of that research is out there, ready to be cherry-picked, the hard work already done by someone else. Authors are chameleons. Pretenders. Poseurs.

The frightening result: a villain who can do anything.

That night, Emma's killer wouldn't be limited by his background or his skill set. With a little prep time, he could be whatever he wished to be. He was a dangerous unknown, a Swiss Army Knife, a shapeshifter, the sum of the internet's deepest, darkest knowledge.

How to pick a lock?

How to tie a clove hitch?

How to slice a carotid artery?

How to pass a police polygraph test?

This was his greatest power. As username HGKaneOfficial always liked to say in his online writing group: *In a story, the author is God.*

"OH, *COME ON.*"

She twists the key again and again. Her heartbeat thuds in her eardrums. Laika watches from the back seat.

Mom. What's wrong?

She punches the steering wheel. Rain falls in sheets now, clattering against the Toyota's metal roof, blurring the house lights through glass.

Why are you afraid?

She knows she's wasting valuable time. She tells herself to stay calm, to work the problems. An unseen psychopath. A dog that may or may not have ingested poison. No car, no Wi-Fi, no cell signal. The killer's prep work is immaculate.

But . . .

She remembers the landline phone inside Jules's house. The author may be God, in his own words, but there's no way he can possibly know about this phone because Emma unplugged it herself more than a month ago. Long before she reviewed *Murder Mountain.*

It's still there. In the pantry.

She eyes the front porch through rain-streaked glass. Taking shelter inside is her only option anyway. There's nothing but acres of grass, open beach, and locked cabins in both directions. Still, she considers ditching the dead car and running for help. Deek's house is a quarter mile away. Can she make it?

Her blood chills with déjà vu. She's read this scene before. Exactly this, somehow.

It's how Psych died. After the ranger's truck failed to start, the young woman gave up on the sputtering engine, slid out the door, and fled back for the cabin. She made it halfway before a high-caliber bullet paralyzed her from the waist down.

She remembers how H. G. Kane described Psych's fall—*as if her spinal cord were snipped by invisible scissors*—and the ghoulish fascination as he marinated in the small horrors of her malfunctioning body. The bone fragments on her jacket. The spreading pool of urine. The way she kept dragging her limp lower body on shredded elbows with tears sparkling in her eyes, still begging him to let her go, not yet grasping the permanence of her injury.

She can hear the author's breathy whisper, like he's inside the car with her. Her skin tingles and she checks the back seat again—only Laika's white face.

It's just her and her dog.

She reminds herself to stay calm.

Fleeing on foot isn't an option. He's almost certainly guarding the grassy open space with a firearm. In *Murder Mountain,* the unnamed killer carried a Savage AXIS .30-06 bolt-action with an infrared night scope, lethal to half a mile. Twice the distance to Deek's house. If she tries to escape his perimeter, he'll kill her. No question.

A quarter mile is a death sentence.

But . . . hopefully twenty feet isn't.

"We're running to the house," she whispers. "Get ready."

To Laika. To herself.

Mostly to herself.

She releases the door's lock. She pushes it open with her fingertips and steps outside into the rain. It's a downpour now, rock-hard, loud enough to drown out approaching footsteps. She twists open the back door to let Laika out. No time to be afraid.

She races for the front porch, her palms slicing the air, icy droplets exploding off her shoulders. Laika pounds beside her, panting.

As she runs, she braces for a high-caliber bullet to the lower back.

He shot Emma Carpenter in the spine—

It never comes.

She reaches the porch. Key chain in hand, she fumbles for the slippery lock—"Shit!"—and senses a dark form climbing the cedar steps behind her as she jams the key inside and twists, *twists* with slick fingers and rising dread as his gloved hands reach behind her to clamp onto her throat—but then the door bangs open. She crashes into warmth, into safety. She almost smashes Laika's tail in the door behind her.

She whirls, locking the latch.

Through the peephole, the front steps are empty. Was he really there?

Where *is* he?

Doesn't matter. Getting back inside is a victory. There's safety in close quarters. The night vision rifle from *Murder Mountain* will be cumbersome indoors. She flicks on every light on the main floor, revealing every unknown space—no crouched figure in the coat closet, no deadly ambush behind the kitchen island—and with her wet shoes squealing, she races to the pantry and finds Jules's ancient Trimline telephone sitting on a shelf exactly where she left it weeks ago, still wrapped in its black spiral cord. Untouched.

He's sabotaged her car.

He's blocked her cable modem, her cell signal.

But he can't possibly know about this, Emma's twentieth-century surprise, as she plugs the cord into the wall and mashes 911 on the spongy keypad.

He cut the phone lines, too.

"FUCKING *SERIOUSLY*?" SHE HURLS THE PHONE AT THE wall.

All homes built in the last century are linked with standardized telephone cables, which, courtesy of Google, he understood to be buried twelve to eighteen inches deep alongside the nearest county road (which was obviously Wave Drive, a quarter mile from Emma's front door). All it took was a small shovel and a wire cutter.

Emma was grasping it now. The convenient horror "tropes" for which she'd one-starred *Murder Mountain* were now her inarguable reality.

No gun.

No car.

No phone.

There could be no escape for this story's victim, no lifeline to police or outside help. In *Murder Canyon*, a remote trailhead inaccessible by vehicle. In *Murder Forest*, a campsite unpatrolled by park rangers. In *Murder Lake,* the body of water itself is the barrier.

Tonight was different, though.

Emma had already performed most of *Murder Beach*'s prep work herself. He didn't need to wait weeks for her to take a camping trip or drive across the state alone. She had no family, friends, or meaningful human relationships to complicate the hunt. She'd willingly isolated herself on this rainy island, and he took no chances in severing the few remaining strings that linked Emma to the outside world.

She wanted isolation?

She got it.

By this point in an H. G. Kane novel, the victims are often trembling and sobbing. They're reactive, prey animals without agency. They rarely show grit or determination before they die their lovingly detailed deaths. But Emma Carpenter was different.

In the living room, a flicker of orange light surprised him.

She'd . . . lit a cigarette.

Smoking: the ultimate deal-breaker on the homeowner's waiver. Not that it mattered now, and Emma damn well knew it. No Dollar Tree fan this time. Puffing with a trembling hand, she approached the windows and stared outside through blurry sheets of rainwater. She cupped her fingers to the glass, squinting out into acres of coastal prairie. Searching for her killer.

She scanned left to right, across the tall

grass to the snarling breakers and back, and for just a moment her gaze passed over her concealed killer's form in the grass—something resembling eye contact. For just a split second, by pure accident, she looked directly at the shrouded form of the person who was here to take her life.

Then her gaze moved on.

She had no idea.

SHE KNOWS HE'S OUT THERE.

Somewhere in that sea of waist-high grass, invisible to her.

Staring back at me.

The motion sensors haven't tripped, and in a way the darkness is comforting. It shows a perimeter of safety. For now. With her cigarette in her gritted teeth, she moves to the whiteboard and uncaps a dry-erase marker. HELP, she writes to Deek. CALL 911.

His faraway house is dark, near invisible on the horizon. Only the faint glow of a bedroom lamp in an upper window. The old man is probably in bed, reading or drinking or both. He'd promised to keep an eye out—but it might be hours before he wanders downstairs to check his telescope. If he even remembers to.

"Shit." She hurls her marker.

Two spaceships. Alone in the void.

In the meantime, she's memorized every entry point in the house. She chews on her cigarette and runs down her mental checklist: two locked doors on the main floor, plus two windows that can't be opened. But he—whoever *he* really is—has already entered the house freely. He's the author of tonight's story and he carries every key. She's barricaded the front door with a tipped end table, but it doesn't feel like enough.

She takes a breath.

And lets it out.

She can't help but wonder—how will H. G. Kane write her story in *Murder Beach*? Will he use her real name? How will he describe her appearance, her actions, her personality? Being *seen* makes her skin crawl.

He's outside. Somewhere.

In her right hand she hefts Jules's kitchen knife, getting a feel for the balance. She can stab. She can slash. With some luck tonight, she might still ensure *Murder Beach* is never written at all.

Some serious luck.

For better or worse, Emma knows she possesses two advantages that those poor Appalachian hikers Prelaw and Psych didn't. First, she knows she's in H. G. Kane's book. She understands the motivations of the deranged man outside, at least in some part.

And second?

It hurts to face this, but Emma doesn't mind if she dies tonight. Not fully. Not quite. She's invested, yes, but only in the same mild way she hopes a horror-movie heroine survives the house full of malevolent ghosts. For months, her grief has locked her into a death spiral, a stalled plane in a slow, inexorable glide. But tonight, in a grimly upside-down way, that gives her an edge.

An edge he won't expect.

As she tosses her cigarette in the sink, she thinks: *I'm not afraid of you.*

10

THE BIRD THAT HIT THE WINDOW DAYS AGO IS STARTING TO feel like an omen. It hit the very microsecond she'd clicked to submit her fateful review of H. G. Kane's *Murder Mountain*—a fleshy and startling thud against glass, as if on cue.

Emma doesn't believe in the supernatural.

Usually.

But she remembers sitting on the porch with Shawn four years ago, watching an orange sun rise over the Wasatch Range. Sipping ginger tea in oversize mugs, red-eyed and fuzzy-headed from last night's Halloween party. She still had black Catwoman eyeliner gooped on her eyelids. They'd discussed kids before, sometimes in jest, sometimes approaching sincerity, always softened with *if* and *when* and *maybe*. But this time, on this clear and cold morning, her husband rubbed his hair, mussed from sleeping in his Batman cowl, took a long sip of his steaming tea, and spoke plainly.

I want kids, he said. *With you.*

Let's make a family, Em.

To this, she can't remember what she said—if she'd agreed or joked or said nothing at all—but she remembers how she felt. In the end, you'll remember feelings more than words, and in that moment, as hungover Batman and Catwoman watching the sun rise on a blistered front porch, her heart felt like it would swell out of her chest.

That's when it happened.

A gruesome *thud* on the window directly between them, and gray-brown feathers wafted over the deck. The precision in its timing felt deliberate, like that suicidal little finch knew exactly what lay ahead for Emma and Shawn. Years of trying and failing to conceive. The sympathetic doctors. The chalky-tasting vitamins. The empty baby room. The ovulation tracker with the stupid pink flower petals. The arguments. The aching, vacuous *uncertainty,* the future held hostage by the present. The nights of telling him her stomach hurt so she could cry privately on the toilet. Even in the moment, they'd recognized the eeriness with nervous laughter.

Hope that wasn't a sign, Shawn had said.

She can't remember if they buried the dead finch in the backyard, but she hopes they did. And here on the Strand, years later, after that (larger and more colorful) coastal bird slammed meatily into Jules's window, she'd taken care to bury it in the backyard by the firepit. The handbook on the windowsill had identified the dead bird as a *red-breasted sapsucker,* native to the Washington coast.

But this was also a troubling revelation, because of H. G. Kane's words that very day. His bizarre response online; some bullshit non sequitur about *little sapsuckers like you.*

Sapsucker.

The bird that died at her window. Just minutes prior.

Since that day, Emma had assured herself it was just a coincidence, that the author's insult had aligned perfectly with an unrelated incident he should have no knowledge of. But tonight, maybe she knows better. H. G. Kane has been toying with her, hinting—in his own devilish way—that he's closer than she realizes. That he commands an omniscient power. That she's trapped in his story, where not even a sapsucker falls without his knowing.

Her stomach swirls. It should be impossible.

And she can't lose her grip on reality. Not now.

But . . . how else could he *know*?

SHE NEEDS TO KNOW WHAT THE CREATURE OUTSIDE LOOKS like.

What gear he's brought. What weaponry he's carrying. She needs to see his *face,* without a mask, to make him something human.

The blackness outside is as solid as painted concrete, impenetrable. Standing at the window, she's aware of how exposed she is to gunfire. But, she reminds herself, guns aren't the preferred tools of H. G. Kane. In *Murder Mountain,* the villain fired his rifle only when the hikers were on the verge of escape. Maybe guns aren't gory enough, or maybe they kill too quickly. Either way, Emma can use this against him.

Walking room to room, she switches off every light and lamp on the main floor. She hopes the killer is surprised by this. Then she returns to the living room window and waits in silence, letting her pupils adjust to the low light.

For this, she needs darkness.

"Let's see what you are."

She presses the Polaroid—Jules's vintage camera, snatched from the bookshelf—flat to the glass. She thumbs the flash shutter button halfway and waits for the green light. Then she presses hard, a satisfying *click-crunch.*

The camera blasts an X-ray of light. A freeze-frame of raindrops captured mid-fall, a chain link fence, and farther out, the sandy trail's edge. Then blackness again, and the afterimage lingers in her eyes like a negative.

No sign of him.

The instant photo drops out of the camera and slaps to the floor at her feet. Laika whimpers beside her, as if sensing the tension.

"It's okay," she lies.

She tiptoes to the next window. Again, she holds the shutter button halfway, waits for the green light, and snaps another photo. Another vivid flash pierces the darkness. She sees Jules's muddy lawn, overgrown rhododendrons, and acres of yellow dune grass beyond. Another bright blizzard of paused raindrops.

No intruder.

"Where *are* you?"

He's been a step ahead of her for days. He's anticipated her moves with unsettling precision. In a novel, the author may very well be God.

But in the real world, Emma is confident God doesn't exist. It's just a man out there.

Right?

Right. Another photo slaps to the hardwood at her feet. Laika sniffs it.

Maybe he's just trying to scare me. Maybe he's giving up and leaving—

No. She won't dare hope for that. H. G. Kane didn't drive all the way to Washington to teach her a cautionary lesson about writing mean-spirited reviews.

Last window.

Laika whines with dread.

"Come on." Emma presses the camera flat against the glass. She presses the flash shutter button a final time, trying not to consider other possibilities (*what if he's already inside the house?*), and before igniting the darkness she can't help but imagine illuminating the author's face just inches from hers behind the glass, every detail exposed in IMAX clarity. Eye to eye with her own murderer, a heartbeat before he punches a gloved fist through the glass and grabs her windpipe.

Click-crunch. A seizure of bright light.

In the frozen microsecond, Emma can see the space in front of her is clear, the planters are clear, the empty firepit is clear, the old chairs are—

There he is.

Her chest tightens. The details are already gone, the imprint fading from her retinas, but she knows what she saw, what she's photographed: a crouched figure.

"Found you."

He's closer than she expected. If Jules's motion sensors have a detection range of thirty feet, he's exactly one foot farther. It's unsettling how confidently he's mapped the home's defenses. He understands precisely how close he can creep without—

The photo lands at her feet, startling her.

It'll take a few minutes to develop. She kneels to grab it, and with her free hand she charges and snaps again—*click-crunch*—illuminating the grass outside.

The figure is gone.

"Shit."

But she refuses to betray her frustration. She knows she needs to lock herself and Laika in a defensible room, to prepare for the attack she knows is coming. But first she has to say one final thing to the lurker outside. He seems to have learned every nuance of her solitary life, every weakness, every private inch of her. But she's been paying attention, too.

She breathes into the window, fogging the glass. Then with her index finger, she traces one word in reversed letters:

AMATEUR

PLEASE DON'T KILL ME, she wrote on the glass.

   PLEASE

Watching the terrified woman beg for her own life pleased him. Inside that glass house, Emma Carpenter was starting to understand the reality of her situation, that by barricading the front and back doors she'd only managed to buy herself time. A handful of minutes and seconds. He'd find another way inside, or he'd make one. He'd wriggle through the crawl space like a fleshy python or scale the drainpipe.

Begging wouldn't save her.

Or her dog.

"COME ON, LAIKA."

With her knife in hand, she tugs the animal upstairs into Jules's master bedroom and shuts the door behind them. No lock. Still, this is the safest room in the house. There's only one entry point—this door—which can be blocked. And two possible escape routes: a second-story window and a laundry chute leading downstairs. If she has to, Emma is mostly certain she can fit her malnourished ass through it.

Mostly.

With her free hand, she shakes her photograph—a plasticky *whap-whap-whap*—but the image is still developing. Too murky to see the killer.

Laika whines with fear.

"It's okay," Emma whispers. "It's fine—"

Lights trigger outside. He's within thirty feet of the house, coming from the west. Emma races to the bedroom window and swipes the curtains aside, hoping to catch a glimpse—but the backyard goes dark again. She hears a strange *click,* sharp and percussive. Like a golf club striking a ball, followed by a gentle sprinkle of falling glass.

The light is out.

She crouches by the windowsill, feeling exposed again. She can't place the sound—what the hell was that? It wasn't a gunshot. The report was too hollow, too oddly muffled.

Laika sits rigidly with her ears perked.

Mom. What was that?

"I don't know."

Then another blaze of light, this time to the north. Another motion sensor is tripped. And then—another bony *click*—darkness again.

Laika whimpers.

He's shooting the lights out one by one. Savoring his power over her. But with what? It's far too quiet to be a gun, unless he has a silencer. In *Murder Mountain,* H. G. Kane didn't bother with stealth because he didn't need to. As isolated as Emma is on the Strand, there's still one neighbor close enough to hear a gunshot.

But . . . these unearthly clicks seem too quiet even for silenced gunfire. Movies lie about silencers; a gunshot is still a controlled explosion. You can't mute physics. Unless H. G. Kane really is magic? Unless this is his story and his rules—

Don't lose it, Emma.

Not now.

Anticipation is worse than reality, Shawn always used to remind her while she pored over her lesson plans at night. She could never improvise like other teachers. She wrote a script and memorized it. Even her jokes were rehearsed. If Ms. Carpenter wasn't the worst math teacher in Utah, she had to be the shyest.

Stop overthinking. Anticipation is always worse than reality.

Always.

Maybe tonight she'll finally prove her husband wrong. In her hand, the Polaroid photograph has finally developed, its image sharpened into detail.

She sees him.

Emma's photograph is now famous.

In the shivery terror of the moment, she couldn't possibly have known that her Polaroid, half-focused and snapped through a window beaded with raindrops, would someday be seen by millions. Although many (bloodier) photographs of the ensuing murder scene in the living room have circulated the web's darker fringes, Emma's is the iconic image of the Strand Beach massacre. At the time of this writing, it has appeared in *Newsweek,* the *Washington Post,* and the *New York Times*. It's rare for a victim to capture a snapshot of her own killer, and that's certainly part of its mystique. It speaks from beyond the grave.

It's an undeniably haunting image, and a prelude to the horrors that made that December night famous: the amputations, the asphyxiations, the impalements, the gunshots. And, as readers are well aware, it would herald the imminent deaths of four people.

Including Emma herself.

HIS FACE IS UNMASKED.

His exposed skin has a strange pallor, as if waterlogged. His eyeglasses reflect the bright camera flash. This corpse-like visage stares back at her from the moment she snapped the photo, his expression impossible to read. He wears a trench coat glistening with rain, black gloves, black cargo pants, and a rimmed fedora. An incongruous mismatch of styles and times: the hat of a 1930s newsman and the shiny leather of *Hellraiser* wrapped around the clammy gray flesh of a raw oyster. This figure is freeze-framed crouching in the tall grass, looking almost oafish, like a pervert caught outside a child's window.

The dark fedora is familiar. She recognizes the hat's rimmed outline from his very first appearance in her bedroom. She really *had* seen him. All along. She can't make out any weapons in his gloved hands, but something hangs suspiciously at his waist. *Is that a gun? Is that what he's shooting out the lights with?*

Too dim. Too blurry.

She shakes the photo again—*whap-whap*—and squints closer. It's not a rifle—or at least, it's no rifle she's seen in any movie. It's a slender black shape, catching a crescent of reflected light, held just under his right hand. It's a strangely dignified pose, fey and delicate. Like a cane or an umbrella—but it's neither of those, either. She has one guess, which she immediately dismisses. That would be impossible.

Behind her, Laika whines again. *Mom*—

"Quiet," she hisses, shaking the photo harder. She needs to know more.

Whap-whap.

No use. The film is fully developed. She squints again, trying to decode the bizarre shape at the pale man's side, yet all she has is her first thought, the one too nightmarish to believe. That it looks like he's *carrying a*—

Laika cries again, an earsplitting pitch, and vomits a warm splash on hardwood. Emma turns and recognizes another slab of pale flesh. A chewed chicken breast, identical to the one she dug out of the retriever's throat with her fingernail just minutes ago.

Disbelief—*there was more than one?*—becomes horror.

There was more than one.

She hasn't saved Laika's life after all. With trembling fingers she lifts the glob and searches for those telltale red pellets embedded in the meat. She finds one. Two. And a few more floating in syrupy bile, *which means . . .*

"Oh, no."

More are still in Laika's stomach. Right now.

A fatal dose.

LAIKA'S NAME HAS A DARK SIDE.

It's often overlooked, but 1957's first dog in space didn't actually survive her world-famous journey. Shawn had been shocked to learn this.

Wait. Really?

Yes, really. History's first canine cosmonaut died within hours of launch due to a mechanical failure. The poor animal burned to death inside the metal capsule of Sputnik 2, which would continue to orbit the earth for another five months with Laika's body still inside it.

Shawn had sighed. *Wow. That's . . . truly awful.*

But wait, there's more! Those asshole scientists never even planned for Laika to return home. It was always meant to be a suicide mission. Laika's rocket-powered coffin was stocked with seven days' worth of dog food to be automatically dispensed, with the final day's meal laced with poison. Of course, they screwed it up and broiled her to death on day one.

You sure do love to ruin a sweet moment, Em.

At this, she smiled.

It's what I do.

"SHIT." SHE PUNCHES THE FLOOR. "SHIT, *SHIT*."

Those black eyes watch her.

Sorry, Mom.

Outside, the east floodlight triggers. Then, with another spine-tingling *click*—darkness again. He's circling the house. Emma clasps her hands to her temples and tries to think, to cut through the distractions and *focus*. She needs to make Laika vomit now, immediately, before the pellets dissolve in her stomach. Just making her gag won't be enough. It needs to be a full-on purge. She has minutes, or maybe less. Maybe it's already too late? How long ago did she eat it?

I ate a bad thing, Mom.

She grips the sides of Laika's face. "You dumbass."

Hydrogen peroxide? Yes. She used it a few nights ago to clean Laika's slashed gums. Peroxide is the fastest way to induce vomiting. Right now. Before the author breaks inside. She knows she's running out of time.

Dying tonight?

Fine.

Having her death immortalized in a shitty e-book?

Also fine.

Letting Laika die, too?

Fucking *unacceptable*.

She stands up. She knows what she needs to do. She knows there's a bottle of hydrogen peroxide under the kitchen sink downstairs, exactly where she left it. She can envision it now: brown bottle, white cap. She opens the bedroom door and peers down the hall.

Perfect darkness.

She glances back one last time to Laika's white face as the fourth and final motion light shatters outside with a piercing *click*.

"I *will* save you."

11

SHE DESCENDS THE STAIRS.

The main floor is laid out like a dark diorama. Raindrops rattle against glass and shingle. The temperature down here seems to have dropped.

Kitchen, her mind whispers. *Under the sink.*

She tiptoes toward it.

On her way there, she scans the windows to her left. It feels like the house is plunging underwater, already miles below the surface and still dropping. Millions of gallons of frigid seawater on all sides. Pressure rising. Her nightmare brought to life.

He's not there.

She remembers to breathe. There's a light switch somewhere to her right, but she knows she must preserve her night vision at all costs. She guides herself along the wood-paneled wall, past the ticking grandfather clock, feeling with an outstretched palm. Rounding the corner, entering the kitchen, she braces for gloved fingers to grasp her throat.

Nothing.

The kitchen is pitch-black. He might be standing directly in front of her. She takes another step forward—an explosive, jangling clatter. Her heart leaps, but she already knows exactly what it is. Laika's metal food bowl.

"Jesus." She steps over it.

No way he didn't hear that.

Upstairs, Laika barks. She's heard it, too—or maybe she's feeling the first painful cramps as the poison enters her bloodstream? Emma doesn't know how many minutes or seconds are left. It all depends on the type of poison in play. Anticoagulant? Arsenic? Bromethalin? She considers trying to bargain with the psychopath. *You can do whatever you want to me, but please promise you'll drive my dog to the veterinarian afterward?*

Not happening.

She reaches for the light switch but reconsiders—those kitchen fluorescents will be a beacon in the dark house. They'll be the brightest thing for miles. He'll close in on her immediately. If she fails to deliver the peroxide to Laika upstairs, all is lost.

Emma can die *after*.

Not *before*.

Her hip bumps into the kitchen island—almost there—and then she guides herself along the counter's edge toward the sink. She finds the cabinet underneath, where she remembers returning the peroxide bottle. Through the window, she scans the darkness outside. Still no trace of the author—but on the horizon, she can see Deek's house. His bedroom light is still on. It's barely past eight, and he's surely still awake. Drunk, but awake.

Please, she thinks. *Please check your telescope.*

She studies the warm glow in her neighbor's window for a moment longer, grateful for another spaceship in the night.

But she can't afford to wait. Every second counts.

She tries not to think about the unknown weapon she photographed at the attacker's waist outside. It shouldn't be, it *can't* be, but it is—she's certain he was carrying a sword. A medieval sword, three feet of curved steel, as poised and deadly as the samurai warrior's blade depicted on that strange poster in the teenager's bedroom Emma fears to enter.

Come to think of it . . . the curved swords might even be an exact match. As if brought to life from that stylized poster. What are the odds? It's a bizarre coincidence, deeply unsettling, and Emma fears she's losing her mind.

Coincidences are fine in real life.

But in fiction?

Bad writing.

SHE OPENS THE CABINET DOORS UNDER THE KITCHEN SINK. They squeak on corroded hinges, excruciatingly loud. Saving Space Dog is all that matters.

"Come on. Come on—"

She pulls out a trash bin. Dish detergent. Hand soap. Drain cleaner—

Laika whines upstairs. A heartbreaking cry.

"Where is it?"

She keeps pulling out more and more, hurling useless objects aside—bug spray, garbage bags, mop pads, a miniature fire extinguisher, more crap than she can ever remember seeing stored under Jules's sink, until the dark space is emptied.

No hydrogen peroxide at all.

It's *gone.*

But she's certain she left it there. Just days ago, after cleaning Laika's cut with antiseptic, she stored the bottle under the sink. *Am I misremembering?* As panic rises within her, she fears the author outside has anticipated this too, somehow, that she's trapped in the shifting rules of H. G. Kane's *Murder Beach*—

In the living room, a window shatters.

12

To this day, there is vigorous debate as to how exactly he managed to shatter reinforced glass with such speed and ease. Engineers and glass-makers have asserted that even a sword as finely forged as his limited-edition Thaitsuki Tonbo Sanmai Katana (his now-infamous calling card) should have taken several bludgeoning strikes to weaken the glass's integrity. Some conspiracy theorists like to cite this as evidence that a second killer was involved, or that the Strand Beach authorities were somehow remiss in their management of the crime scene. Sadly, Emma Carpenter herself is deceased and unable to comment. That leaves me. And you're reading this book, dearest readers, because you want the truth. You can find speculation anywhere. Take it from the man who was literally there.

He didn't strike the glass. That's what the armchair CSI agents don't understand.

He *impaled* it.

A driving, two-handed thrust delivered from

an impressive core of physical strength. Thousands of newtons of kinetic energy concentrated into a single pointed tip just molecules wide. A panel of the living room's sea-facing windows, six feet by twelve, disintegrated instantly. A waterfall of shards crashed to the flowerbeds at his feet.

Then he climbed inside.

Crushing a windowsill of jagged glass teeth beneath his latex-gloved palm, he vaulted up onto the home's main floor. At two hundred and sixty-eight pounds he was hefty but undeniably powerful, and capable of feats of catlike agility. This maneuver didn't even wind him. His tactical boots landed on glass fragments—crunch, crunch—and he searched the dark interior for the woman he was here to murder.

On his way inside, he kicked aside a coffee table. Emma's e-reader hit the floor and a glass nautical ball shattered. He was aflame with adrenaline, his skin flushed hot, his heart slamming. This was the blood rush before the kill, the climax of many days of methodical buildup. He'd studied his victim's solitary habits and had drawn his plans. He'd dug up phone lines with a garden shovel and packed poison pellets into raw chicken breasts. And just like him, his readers had eaten their vegetables—the stage setting, the backstory, the character development—and would now be rewarded for their patience. Finally, for reader and writer alike, the action could commence.

The grisly *good* stuff.

The guts. The screams and sinew. The money shots.

He inhaled the room's air. A familiar cocktail of scents: stale blankets, dog fur, mothballs, and the subtle odor of Emma herself. He knew it all.

Above, he heard skittering movement. He recognized this, too—Emma's golden retriever was in the upstairs bedroom, pacing and crying with gopher poison in her stomach. He knew his victim wasn't up there, though.

Emma was in the kitchen.

He crept deeper into the house—his footsteps quieting on a bearskin rug—with his katana at the ready. He gripped the sword's battle-wrapped handle (the tsuka) in an arched pose, edge out. This was a textbook display of the versatile ch□dan-no-kamae stance. The katana, as he knew, is among the most fatal armaments ever conceived, a cutting instrument capable of severing muscle, tendon, and ligament in a split second. A single slice can dwarf the damage of most high-caliber gunshots, and even when wielded by an amateur, a katana can easily amputate a human limb or head.

He was no amateur.

This weapon's nightmarish power is difficult to overstate. It is also, perhaps, difficult to fully convey to readers who have never held one. But one of his all-time favorite jokes might help, as often quoted by username HGKaneOfficial in his online writing critique group:

Two samurai warriors sit around a campfire and argue over who is the finer swordsman. The first samurai sees a housefly buzz
past and decides to settle the argument.
He slashes his katana in a sudden blur, bisecting the insect in midair.

"See?" he says. "Can you do that?"

The second samurai acknowledges that
the feat is indeed impressive. And when a
second fly appears, he wields his own katana
as well.

The fly buzzes past, seemingly unharmed.

The first samurai laughs. "You missed."

"No," the second insists. "I didn't."

"But your fly is still alive!"

"That's true," the second says. "But he
will never have children."

Now his tactical boots clicked on tile.

He'd reached the kitchen.

The dark room was empty. No trace of Emma. He
stood still, dripping with rainwater, and listened for creaks, whimpers, or even a heartbeat.
His hearing had always been acute, bordering on
the supernatural. His childhood doctor once told
him he had "golden ears," another blessing for a
human apex predator.

Still, he heard nothing.

Not even a breath.

From where he stood, he could see the entire
room—the row of barstools, the stainless-steel
fridge and electric stove, the hastily searched

cabinets under the sink, and six feet away, in the room's exact center, the kitchen island.

EMMA IS CROUCHED BEHIND IT.

Rigidly still, with her back pressed to the wood cabinet.

Don't breathe.

She knows he's standing in the room with her. Just six feet away. She can't see him, but she can hear his huffing breaths, still winded from climbing through the shattered window. His panting is hoarse. Raking. Animalistic. Rainwater drips off his clothes and taps tile. She hears the shriek of wet boots as he takes another step forward.

She clasps a hand over her mouth.

Don't you dare breathe.

But she can't hold it any longer. It's going to explode out of her chest. She feels it bubbling up her throat, unstoppable. She's thinking about Laika, poor innocent Laika, waiting upstairs with poison in her stomach while Emma hides in the kitchen with a sword-wielding psychopath standing just feet away—

Another wet footstep. Closer.

How could he have known about the hydrogen peroxide? Did he foresee this exact situation and steal the bottle during one of his nighttime infiltrations? Did he write it out of existence? H. G. Kane is *cheating,* somehow.

She hears his sword rise—a whisper of sliced air. It seems to slip between molecules. Then an earsplitting crash, and she flinches (*don't gasp, he'll hear you*) as ceramic shards scatter across the floor. One piece lands beside her. On it, a bulging black eyeball. RIP to Jules's Chihuahua Stewie.

She struggles to focus. She's seconds away from passing out or exhaling an involuntary gasp, and either way, he'll hear her and raise his sword and—

Work the problem. She tries to pin her thoughts down, like wriggling snakes.

If I die here, so does Laika—

Jules's wine bottle drops, too, with a wet shatter. A tendril of red liquid inches past Emma's right ankle. Silently, she lifts her shoe away from it.

He's playing, tipping things off the counter with his sword. Like a school shooter wandering a locked-down campus, searching for stragglers to kill, amusing himself with small acts of destruction. Or maybe he's smarter than that. Maybe he's trying to startle Emma into gasping, into revealing herself—

Stay calm.

She can't. She can't breathe. She's cornered. And Laika is going to die upstairs—

Focus.

She clasps a palm to her mouth, parts her lips, and quietly exhales through gritted teeth. Letting her lungs depressurize, muffled by her fingers. Every muscle in her chest is taut. Equalizing pressure is a slow and agonizing process.

With a rain-soaked killer standing just *feet* away. Listening for her.

Finally it's over. Her lungs are empty.

Good. Now inhale.

Upstairs, Laika whines a pained yelp, and Emma's thoughts race frantically again: *What if it's already too late? What if my efforts are in vain and Laika is already dying—*

A shrill grinding screech. It seems to fill her brain, crowding out every other thought. He's running his blade edge along the stainless-steel fridge now. Jules's magnets drop to the floor, click-clattering like loose teeth—

Stay calm.

His boot lands beside her hand. Almost stepping on her fingers.

Silence.

He's stopped there. Right around the island's edge, towering above her. Over the grape odor of the wine, she can smell his breath. Mtn Dew. Stale body odor. And something else, dense and overwhelming in its strange clarity, dwarfing all others . . . the scent of *butter*?

If he looks down, she knows, *he'll see me.*

Even in darkness, she can see his boot with perfect clarity. The black laces, double-knotted. The treads crusted with gritty sand, slivers of wet grass. Slowly she draws her hand away.

She waits with ice-cold sweat on her skin.

But her stomach hardens into a cast-iron ball as she realizes he's not searching anymore. He's found her already, somehow, homing in with a strange animal cunning. He's about to peer over the countertop and raise his sword. It's all over.

He knows where I am.

Behind the island counter.

He sensed Emma was crouched against it, just inches away. He had a preternatural sort of aware-ness, a gift for anticipating the movements of his prey. The front door was blocked by a tipped end table. No tertiary rooms to cut through. He'd searched the living and dining rooms. By elimi-nation, he'd pinpointed her here.

He sidestepped the kitchen island, raising both arms for a cleaving downward strike. With such force, the katana's carbon steel edge would slice through the soft flesh of the crouched woman's shoulder, bisecting her collarbone, ampu-tating every nerve and tendon to her right arm, and driving all the way down to her ribs.

 Instead, his blade swished through empty space
 and dug into a cabinet door.

EMMA CRAWLS AROUND THE ISLAND.

Go. Go. Go—

Behind her, a huffed grunt. "I see you—"

And a hoarse wooden scrape—*he's tugging his sword free*—as Emma scrambles into a sprint. Through the living room, rounding a corner and climbing the stairs two steps at a time. His thick voice howls after her: "I *see* you, Emma—"

From the kitchen, a thunderous crash—ripping his sword out must have torn the cabinet door off its hinges. He's frighteningly strong. And he's following her—*I see you*—stomping through the living room now. But Emma is too quick. She's already upstairs.

She crashes through the bedroom door, bruising an elbow. Whirling, slamming the door shut, still wishing for a damn lock. Inside, Laika turns to face her.

Mom. You're back.

No time. She can hear the author's tactical boots climbing the stairs after her now, brittle rising creaks. Carrying that horrific steel sword.

Down the hallway.

To the door.

Her heart flutters: the *unlocked* bedroom door.

The heaviest furniture nearby is an oak armoire stuffed with Jules's summer clothes. A hundred pounds, at least. Emma wraps her arms around it in a frantic bear hug and rocks it, one ancient leg to the other, tipping the monstrous thing toward the door, but she's already too late. To her horror, the doorknob turns.

The door opens—

As the armoire crashes down against it.

The vanity mirror shatters on its way down, spilling razor-sharp shards to the floor. Emma steps back from the improvised barricade, her heart slamming in her chest. Watching the doorknob rattle furiously. Blocked.

Backing away, she grabs Laika in a bracing hug.

"I love you."

Then she grips the animal's throat vise-tight, and in her other hand, she raises the object she snatched from the kitchen countertop: a clear glass saltshaker. She thumbs off the cap.

"Sorry, Space Dog—"

As she pours it down Laika's throat. All of it. The retriever struggles, gagging, sputtering, but Emma forces most of it down. H. G. Kane may have removed hydrogen peroxide from tonight's story, but he overlooked salt. A few tablespoons of cooking salt can induce vomiting in a dog almost as surely as peroxide, and she's force-fed Laika at least half the shaker.

So . . . bombs away.

Laika coughs, licking her lips. *Mom. What the hell?*

Behind her, the door bashes inward. A violent jolt; the shock rattles Emma's teeth. The author is brute-forcing his way inside, and he's even stronger than she feared—Jules's hundred-pound armoire scrapes impossibly across hardwood, and Emma's heart hitches with terror as the bedroom door inches open anyway—

Then the armoire thuds against the bed.

Definitely blocked.

She allows herself to breathe again. It comes out as a gasp. Gripping Laika's white fur with her knuckles, she listens as he jostles the bedroom door one last time before giving up. The doorknob jangles a final time, released.

Then silence.

Outside, the wind growls.

Laika whimpers again—with that aching bellyful of salt, she's going to detonate any minute—but Emma holds her close, listening for the man's footsteps in the hall outside. The rustle of his trench coat. The swish of his bizarre sword. Any sign of what he's doing next.

She hears nothing.

It's like he's evaporated. And in the growing silence, something else rises to the surface in her mind. The intruder's smell. That strange and oily odor that radiated off him in the kitchen. She's certain she's smelled this same odor in the house before, ever since she first arrived on the Strand, weeks before she one-starred *Murder Mountain*. Weeks before she summoned H. G. Kane to this isolated coast. It's impossible. She can't trust her own memory. She can't trust time.

Like the dead bird at her window, this alien figure controls it all.

In a story, the author is God.

13

EMMA BACKS AWAY FROM THE BEDROOM DOOR, AFRAID TO take her eyes off it, bracing for another crash. She tugs Laika into the bathroom, past the dual vanity sinks, past her own disheartening reflection. She looks thinner and weaker than ever.

There's nowhere to retreat further, so she crouches in the slippery bathtub. Watching the door. One palm gripping the porcelain edge. The phrase *having your back to the wall* has a negative connotation, but she remembers Shawn once admitting that he'd gone most of his life thinking it was a positive statement. When your back is against a wall, he'd reasoned, nothing can attack you from behind. You have a ruthless clarity: whatever you're up against, you'll see it coming.

Here, now, crouched in a stranger's bathtub with her golden retriever and a kitchen knife in her trembling hand, Emma Carpenter is literally in this position, her back to a wall.

"Shawn," she whispers, "I can't do this."

Yes, you can.

She tries to picture her husband's face, but even her own memory fights her. Her thoughts are liquid, impossible to hold on to.

"I miss you."

I miss you, too.

So much.

It's okay. I'll meet you there, Em.

There it is. A single sentence. Four words that joined their lives.

I'll meet you there.

If only.

She's still straining to remember the nuances in her husband's face, the scent of his hair, the timbre of his voice. But she can recall every inch of his model railroad layout.

You can do it.

Yes, she can draw it all from memory. The figure-eight track crossing over itself with a truss bridge. An outer oval loop follows the perimeter, encircling a town of immaculately detailed buildings—*Farwell,* Shawn named it, after his grandfather's hometown—nestled in the shadow of a five-foot plaster mountain. Even in one one-hundred-and-sixtieth scale, it's a towering landmass that climbs the basement wall, cloaked with pines and lichen foliage.

I know you can do it. I believe in you.

Painting the mountain's plaster-mold rock faces was fun. Emma honestly loved it. There were no lines to follow, like the fussy little storefronts Shawn slaved over with a magnifying glass. Natural scenery is more about instinct. You let the paint fill the plaster crevices on its own accord, first charcoal gray and then lighter colors like yellow ocher. (*Don't forget a touch of burnt umber, too, as the rock oxidizes.*)

But then came the hard part: gluing those painted rock outcroppings into place on the mountain's slopes. It's harder than it sounds. The rock molds can't look *glued on;* they have to feel like they've been buried under the soil all along and are only now exposed by erosion. It's a delicate trick, burying something that isn't buried at all, and the eye knows the difference.

You can do it, Em. He was making trees as he said this, a shake-and-bake assembly line.

I don't think I can.

This was a major gesture of her husband's trust. If you screw up a tree or even a building, you can just scrap it and make another. But the rock faces are an integral piece of the layout. Create an eyesore, and it's there forever.

I shouldn't. I don't know what I'm doing. She held out a hand. *Let me make some trees.*

Trust yourself.

No. I'm going to mess it up.

She could tell how much he *wanted* her to do it, and that just broke her heart all the more. Finally Shawn said: *If you build the mountain, you can name it.*

She thought. *Anything I want?*

Anything.

You're sure?

Call it whatever you want.

This gave her a small rush, being invited to participate in the fiction. Maybe it's why she's always loved to read and why she vanished so utterly into her books after the funeral. There's joy in it. Every last detail is handcrafted.

Every inch.

Every building, clump of foliage, and convincing (or unconvincing) rock face.

Okay, she decided. *I'll do it.*

And she did. Without doubt, without fear. That evening, Shawn ran an inaugural locomotive and a few boxcars while they held hands and sipped wine, watching the small train wind through and around the majestic plaster slopes of Mount Buttfuck.

He snorted Cabernet in his lap. *Really, Em?*

You said anything.

SHE LISTENS FOR THE KILLER BUT HEARS NOTHING.

She can't tell if he's downstairs or if he's left the house or if he's waiting just outside the bedroom door. The silence builds. She can feel her pulse in her throat.

Emma isn't a religious person, but she can't help wondering if it's a coincidence that the author first appeared in a mouthless horned mask.

A demon.

Maybe she's already done it—slipped her green Osprey backpack over her shoulders and walked out into the rolling waves. Maybe she's ten feet underwater right now, with those straps gripping her shoulders in a fatal embrace as icy seawater bloats her lungs. Maybe her recurring nightmare of drowning is actually *real life,* and everything else has only been the fever dream of death, the last oxygen-starved synapses in her brain exploding like Deek's fireworks. Maybe the devil has come to the Strand to collect her soul personally. Maybe centuries of biblical imagery are wrong and Satan carries a sword and wears a stupid-looking fedora. Who's to say?

She grips the bathtub, knuckles white with the strain. Stares at the door.

Anticipation is worse than reality.

Trust yourself.

"I'm not dead," she whispers. "Not yet."

Because Emma Carpenter is now dead, it's impossible to determine exactly what she was thinking while she took refuge inside the barricaded second-floor bedroom with her dog. Her mind had to be racing. She'd narrowly survived his attack downstairs. Escaping the kitchen was a victory, albeit a lucky one.

He wasn't concerned.

Not remotely. He knew every inch of the house. Every variable was under his thumb. He would simply press his advantage and attack her again from a new angle. And the time was only 8:51 P.M.— she'd survived barely an hour.

He had all night.

Under the kitchen fluorescents, he quickly checked his sword for damage. As powerful as the katana is, it's also famously fragile if misused. Those Hollywood sword fights where the hero's and the villain's blades parry and clack are pure fiction. Real samurai were slavishly careful with their armaments, as anything tougher than human flesh risks chipping the brittle steel—or even shattering it. He wiped away rainwater with his sleeve (rust is another foe), and before leaving the kitchen, he peeled Emma's cigarette butt out of the sink and licked it. This was the closest he'd gotten—thus far—to tasting the woman's lips.

And it saved his life.

If he hadn't, he wouldn't have noticed the light outside.

A STRANGE GLOW SHINES THROUGH THE FROSTED GLASS over the bathtub, as startling as a flying saucer landing on the front lawn. At first Emma can't believe it's real. With her free hand she slides the tiny window open. It scrapes only a few inches, and it faces south, away from the unknown light. But she can listen.

Ice-cold rainwater leaks inside as the glow slowly brightens, shadows bending through the tall grass as the light source moves. *Headlights.*

She hears gravel crunch under tires. The whine of brakes. This new vehicle is parking in the driveway just in front of the house, out of her view. She waits with a breath swollen in her chest, crouched under the bathroom window with Laika in her arms.

A car door creaks open.

It slams shut.

A voice booms: "POLICE."

Yes!

She collapses into the tub, exhaling hard. Yes, this confirms it. Deek stayed awake to keep watch, just as he promised, and he saw her whiteboard message and called 911 exactly as she asked, thank God, *thank God—*

She hears motion outside—a slithering rustle of wet grass. Panicked footsteps. The author has exited the house and he's now running, but not fast enough—

"HEY."

The footsteps halt.

"YES, YOU. DON'T MOVE."

Silence.

Emma feels an evil grin sting her cheeks. It's almost hilarious how sharply the night has turned against H. G. Kane. Belly laughs convulse up her throat, but she fights them. She knows the danger hasn't passed yet. Not even close.

The police are here—but the author is a ruthless dog-killer. His attack has been premeditated for days. He's planned everything, and surely he's planned for this.

"LIE DOWN," the officer commands. "OR I SHOOT."

He sounds young and nervous, and he should be. H. G. Kane might be only feigning surrender, letting the poor rookie in close before a surprise slash to the carotid. Or a bloody decapitation. That's how it would unfold in an H. G. Kane novel. It sits in Emma's stomach like an ulcer; she can't trust this new development. *It can't possibly be this easy.*

Can it?

Silence.

She tilts her head toward the window, holds her breath, and listens—until finally she hears knees on gravel. The sound of kneeling. Compliance.

"GOOD." The officer sounds relieved, too. "HANDS BE-HIND YOUR BACK."

Just like that.

It's all happened so fast. In an instant, H. G. Kane is mortal again and stripped of all magic and mystery—just a human man with a sword, now belly-down with a cop's knee pressed to his back. They got him. It's over.

Deek, *for the win.*

Calming now, Laika looks up at her. Black eyes lock onto hers.

"You did good," Emma sighs.

I love you, Mom.

"I love you, too, Space Dog."

Then the retriever stiffens in her arms and unhinges her jaw in a gurgling belch—

"Oh." She forgot. "Oh, *shit*—"

It happens. All over her lap.

Emma breathes through her teeth and stares up at the bathroom ceiling, ignoring the eye-watering odor as Laika empties her stomach. Despite herself, despite everything, sitting in a stranger's bathtub with dog puke all over her lap, Emma begins to chuckle again. Giddy, stupid laughter. She's fended off her killer. She's saved Laika's life. And now with armed authorities arriving on-scene, H. G. Kane is captured with handcuffs biting into his wrists. He can't possibly write his way out of this.

"Thank you, Deek," she whispers. "Thank you."

When she sees the old man again, she'll bear-hug him, squeeze his bony little shoulders until they snap. They'll have coffee or tea in person. She'll *talk* to him, for real, face-to-face. No more whiteboards. No more excuses. And Emma is realizing something else, a new sensation that brings a fresh wave of exhausted tears to her eyes: for the first time in months, the thought of a day after this one excites her. She wants to see what happens next.

She *wants* a tomorrow.

With shivering teeth, she cranes her neck up to the window and shouts one more thing outside to the man who calls himself H. G. Kane, now in police custody.

"Have fun writing this chapter, *asshole*."

14

He drove his knee into the man's spine, forcing him prone into the wet gravel. He'd given his most convincing police voice. Deep. Authoritative.

And it worked.

The delivery driver complied immediately, dropping to his knees and surrendering to the commanding voice behind him.

Thirty-one-year-old Jake Stanford was a lifelong Washington resident, father of two, and a FedEx employee of three years. His surviving family describe the former Navy truck driver as a natural go-getter; a jack-of-all-trades who was as comfortable deep-sea sturgeon fishing as he was volunteering at Grundy's annual canned food drive. Tragically, Jake's single infraction against company policy that evening, during the final stop on his route, likely contributed to his capture. While delivering parcels on foot, Jake would often switch from phone speakers to his Bluetooth earbuds to avoid breaking rhythm

in his music, and this likely dulled his situa-
tional awareness. He didn't hear the footsteps
behind him—only the voice.

By the time Jake realized that voice was only
impersonating a police officer, he was already
prone on the driveway, unable to fight back. The
katana was already raising for a fatal thrust—
until the carbon steel glinted with a bright new
light source.

Thirty feet away, the house's front door had
opened.

Emma's voice.

"Stop."

THERE HE STANDS.

Spotlighted by the delivery van's headlights, towering over
his new hostage in the downpour. It shouldn't be possible. He's
cheated again, *somehow,* and all of Emma's hard-fought confi-
dence has drained out of her body. It's wrenching, hollowing.

The pale visage of H. G. Kane is finally in clear view.

His face is freckled and stubbled with curly ginger neckbeard. His cheeks are plump, boyish, hanging over fleshy jowls.
His mouth is a small and dirty-looking orifice, as puckered as
an asshole. Behind his fedora, she can see the author's red hair
is worn long and greasy. He must be at least six-three and two
hundred and fifty pounds, oversize in a clumsy and sad way. His
trench coat is pulled taut to contain his cauldron belly. His cargo
pants bulge in odd places. None of his clothes fit quite right.

She expected Jason Voorhees. She got a life-size Chucky doll.
Somehow, this is *still* worse.

His victim, a young man in a FedEx uniform, writhes under the sword's edge and cranes his neck to look up at her with

wide eyes. This makes the danger real in a way Emma can't describe—up until now, H. G. Kane has been her private demon.

This is really happening.

Her stomach heaves.

"Let him go." She doesn't recognize her own voice. "This is between us."

The wind growls between them.

He glances at her, then down to his hostage. He can end a human life with a single thrust. His glasses shine with reflected light, rendering his eyes unreadable. Like glowing canine irises. Slowly he points a black-gloved hand at Emma's kitchen knife.

This is a clear message: *Drop it.*

The FedEx driver shakes his head—"Wait, don't"—as Emma underhands the knife into the dark yard. She knows it's useless here.

"Good girl," the figure says.

Good girl. Like praising a puppy.

Then, with his other hand, he reaches into his trench coat and pulls out a semiautomatic pistol. Emma's gut stirs with horror at the sight of it. Like a tumor in an X-ray, like a motionless body inside a wrecked car, it's Bad News concentrated to its purest form. And strangely, the firearm seems to be rattling, vibrating in the killer's grip.

He's trying to fight it.

But his hand is trembling.

His hand was perfectly still.

His nerves were stone-steady. His veins ran with ice water. He had adapted to the delivery driver's unexpected arrival, dominating Jake Stanford in seconds. He was a sociopath in the

truest sense, a clean-burning machine unfet-
tered by empathy.

With this new development, his plans had
changed dramatically.

He was on the Strand to murder one person,
and now it would be two. Stressful as it was,
in his view it was also worthwhile to supple-
ment the body count of *Murder Beach*. Username
HGKaneOfficial often mused that fiction was in its
own way sociopathic, a created world where some
deaths matter and some really don't. Did anyone
truly care when the gun store owner got blown
away by Arnie in the opening act of *The Termi-
nator*? No, he'd reason, because we're invested
only in Sarah Connor and Kyle Reese, characters
with names. As readers and viewers, we're stin-
gier with our empathy than we'd like to admit,
and that December night, a young father of two
died on his knees to serve a supporting role in
someone else's story.

He studied Emma in the bright headlights.

He couldn't help but admire her.

HIS LIPS CURL INTO A FLESHY GRIN.

Again, Emma feels insects crawling on her skin.

"You talk in your sleep," he says. "You said a name while
you tossed and turned in your bed. The same name, over and
over."

She braces for it.

"*Shawn.*"

It hits her like buckshot to the heart. Her husband's name

feels obscene, violated, coming from those hairy lips. He has no right. Still she says nothing, unblinking.

The chubby smile grows. "Shawn's dead, huh?"

Fuck you, she thinks.

"In your locket." He points at her neck. "I bet there's a picture of him?"

Fuck-you-fuck-you-fuck-you—

"Grieving widow, living alone in a beach house? Bit of a cliché, honestly."

You don't know me, she thinks.

You only think you do—

"You might be surprised," he says abruptly.

This startles her. She can almost feel his dirty fingernails inside her brain, picking through her thoughts. She takes a breath. "Who are you?"

"The devil."

"Who are you really?"

"I'm here to do what you've been trying to do for months, Emma." He cocks his head and his hairy throat flesh jiggles, oddly birdlike. "I'm actually here to *help* you, strange as it sounds. I know why you're here. I know what you're struggling with. I saw your backpack by the door, all loaded up with rocks."

In her peripheral vision, Emma senses new light.

It's coming from Deek's house. If the old man is in his living room, he might check his telescope. Or—better yet—he might be watching the standoff right now. She keeps the light at the edge of her vision. She can't tilt her head. If the author sees it, too, he might panic and execute his hostage.

Don't look at it.

The FedEx driver noticed it, too. Her chest flutters with panic as he cranes his neck—

"*Hey,*" the author snarls, shockingly loud: "Don't look up. Don't look at my face." He slashes in reflex, his wrist barely seeming to move, the sword not making a sound at all—but the hostage cries out in blood-curdling pain. Emma grips her locket in a tight fist just below her collarbone. She has to squeeze something.

"Look down." He jams his pistol into the back of the man's neck and twists hard, a cruel screwdriver motion. "Don't look at me. Do you understand?"

The hostage nods, clutching his ear. From here, Emma can't see the injury. Blood runs between his trembling fingers and mixes pink with rainwater. For some reason his blood doesn't look exactly real to her. None of this feels real. How can H. G. Kane know her so intimately?

In a story, the author is God.

Or the devil.

She notices the FedEx driver's right hand is slowly moving, unseen by the author. She tries not to look directly at it, either, or he'll notice—but she follows the man's hand across wet gravel. His palm rests atop a decorative stone marking the driveway's edge. His bloody fingers clasp around it, spiderlike.

A weapon.

Emma locks eyes with him. *No,* she wants to whisper.

But he tightens his grip on the rock. She shakes her head now, keeping her motions small. A desperate, unspoken plea: *Please, wait. You have no idea how dangerous this man is.*

The driver acknowledges her stare. But he keeps the rock.

Emma knows the standoff is about to boil over. H. G. Kane won't allow any witnesses to leave tonight—especially if he's afraid of being identified without his demon mask. This leaves only one potential way forward. It's a risky one.

Deep breath.

"You can kill me," she tells the author. "But let him go."

He says nothing.

She steps forward, keeping her eyes locked on his through the pouring waterfall created by the overloaded gutter. "He hasn't seen your face." She glances to the hostage. "Right?"

Silence.

"Right?"

Weakly, the man nods. His earlobe nods, too, half-severed.

"And he doesn't know your name. Or why you're here."

He nods again.

"This is between us." Emma reaches the porch's edge. The gutter's waterfall crashes down on her now, ice-cold on her skin, pooling in her sunken clavicles. She fights a shiver in her voice: *"You and me.* So please, let him go."

He admired her attempt to bargain for Jake Stanford's life, but there was simply no room to negotiate. The situation had escalated with this new development, and greatly accelerated his own time frame. He knew he already had hours of forensic evidence to tidy up. He would need to fry Emma's phone, her e-reader, and her laptop. He would need to wipe down every fingerprint and bleach every surface for stray hairs, skin cells, or fibers. To say nothing of the secrets within the walls of the house itself. There could be no living witnesses to his now-infamous Strand Beach massacre.

No deals.

He wouldn't allow a soul to leave alive.

"DEAL," THE AUTHOR TELLS HER. "I'LL LET HIM GO."

Emma releases a trapped breath.

Too easy.

"You're right." He flashes a doughy, vulgar smile. "It's all about you."

She says nothing.

He's lying.

Something is wrong, as wrong as a dislocated limb. She can't take him at his word. His words are worse than meaningless. In the silence, she stares back at his unreadable glasses and braces for violence. She knows it's coming. She knows he's about to do *something* to the innocent man before her eyes, just to prove he can, that H. G. Kane is in full control of her nightmare.

Nothing happens.

Instead, the human Chucky doll stuffs his pistol into his trench coat and steps back, still grinning, and—true to his word—gives his hostage space to stand up.

What the hell?

The FedEx driver—his uniform soaked and stained with blood—pushes himself upright into a sitting position, still clutching his ear, still afraid to stand. Afraid to leave. He's as shaken and deeply confused as Emma is.

"Run," she hisses to him. "Please, run."

Before he changes his mind.

Even still, she's certain the author is lying. He's playing cruel games, savoring his power over them. Why would he allow a witness to leave? His smile is fading now, darkening, turning like rotten mayonnaise. "I wanted to save you, Emma."

Silence.

She hesitates. "W . . . What?"

"I wanted to save you." He waits expectantly, maybe even desperately, as if giving her a chance to express gratitude. "He told me I had to kill you. And I stood up for you—"

Her mouth instantly dries. *"Who?"*

The author stops himself. As if realizing he's said too much.

"Who told you to kill me?"

He tips his fedora at her. A chivalrous gesture: *M'lady.*

"Answer me."

Still smirking, he glances out at the windswept grass and the breakers beyond. As if he's soliciting the permission of someone unseen, someone watching.

She turns, too.

It's too dark to see. Just rain and wind.

He told me I had to kill you.

With her spine tingling, she remembers Demon Face in Jules's night vision camera. Every time she's seen H. G. Kane thus far, he's worn that fedora. But Demon Face wore no such hat—and he had a lighter coat, like a windbreaker. What if there are two intruders out there?

A twin brother?

A cowriter?

A crazed fan?

"Tell me," Emma hisses. "Who *else* is out there?"

Before the author can answer, she notices the kneeling FedEx driver has shifted his weight forward. His eyes hardening. His jaw setting. His muscles tensing.

He's made up his mind.

No.

She screams—too late—as he swings his rock at H. G. Kane's face.

To say he was a skilled swordsman would be a gross understatement.

Outside of his prolific writing, he lived and breathed by the blade. His apartment walls were a library of Japanese and Chinese combat swords carefully mounted on brackets. A Global Gear Makaze. A Hanwei Practical Pro. On the shelf beside his gaming PC's ultrawide monitors sat a wicked Cheness Cutlery Kaze. In the bathroom above his toilet, a small but deadly tantō dagger encased in glass (to keep out moisture).

And on the bedroom wall over his king-size mattress, within arm's reach in the event of a home invasion, was his pride and joy: the now-infamous twenty-eight-inch Thaitsuki Tonbo San-mai Katana. He owned rarer and finer swords, but this one held special value. His mother bought it for him as a gift on his eighteenth birthday to celebrate his first self-published novel. Accordingly, it was the blade he chose to carry on the night of the Strand Beach massacre.

Aching for its first "blooding."

Four years earlier, he'd uploaded the most popular video on his (now demonetized and defunct) YouTube channel HGKANEOfficial. Prior to his profile's deletion, the video had garnered more than two million views. He'd tried many times to replicate its success.

At one minute and fifty-eight seconds, the recording shows him filling a two-liter Mtn Dew Code Red bottle with water from the hose and placing it upright atop a black card table. The setting: nondescript suburbia. There's a garage door with peeling paint in the background. The sky is hard blue. Somewhere far away a lawn mower rumbles. Somewhere much closer, a dog yaps incessantly, crackling the microphone.

"Shut up, rat."

He's always hated his mother's nervous little dogs.

In this video he's two years younger, his chin freshly shaved with ginger stubble. He wears a black T-shirt featuring Pepe the Frog, khaki cargo shorts, and New Balance sandals with black socks. And of course, his wool felt fedora—a chic testament to his strength and unwillingness to take no for an answer.

He leans offscreen—ensuring the iPhone is filming—and then he stands in the foreground beside the two-liter Mtn Dew bottle.

He says nothing.

He only stares into the camera, squinting in the afternoon sun. His right hand slides down to his hip, to the black saya hanging at his waist, which most viewers do not notice until now. His thumb pops the katana's hilt collar a few centimeters free with a wooden click. He glances left, then right. Choosing his moment.

He waits.

So must we.

A passenger jet passes overhead. The faraway lawn mower changes pitch.

Somehow we're still not ready for it when it happens. A blur, a glint of white-hot sunlight, a hiss of friction. By the time the sound has registered on-camera, he's already completed the motion and he's smoothly twirling his katana back into its battle-wrapped saya. To his right, as if blasted by an offscreen bullet, the two-liter Mtn Dew bottle explodes in half, two diagonal pieces sliding apart with clean-cut edges.

He looks back at the camera as water dribbles

off the table. He doesn't smile. The sun is in his eyes anyway.

In the distance, the neighbor's lawn mower ceases. So, too, does the small dog's barking. Just a coincidence, but this creates a strange stillness, an expectant gulf of negative space, as he reaches for his sheathed weapon again. He performs the same maneuver for us, perhaps even faster—the glint, the blur, a bony crack—and again, the blade is back at his waist. A viewer might wonder if his stroke hit anything at all. The Mtn Dew bottle's plastic halves tremble in shock, but remain untouched on the table.

The last of the water finally trickles away.

Airy silence.

Then the card table itself falls apart. Each bisected half topples on two legs, landing in the grass. The dog resumes yapping and the far-away lawn mower starts up again, but he keeps staring into the camera with his right palm over his lacquered wood scabbard, resting delicately, almost lovingly, on the terrible power carried there.

Offscreen, someone claps. This individual is never identified.

Now, finally, he grins.

THE BLADE MOVES TOO FAST FOR EMMA TO DISCERN. SHE sees nothing but its effect. The man's right hand—swinging the clutched rock—twirls away freely. Then another piece of him flies off. Another. He flutters apart with every razor stroke and

Emma can feel every near-silent cut in her bones. A human body is dismantled by whispers.

She staggers back inside the house.

Missing a step. She falls.

She kicks the front door shut behind her and screams into the floor.

15

SHE HAS SEEN ONLY ONE PERSON DIE BEFORE.

Five months ago.

It wrecked her. It built a great wall in her life between Before and After. She'd considered herself desensitized by witnessing thousands of fictional deaths, but somehow this made her even less prepared for the real thing. And now this—what just happened in the driveway—is gut-wrenching in its speed and precision and near silence.

Get up.

She's in the kitchen now. On her elbows. She can't remember crawling here. Her phone is in her right hand. She checks it again, praying for a different answer.

Get up, Em. Right now.

As she pushes herself upright from the tile, something thuds loudly against the kitchen window. She cries out in shock. It sounds like that dead bird from days ago—but it's heavier, damp and oddly fleshy, hurled from the darkness beyond.

It left a smear on the glass. Red butterfly wings.

Ignore it.

She twists her head away, nauseated. Nothing can be done for him now. And something else—she hears it echo from the night, a human male voice but warped over open space. A strange raw scream. No syllables, no melody. The piercing intensity of it brings tears to her eyes. She can't imagine the poor man still being alive, nor what kind of agony he must be in, nor how much longer he'll feel it.

The man's scream goes on and on.

Ignore it. It's just a distraction—

Until she realizes it doesn't belong to the slaughtered FedEx driver at all. He's already dead. And in the cry, she detects a new emotion with rising clarity.

Rage.

The author isn't used to collateral damage. Maybe he was being honest after all, and he didn't wish to kill anyone else. His novels are controlled scenarios, small stages immaculately managed for slasher and victim to dance their dance. When he describes tonight's events in *Murder Beach,* he'll probably lie and pretend he was pleased to kill more than he intended and increase the night's body count. But she knows the truth—H. G. Kane screwed up.

He'll be even more dangerous now.

More than ever, Emma misses the stars. She wishes she could see through the rain clouds and be assured that Aries and Gemini and Messier 31 are still out there. Even the constellations will wander and drift apart, if you could live long enough to see it happen.

Even the stars will die.

This has always made her feel like that panic-stricken high schooler again, retreating into the cube-like walls of a restroom that smells like bleach, the only space in which she feels safe. Where the hidden eyes can't see her, where no classmates will speak to her. Where she can quietly die and rot in peace. Because someday even the universe will be a boneyard, and as Immortal Shawn knows, there are fates far worse than nonexistence.

She's starting to grasp it now: the true depth of what she's up against tonight. She's known it in her soul for hours. This isn't a surprise, and it shouldn't jolt her.

It was all real.

Psych paralyzed by a bullet to the spine. Prelaw's intestines unraveling from her belly. A human head kept in a duffel bag. A novel Emma herself had so casually one-starred days ago, and from the comfort of her reading sofa, judged to be *unrealistic*. All as chillingly real as the rodent poison Laika vomited, as the unidentified piece of a human body that just hit the kitchen window. Real murders. Real, innocent people reduced to meat for his designs.

So *many* of them.

She tries to remember, her thoughts thickening with another wave of paralyzing horror—how many books has H. G. Kane self-published?

Sixteen.

His first murder was a high school classmate named Laura Birch.

No H. G. Kane novel was written to tell the tale of Laura's death. It was too raw, too personal, and his own emotions were too tangled up in it.

He'd been friends with Laura since junior high. They shared two classes and a homeroom. On Fridays they'd stay after school for game club, where they played Magic: The Gathering, Pandemic, and Settlers of Catan. On weekends, they sometimes met at the local museum (the closest thing the small town had to a youth hangout). Their relationship never became romantic, despite his best efforts.

Laura was a bright girl, tall and blond with a shy smile. She was a Math Olympiad star whose SAT scores fast-tracked her for a prestigious college out of state. Her parents recalled her particular fascination with her AP Government class that year, and her expressed interest in being a lawyer or lobbyist in the battle to address climate change.

He loved her.

For years, one way or another, he loved her.

He'd shared his own aspirations and shown Laura his writings before—fragmented short stories, soggy attempts at poetry, even an incomplete graphic novel about modern-day samurai—but his junior year was a turning point. He'd just completed his first "real" novel. And it was a decided improvement over *Propeller Head*.

Titled *Semiautomatic,* the 110,000-word opus centered on a school shooting at Montana Valley High, a barely concealed facsimile of their own Monsanto Valley High. All through the admittedly overlong novel, the main character—a quiet, intelligent, and frequently bullied boy named Henry—attempts to stop an unnamed classmate's bloody rampage with an AR-15. Instead of hiding under a table, Henry follows the shooter as he stalks room by room through the evacuating campus, waiting for his moment to heroically intervene. As he does, Henry observes the shooter's rage is focused on a half-dozen classmates for specific grievances. Each flashback-heavy chapter is titled by a target's name, many with real-life parallels (the laziest being algebra teacher Mr. Carlson recast as Mr. Karlson).

Eventually, a plot twist: Henry and the school shooter are the same person. Henry is his own mortified conscience.

And Laura Birch had an alter ego, too—creatively named Liza, whose cardinal sin is cheating on Henry—and during the climactic Liza chapter inside the bullet-riddled library, Henry/the shooter heroically lowers his AR-15 and chooses to spare the girl's life. This is treated as a moment of redemption. "I may be a monster," Henry monologues as the SWAT team closes in, "but you all abandoned me and attacked me and ignored me. Today's blood is on everyone's hands." It ends with an ambiguous gunshot. Did Henry kill himself? Did the police gun him down?

His always supportive mother was excited to read his first full-length novel.

He refused.

Instead, he printed *Semiautomatic* on double-sided paper (like a proper book), bound it with brass brads, and presented it to Laura one Friday afternoon on the bus ride home from game club. She accepted the bulging manuscript and agreed to read it.

He gave her the weekend.

Then the rest of the week.

A month passed.

He noticed Laura seemed to be avoiding him. She stopped speaking to him. She also stopped attending game club, ostensibly to focus on her homework. It's unknown how much of *Semiautomatic* she actually read, or if she even made it past the first page. It's probable she considered notifying law enforcement but felt conflicted about doing so.

Finally, on Wednesday, November 9, 2011, he confronted Laura one rainy afternoon on her long walk home from the school bus stop. He'd been waiting on tenterhooks, he'd opened his heart to her, he'd shared dark and vulnerable parts of himself. He followed her down the long prairie road and asked her to get into his mother's black Lincoln. Maybe it was his friendly offer of a ride. Maybe it was his begging or his cajoling or his threatening. In the end, it doesn't matter which tactic finally worked.

She got in.

No one ever saw Laura Birch again.

Her disappearance rocked the school, stymied local law enforcement, and set the small community on edge. There were no witnesses. No classmates or family Laura had confided in. The manuscript was never recovered. He spoke to detectives on several occasions, feeding them just enough information about Laura to seem helpful. In truth, he was probably much more of a suspect than he realized at the time. It was well known by his classmates that he'd nurtured a crush on Laura and that it was almost certainly unrequited. For a few nerve-racking days, an arrest felt all but certain.

But Christmas break came and went.

Then midwinter.

Then spring.

At last, the dog days of summer.

He was starting to feel invincible. Soon it was his senior year, Laura Birch's disappearance was still unsolved, and rumor had it someone on her Math Olympiad team had spoken to Laura in a chat room and she'd claimed to be in Mexico living with a new boyfriend. He had exactly nothing to do with this, but it was a helpful red herring. Although thousands of people go missing every year, when it's a pretty white girl with a scholarship, it takes considerably longer for the embers to burn out. But that year they finally did, and he was on top of the world. His college applications had been yielding promising returns, and to his mother's delight, he'd been accepted into prestigious Caltech.

As much as he'd dreamed of being an author like his idol, his mother insisted he pick a steadier occupation first. Being naturally gifted with numbers, he learned to write software code. Within a year of graduating from college he was gainfully employed and could afford any swords, airsoft guns, or video games he wished for. Still, he never gave up on his true passion, toiling away at his horror novels on mornings, evenings, and weekends.

He wasn't especially proud of *Semiautomatic*—in fact, his adolescent work embarrassed him now—but he would never rewrite it. He didn't believe in rewriting.

Meanwhile inside his childhood home, unbeknownst to his mother, he kept a secret decade-old stash. Inside the cavity of a hollow wall behind a poster, he kept thirty-six grisly Polaroid photographs, a lock of Laura's hair, a clear pillbox containing her teeth and earrings, and the long knife he used to dismember Laura's body before he dumped her in the sea piece by piece—a twelve-inch Japanese wakizashi sword.

Wrapped in plastic.

Pitted with rust.

Still browned with Laura's dried blood.

DEEK IS AWAKE.

Thank God.

Even without magnification, Emma can see her neighbor's tiny figure backing away from his own living room window a quarter mile off, mortified, bumping a stack of his own books and nearly falling. He's witnessed everything.

Now he scrambles to his feet.

"Go," she hisses. "Call police."

And across his crowded living room, disappearing from one window and reappearing in another, past a closet door and bumping it open—

"Go, go, *go*—"

The tiny man rips the corded receiver off his wall. Behind him, the door opens—Emma's heart flutters with alarm—but it's still swinging from when he bumped it. Revealing darkness inside; a barely visible mass of sunken cardboard boxes and musty hanging coats. H. G. Kane can't possibly be hiding inside there, but it still grips her stomach; a dire certainty that something dangerous lurks just out of view.

Gripping his phone, with his back to the open door, Deek mashes keys.

Nine.

One.

One.

SHE WATCHES HIM SCREAM SILENTLY INTO HIS PHONE. HE checks the plug, then redials once, twice, before hurling it across his living room. A mountain of dog-eared binders topples over. She knew it was too good to be true.

It's soul-crushing, all the same.

CUT MY PHONE, he writes on his whiteboard.

Join the club.

He writes more: EMMA, YOU NEED TO RUN

If only.

That sword may be H. G. Kane's primary weapon, but he carries a gun, too. As reluctant as he may be to fire it, the instant she runs into the open dunes, she'll give him no choice. At least Prelaw had trees and boulders to hide behind—this far up the Strand, there's no cover at all. Just acres of waist-high grass.

Deek is wrong. Running is *not* an option. It's ten miles to town, and even if she survives the long trek—even if the author miraculously misses with every round in his magazine, and she outruns him—she'll still be leaving Laika behind in the bedroom upstairs. He'll return to the house furious. He'll find Laika. And with no other means to resolve *Murder Beach,* he'll score the last cruel point he can.

You love that golden retriever too much, he'd lectured her.

It's unhealthy.

But . . . she remembers the silver revolver Deek has always kept mounted above his fireplace. Now would be a hell of a good time to dust it off. In her neighbor's view, she points and makes a gun with her thumb and index finger. *Bang?*

He shakes his head.

NO BULLETS

"Of course."

All too good to be true. The night is only beginning. And worrying unknowns scratch at the back of her mind. The author's next words to her, seconds before he butchered an innocent man: *I wanted to save you.*

He told me I had to kill you.

The wind growls outside. The storm is intensifying.

Maybe H. G. Kane is a pen name shared by multiple writers? One might write the books, while the other commits the atrocities. If so, which one has she met? Which one is Demon Face? Maybe he has a twin brother, and there's always been two life-size Chucky dolls stalking her from the tall grass outside.

The most troubling possibility she keeps buried within herself. She tries not to even consider it. Because she's already concluded Deek is too small to be Demon Face. The figure photographed by Jules's doorbell camera several nights ago was too big, too barrel-chested to be the frail old man in a rubber mask.

Right?

Right?

She hopes to God she can trust her Hangman buddy. Right now, Deacon Cowl might be her last friend alive on earth—a man whose voice she's never even heard.

WHERE IS HE?

THE GREEN DRY-ERASE MARKER TREMBLES IN HER HAND AS she writes. She's barely looking at the whiteboard; her eyes scan the darkness outside. Then she leans to her telescope, still aimed at Deek's window. Pressing her face to the eye cup makes her feel achingly vulnerable. She hates sacrificing her peripheral vision.

In the curved glass, she finds Deek. He swivels his own telescope to scan left, then right. A long sweep, searching the grass. This worries her.

Where the hell is he?

The hairs on her arms prickle. She checks over her own shoulder—nothing in the room with her. Just the wind and the downpour, clearly audible through the broken window.

The *broken window.*

Moving fast, Emma tips her reading sofa over and pushes it—gasping with exertion—to block the empty window frame. The bearskin rug bunches up underneath. It's more an inconvenience than an obstacle. When the author attacks again, he'll easily push it aside. But this will make noise. Emma will hear it. She'll know where the attack is coming from and she'll have a few seconds to act.

It's a razor-thin advantage, but it's something.

In the faraway window, she can see Deek has paused his search. He grabs his marker.

GARAGE, he writes.

Somehow it's scarier to know only the author's general area. Like he's immaterial, omniscient. She wonders how he'll describe the night's events in *Murder Beach*. Will he cast himself as a perfect, infallible predator? Will he gloss over Emma's small victories?

Now Deek points left.

BACKYARD

He's moving. Circling the house.

Emma hates communicating like this, but it's the only option left. The killer can read a whiteboard, too. He might already be eavesdropping.

She senses the author's motives have changed. The stakes have escalated. The dead FedEx driver will soon be reported missing. H. G. Kane is operating on a ticking clock now and he's probing the house for another entry point, deciding on his next angle of attack. This means that right now, while he's focused on Emma, is Deek's best chance to escape. Once he realizes there's another witness involved (if he hasn't already), he'll be forced to kill again.

TAKE YOUR JEEP, she writes to her neighbor. DRIVE, GET HELP.

He'd already ensured both vehicles were disabled.

SHE ERASES AND WRITES: RUN ON FOOT.

Emma had to know that an unarmed arthritic man in his mid-sixties couldn't possibly outrun a killer through a quagmire of wet sand and thick grass. To say nothing of the simple geographic problem posed by the Strand itself—the town and whatever few summer homes were still occupied in late December were all to the south.

Any direct route of escape would cut directly past Emma's house, through his sights.

"DAMN IT." SHE FORGOT ABOUT THAT.

But . . . there are homes north of Deek's, too. A few dozen farther up the beach, toward the rocky seawall. She knows the cabins are all unoccupied, yes. But still useful.

She erases—again—and writes: RUN NORTH, BREAK INTO A HOUSE, USE PHONE.

Not an option.

When he dug up the neighborhood's phone lines buried beside Wave Drive, he'd been unable to tell which black cable served Emma's house. They were unmarked and seemed to splice together in a way that his preliminary Google research hadn't prepared him for. So he made the decision

to cut them all, cleanly severing landline communication with every single residence to the
north—

"FUCK." **SHE WANTS TO THROW HER MARKER. RUNNING IN**
any direction is too risky, and Deek won't stand a chance if he's
spotted.

The old man has written a new message. He stares across the
gulf at her with grave eyes.

WE NEED TO FIGHT HIM

"Yeah. I know."
He underlines: FIGHT HIM
"Agreed."
He adds: HAVE WEAPONS?
Her best kitchen knife is gone. The others are either too dull
or too flimsy. What else? She opens drawers clattering with butter knives, spoons, measuring cups. Nothing sharp enough to
stab or solid enough to swing. But she has an idea. From the
lower cupboard—where the author's sword ripped away the cabinet door—she grabs Jules's largest cooking pan, drops it in the
sink, and twists the faucet to full blast.

Through the kitchen window marked with smeared blood,
she scans the darkness outside. Just sheets of rain and wind-
whipped grass.

I'M COMING OVER, Deek writes. CAN HELP

No. She shakes her head. She won't allow another bystander
to die tonight. Deek is an old man. He might be a bit drunk.
He won't hold up in a fight. And if he comes over, he'll sacrifice
their only advantage: his telescopic view of Emma's house.

STAY THERE, she writes. TELL ME WHEN HE MOVES

Deek nods. Reluctantly.

DON'T LOSE SIGHT OF HIM

He nods again.

Emma is afraid to write more. She has to assume that every word she writes is being read by the killer, too. She has to be careful.

Resigned to his supporting role, Deek answers: WILL HELP AS MUCH AS I CAN

"Thanks."

WE'LL THINK OF SOMETHING

"Love your optimism."

Two shut-ins, communicating by whiteboard as a murderer circles in the tall grass outside. No cars. No guns. No phones.

Emma has spent weeks envisioning her own death, and it doesn't alarm her that she will almost certainly die tonight. There's no point sugarcoating it. And Deek's odds aren't great, either. But another razor-thin advantage surfaces in her mind: the author can monitor their communications but can't attack Deek without leaving Emma's house unguarded. And vice versa. For all of H. G. Kane's power, he can only be in one place at a time.

Assuming there's only one of him.

That, too.

While the pan fills under the kitchen faucet, Emma hurries downstairs into the basement. She hates breaking eyeshot with Deek, but this is a necessary risk. At the bottom of the staircase, she finds the light switch on her first try and searches Jules's toolbox for weapons.

Here in the clammy basement she notices how dizzy she feels. Light-headed. Her mind races without traction, like an uncomfortable high. For weeks she's subsisted on nine hundred calories a day, and even in her best shape, taking on a two-hundred-and-fifty-pound swordsman would be near hopeless. She's a long way from her best shape.

Emma has an alarming thought.

It comes to her uninvited, crawling under the door on tiny spider legs and whispering in her ear. She could go outside, face her killer, and end it.

Right now.

It would be so easy. Easier than putting on a weighted back-pack and walking into the waves, forcing her body to take every miserable ice-cold step. It would be out of her control entirely. She's afraid of how comforting it sounds. How *good*, even.

But . . . she'd be abandoning Laika.

And Deek.

If I die, so do they.

From the rust-eaten toolbox, Emma takes the two best weapons she can find: a screwdriver and a claw hammer.

WHEN SHE RETURNS UPSTAIRS, THE PAN IS OVERFLOWING. She twists off the faucet and carries it—a sloshing gallon at least—to the stove and flicks the burner on high. The coils glow red. Splashing the killer with a face full of scalding water is a hell of an opener.

But it'll take minutes to boil. Minutes she might not have.

Update from Deek: the author has moved again.

DRIVEWAY, he scribbles. HE'S IN THE VAN

The FedEx van.

He adds: DOING SOMETHING

Another disturbing unknown.

The late delivery was a surprise to both sides. She hadn't expected any packages this evening or this week. She hasn't ordered anything at all lately. She's sure of it. But several days ago, despite her protests, she remembers with a flicker of adrenaline . . . Jules did.

Five stars on Amazon, she'd texted gleefully. Batteries included.

An item for Emma's self-defense.

A stun gun.

He studied the three-pound Amazon parcel addressed to EMMA CARPENTER under the Ford Transit's dome light.

Then he tossed it aside.

He didn't know what it was, nor did he care.

He searched the vehicle's glovebox, then the center console, and finally under the seat. He had to make certain there were no firearms. Sometimes, he'd read on the internet, delivery drivers serving rural areas carried guns. Luckily, Jake Stanford didn't.

Then he inserted the stolen Ford key, still slick with Jake's blood, and gave the engine a throaty rev. He shifted into Drive and pulled the van off the gravel driveway, grinding over flowerbeds and rough grass. The suspension bumped and jostled as he idled up behind the garage and parked there. Hiding the vehicle from view.

Just in case any more unplanned guests came down the driveway.

OUTSIDE, SHE HEARS THE ENGINE'S GROWL SUBSIDE.

A door shuts.

Silence.

She figures he's parked the van less than fifty feet from the house, just behind the garage. But even if she could sprint to the vehicle without getting shot, break a window, and rip open the package, the stun gun would require unboxing. Assembly. Reading a manual. The batteries might not even come pre-charged. All things she won't have time to do while he closes in on her.

"Shit."

And she can't tell Deek about it—the author is surely monitoring their whiteboards. She can't afford to tip him off to it. As she waits for the water to boil on the stove, she notices her neighbor is waving urgently for her attention. He's written a new message.

Something has changed.

I'M COMING OVER
HAVE TO TRY TALKING TO HIM

No. Horrible idea.

She shakes her head. "Stay home, Deek. Please—"

He insists: HE IDOLIZES ME, MIGHT LISTEN

This stops her mid-breath.

"*What?*"

In her telescope, he's still writing: I RECOGNIZE HIM

HE WROTE THAT SHITTY BOOK

Yes. The shitty book that Deek himself *recommended* two weeks ago. As a joke.

IT'S MY FAULT
I'M SO SORRY

But Emma barely registers his apology. Her mind is racing, struggling to process this jaw-dropping new coincidence.

The killer doesn't just know Deacon Cowl; Deek personally *knows* the killer, too, somehow. Can she even trust her neighbor? Something about this revelation alarms her. She can't put her finger on it.

The old man is still writing frantically. In the uncomfortable silence, the lull between messages, she recalls H. G. Kane's reedy voice. His quiet desperation. The rage building below his words, seething and white-hot.

Do I sound like a fucking amateur, Emma?

It should all be a joke. People dying for an Amazon review, for imaginary golden stars on the internet. Even the killer's appearance dares you to laugh. His fedora. His tactical boots and gloves. The cringy sight of a pale, neckbearded white guy strutting around with a Japanese samurai sword in a period-authentic scabbard.

Until an innocent man was sliced to pieces before Emma's eyes.

Until a body part thudded wetly against the kitchen window.

HIS REAL NAME IS

Deek finishes his message, and when he finally steps away from his whiteboard, the full name of the man who coalesced inside Emma's bedroom appears one word at a time. The true identity of H. G. Kane reads like a written curse.

HOWARD

GROSVENOR

KLINE

EVERY WRITER HAS AN UNHINGED FAN OR TWO.

But Deacon Cowl's first encounter with Howard Grosvenor Kline—years ago—was disturbing by any standard. Young Howard, as it turned out, was a superfan of *Silent Screams* and hell-bent on soliciting his hero's guidance on his own writing career. When his perfectly normal fan mail went unanswered, he took the perfectly normal next step and appeared at Deek's front door.

STALKED ME + MY DAUGHTERS, he writes. FOR YEARS

Given what Emma knows about Howard thus far, that sounds about right. His needy smile. His perpetual victimhood. His alarming talent for finding people.

KEPT SENDING ME SHIT BOOKS
BEGGING ME TO READ

And . . . those drafts that kept arriving in Deek's mail were probably the vile books that preceded *Murder Mountain*. How will the old man react when he learns the truth? The amateur manuscripts he was ignoring, scoffing at—all depicted real murders. Real victims.

She's not sure she has the heart to tell him.

GOT RESTRAINING ORDER, Deek writes. THOUGHT IT WAS OVER

If only, she thinks.

NOW HE'S BACK, he writes. OLDER

SMARTER

ANGRIER

In the distance, a sonic crash of thunder races over the sea. The storm is growing closer. It jolts Emma's bones, the promise of bad things on the way.

AND, he writes.

STILL THE WORST FUCKING WRITER I'VE EVER READ

He'd always been a gifted writer.

Even as a child, his skills were inarguable. *Propeller Head* was a tour de force, and *Semi-automatic,* for all its teenage angst, was crafted with undeniable skill.

From a young age, Howard wrote with urgency. In his junior year he learned that S. E. Hinton wrote her celebrated 1967 novel *The Outsiders* while she was in high school, and this triggered a race against time in his mind. If S. E. Hinton can be published at age nineteen, why couldn't he? And as any aspiring writer knows, it's a famously carnivorous business. Fewer than one percent of novels written make it to be traditionally published, and even fewer turn a profit—so he reasoned he needed a professional's guidance to stand out amid the cutthroat field.

Who better than the author of his favorite true crime novel?

His messages went unanswered. His delivered manuscript was unread. So one rainy afternoon in Strand Beach, Washington, he arrived on foot. He jimmied the back door with his wakizashi sword and found the home vacant inside. He was unaware that the entire Cowl family was on a five-day vacation to Crater Lake and due to return that evening.

So he waited.

He didn't mind.

As the sky darkened, he spent hours combing through personal items. Studying framed photographs from guest interviews on *The Tonight Show* and *Dateline*. He leafed through Swiss and German editions of *Silent Screams*. He explored the children's bedrooms. He helped himself to two beers from the fridge. He played with the unloaded .38-caliber Smith & Wesson revolver on the wall—a gift presented by the Fort Worth Police Department "with eternal gratitude, in recognition of Deacon R. Cowl's integral role in the apprehension of the Stockyard Slayer."

His only error: leaving the living room lamp on as he waited. This light was visible from the driveway and resulted in a 911 call at 9:31 P.M., thanks to the sharp eyes of Karen Cowl.

His arrest was a mortifying experience.

Caught off guard and carrying his wakizashi sword at the moment police arrived, Howard came within an eyelash of being fatally shot by his arresting officer (his mother later filed a formal complaint about this). The handcuffs bit into his skin. The booking photos were humiliating. The white-brick holding cell was stuffy. This, like his near miss with homicide detectives over Laura Birch's disappearance several months later, would be a formative moment. Anyone can look back on his life and pinpoint key moments of missed course correction. He would be smarter. Quieter. Deadlier. No more mistakes. He was no amateur.

He would enter homes like a stalking shadow. He would train his muscles to remain still for hours, to leave no physical evidence. His victims would wonder if they'd ever seen him at all in their bedroom, or if he was merely a half-remembered dream and a trick of the moonlight. He would be seen only when he chose to.

He would return to the Strand, yes.

But he would return as a different person entirely.

SHE WRITES: WHERE IS HE NOW?

Fear gnaws at her.

In the distant window, Deek scans his telescope right, then left toward the ocean. Searching. Not a good sign. The moment seems to last forever until finally the old man looks up at her and shakes his head.

"Shit."

She writes: WHERE DID U SEE HIM LAST?

He points.

The *driveway*? That's old information. A minute out of date, at least. The author could be anywhere now, creeping low in the darkness.

"You had *one* job, Deek," she mutters in frustration.

He's still frantically searching.

Leaning into his telescope, his balance visibly wavers. She should have figured he's been drinking tonight. Deacon Cowl has a brilliant mind, and like many with brilliant minds, he feels the need to kill it with every substance he can find.

"One *goddamn* job."

She takes mental inventory of the house. Laika is safely upstairs on the second floor. The two doors are barricaded, the first-floor windows are all shut, and the broken one is blocked by a tipped sofa. Nothing is impenetrable. But if H. G. Kane—no, *Howard Grosvenor Kline*—enters through any of these routes, she'll hear him coming.

Right?

She feels like she's forgetting something. It needles her. In the kitchen, the stove burner ticks. The water's temperature is slowly rising.

Her head aches. "Where the hell *is* he?"

SORRY, the old man writes. I'M SO SORRY, I LOST HIM.

But Emma isn't focused on his words at all anymore—because as Deek leans over his whiteboard to write more, he reveals a dark figure standing behind him.

Howard stepped out of shadow, careful not to make a sound. The floorboard barely creaked under the sole of his tactical boot. He gently shifted his weight to his heel, his motions practiced and deliberate to avoid rustling his trench coat.

He let out half a breath.

Then, standing stone-still in the doorway, he raised his katana in two gloved hands. The blade's edge was red with Jake Stanford's blood. With an elevated jōdan-no-kamae stance, he aimed his decapitating swing.

EMMA CAN ONLY WATCH.

"No."

As the storm intensifies, she can just barely see it through rain-blurred glass—a silhouette standing behind Deek inside the open driveway. She recognizes the broad shoulders. The rim of his telltale fedora.

That *awful* hat.

Deek leans back to his telescope, obscuring the doorway again.

She mouths: "Behind you."

The old man only squints at her through watery glass. He can't read Emma's lips, but he can tell something is wrong. Just over his shoulder she glimpses that fedora again—the human shadow that first appeared in her bedroom. Watching with reptilian stillness.

Howard's favorite trick.

And—she now knows—a weakness. He likes to remain undetected and study his prey up close, perhaps to better absorb all the sensory details he'll later write. If he doesn't know he's been seen, he'll remain still. Once his presence is known, he'll attack.

Think, she urges herself. *Think.*

On his whiteboard, Deek draws an impatient question mark. He raises both hands in aggravation. He has no idea his superfan is in the room with him, sharing oxygen with him. Seconds from attacking him, cutting him *into pieces* like the poor delivery driver—

Think.

She inhales a shuddering breath. She lifts her marker. DON'T TURN AROUND, she writes. HE'S BEHIND U.

He stood statuesque with his katana raised, exhaling silently through his nose. He squinted to study Emma's whiteboard, wondering what exactly she was scribbling so urgently for her neighbor's telescope.

An offer?

A request?

Instructions?

From where he stood, he couldn't read Emma's handwriting.

DEEK LEANS INTO HIS TELESCOPE'S EYE CUP TO READ HER message.

Silence.

Quickly, Emma adds: DON'T MOVE

OR HE'LL ATTACK

The silence drags on as he reads, then rereads. Five seconds. Ten. She waits with a swollen breath until finally the old man leans back from his telescope. Somehow, across a quarter mile of rain and darkness, they make grave eye contact.

Yes. He gets it.

Through her lens, she notices Deek's hand is inching low toward his desktop. Keeping his movements subtle, unnoticed by the killer behind him, he lifts a small silver instrument into view. It gleams wickedly sharp.

A letter opener.

No. Emma wants to scream. *Don't try to fight him.*

He'll kill you, too.

The old man slowly rotates the tool underhand, tucked like a prison shiv. He takes an anxious breath, his eyes locked on her. She shakes her head, urgently now—*Stay with me, Deek, and we'll think of something, anything else*—but he's already writing one final word.

RUN

"No."

Then Deek stands up ("No, no, *no*—") with his letter opener in a clenched fist, blade out, whirling to face the doorway behind him.

18

DEEK FLICKS A LIGHT SWITCH. HIS DISTANT LIVING ROOM blazes with illumination and Emma can now see the standing figure in clarity.

Just a coat on a hook.

And a black hat.

Like the discarded skin of a reptile, this silhouette is just the deflated form of Howard Grosvenor Kline pinned to a closet wall. He isn't standing in the darkened doorway behind her neighbor. He never was.

Deek stares at his own hanging clothes. Then back at her.

What the hell, Emma?

She chokes on a bitter laugh and lets out a trapped breath. She hates herself for literally jumping at shadows. Her neighbor is safe. For now.

Deek searches his kitchen, too. Then his bedroom. Still clutching that dinky letter opener for defense. Flipping on more lights, more, until every cluttered window is aglow. The old drunk is paranoid now, checking every square inch of his home.

Then a new breeze tickles Emma's exposed skin, and she smells something close. In the room with her. Waiting silently behind her.

Mtn Dew.

Body odor.

And, pungent and unmistakable: butter.

He grabbed Emma's hair in a gloved fistful.

Then he wrenched her head sharply backward—
she shrieked with a hoarse animal terror—and
with his other hand he raised his blade to her
throat.

19

SHE TWISTS FREE.

Hard.

Her scalp rips. She hears it before the eye-watering pain hits—a sickening crackle, like nailed carpet pulling free—and she drives her body forward, out of his grasp. His finger hooks on Shawn's sterling silver locket. The chain snaps.

Far away, Deek watches, screaming, pounding his window.

She hits the floor. A gloved hand grasps her ankle, sausage-fingers tightening—but she kicks and scoots away from him, knocking the tripod telescope over with a teetering crash. The lens shatters. Her back thuds against the window. Trapped by glass.

The towering Chucky doll advances, his piggy eyes locked on her, still carrying a knot of her hair. With his right hand, he flicks his katana. The three-foot blade whips snakelike, too fast to see, casting a fine spray of blood to the floor at her feet.

In hopeless defense, she raises her own weapon.

A *hammer*.

Then a supernova of light. As blinding as concert stage lights, filling the room with a thousand watts of vivid rainforest-green.

The sound arrives, as sharp as artillery fire. Against her tailbone, she can feel the plate glass vibrate in its frame.

The killer halts mid-swing. He's startled, off-balance. Glancing out the window over her shoulder, toward the sudden and dramatic brightness.

He's puzzled.

Emma isn't.

She knows exactly what it is.

A second starburst explodes over Deek's house: fiery orange. It pierces the night sky, drawing acres of dune grass in perfect detail as sizzling cinders fall back to earth with the rain. Fireworks, her neighbor's last-ditch distraction.

It's enough.

Thank you, Deek—

Howard Grosvenor Kline recovers fast and slashes again, but she's already seized her moment and scrambled away, his blade a half-second behind her. She's running for the kitchen.

Thank you, thank you, thank you—

Fireworks bloomed outside as he chased her toward the kitchen. One thunderous blast after another, a kaleidoscope of racing shadows.

Even in the adrenaline of the moment, he recognized Emma's split-second cleverness. She knew that running farther to the barricaded front door would be a fatal error; that moving the table and unlocking the latch would cost time she didn't have. Her options were tight. Instead she skidded at the kitchen's edge, pivoting hard, and bolted downstairs into the basement. He followed her down into a mouth of clammy blackness, albeit in no great hurry. There was no other exit from the cellar.

She'd cornered herself.

The stairs were rotting, soggy underfoot. At the bottom of the staircase, he knew exactly where to stoop to avoid bumping his head on the low copper pipe. This ill-advised bottom floor was nearly five hundred square feet but crowded with sagging cardboard boxes and generations of furniture mummified in plastic wrap. Moth-eaten relics draped in bags. The foundation walls seemed to sweat odorous water, dripping to a moldy cement floor.

Down here, it was pitch-black. Impossible to see. He knew his prey could be hiding anywhere in the cloying, damp space.

And . . . he knew the basement had a light switch on the wall to his immediate left. Two feet away. Waist height. He didn't need to grope for it; its location was already hardwired into his muscle memory as he reached with a confident hand.

EMMA SWINGS THE CLAW HAMMER WITH ALL HER STRENGTH.

Even in total darkness, she remembers exactly where the light switch is. Which means she knows exactly where he must stand. And, most crucially: exactly where he must place his hand to flip it.

Direct hit.

She swears she can feel the bones in his gloved fingers crunch like dry sticks. The basement lights strobe like lightning. He shrieks through gnashed teeth, a girlish scream.

It barely hurt.

He didn't scream or even grunt. Howard had always been a well-muscled and capable close-quarters fighter with an exceptional pain tolerance. Even while ambushed in the basement, he was already smoothly counterattacking. She'd struck his right hand, yes, but at a fatal cost—she'd forgotten entirely about his left hand. In it, he swung his katana.

Directly into Emma's face.

THE SWORD STOPS INCHES FROM HER CHEEK. HER EARDRUM rings with impact. The steel blade vibrates, lodged at least an inch into the house's load-bearing column beside her.

It looks like luck.

It isn't.

Emma didn't flee to this basement in terror. She *chose* this basement. Right here, in this cramped space where Howard's sword has little room for an uninterrupted swing. She knows she won't stand a chance in a straight-up fight—he's bigger, stronger, and armed. So she's lured him to a setting where she has the advantage, where she can strike from the shadows. Hit and run.

Howard howls in agony, the bones in his right hand hopefully shattered. His good hand leaves the sword's grip—still cleaved deeply into the support column—and plucks his black pistol from his trench coat.

But she's already broken contact and is racing upstairs.

Attack.

Hide.

Repeat.

She hears his injured scream bellowing up the dark staircase after her. He's slowed. Humiliated. Enraged. It's all happened in seconds. He knows he's lost this round despite every advantage, and Emma is already upstairs, preparing her next ambush.

> With his uninjured left hand, he twisted his katana out of the post. The steel edge screeched free. Over years of home training, he'd practiced numerous killing strikes using his nondominant hand. Now he would draw upon those skills.
>
> With gritted teeth, he peeled the Ninja latex glove off his right hand. His fingers were already starting to swell. A later medical examination would determine that his middle digit's proximal phalange was fractured, as well as two metacarpals. Despite Howard's exceptional pain tolerance, it was inarguably one hell of a hit. Perhaps it gives Emma Carpenter some posthumous satisfaction to know that despite her death, her hammer blow in that pitch-black basement couldn't possibly have struck truer.
>
> Upstairs, the battle would continue.

THE LIVING ROOM.

That's where she'll attack him next.

The top of the stairs is too obvious. The kitchen, with the still-warming water on the stove, will be his second focus. By the time he's searched both of those areas, he'll start to worry she's already outside and running to Deek's house for help. On his way into the living room, he'll be focusing on the windows. He'll be vulnerable to an attack from this blind corner.

It's perfect.

Emma stands flat against the wall, controlling her breaths. In her grip now: Jules's rusty flathead screwdriver. When Howard rounds the corner, she'll deliver a piercing stab to the face and end the night for good.

She thinks about Prelaw. And Psych.

Whatever their real names must have been. It's wishful thinking, but she hopes somewhere the two women are looking down on her and smiling. That maybe, somehow, all of Howard's past victims are cheering her on tonight, celebrating her wins, grieving her losses. She must be the first victim to break one of his bones, at least. Worst-case scenario: she'll make *Murder Beach* one hell of an H. G. Kane novel. Best-case: he'll never live to write it at all.

Let's see if you can do better, he'd growled at her through the door.

Indeed.

Let's.

Another artillery crash from Deek's house—the old man must be furiously lighting off his entire stash, one after another. Anything to interfere with the killer's hunt, to confuse his senses, to grant Emma a fighting chance. The room fills with light—marine blue now. Dizzying shadows race over the floor, up the walls. It all feels like a fever dream.

Her heart pounds. Her cheeks are flushed hot.

Standing in silence, she considers running outside and making a break for Deek's house—maybe she's gained enough of a head start—but then she hears wet boots on tile. He's already emerged from the basement. Soon he'll be close enough to smell again.

Another strobe of falling purple light. Then darkness again. She listens to the author's boots squeak through the kitchen, into the dining room. He's just a few steps away. Right around the corner. She hefts her flathead screwdriver, edge out. She knows she'll need to stab *hard*. With her other palm braced behind it.

A quarter mile north, Deek detonates another firework. Bloodred.

In a strobe of arterial light, she can see Howard's black shadow trace across hardwood at her feet. It's startlingly clear. She can see he's walking cautiously, carrying his pistol left-handed. This is good. She's crippled his dominant hand. His accuracy will be lessened.

She holds her breath.

You can do this, Shawn whispers in her ear.

Predator and prey are separated by only a blind corner now. She hears a metal *click,* alarmingly close. It's a pistol's hammer cocking. No more playing with swords. He's slain a bystander, he's wounded, and he's desperate. She's challenged him, all right.

She tightens her grip on the screwdriver.

Don't be afraid. You can do this, Em.

Like painting a plaster mountain. Trust your instincts.

I know you can.

But as always, the reality is more complicated. The model railroad had slowly faded from their lives as the monthly struggle to become pregnant overtook their evenings and arguments. She can't remember the last time she saw Shawn run his trains. Bit by bit, little parts broke and were never glued back together. When the plumbing in the second-floor bathroom burst last April, the tracks rusted and the mountain she helped build collapsed with water damage. Neither of them had dared to examine the full toll. It's easier, to not look.

The last red embers burn out.

The house sinks into darkness. But she can hear the author's boots, creeping closer on brittle floorboards. She waits for the next flash of color. That will be the moment. She'll have one chance to strike his face. She can't miss.

You won't, her husband tells her.

The room falls silent.

Only darkness.

Deek must finally be out of fireworks. This means she'll have to attack Howard in the dark. This is fine. Not ideal, but fine. Now he takes his final step to the corner's edge and stops.

I'll see you again, Shawn whispers. *I'll meet you there.*

Deal, she vows.

It's silent but nonetheless startling when Howard Grosvenor Kline's black form peers around the corner. Inches away. Searching the wide living room, scanning pools of shadow for his prey. Whatever he expects to see, it sure as hell isn't this.

She stabs the flathead screwdriver straight into his face.

"That's for Prelaw and Psych, *asshole.*"

20

HER SCREWDRIVER PLUNGES INTO YIELDING FLESH. HE cries out, a gasping moan. His pistol clatters to the floor and tumbles away.

In the night sky, a final flash. There was one last firework after all. This one burns white. Merciless. A nuclear flash. In the harsh blaze, she's staring into surprised eyes, vine-like blood vessels, inches from her own. The screwdriver has skimmed off his jawbone and gone low, driving deeply into the soft flesh just below his throat. Through her fingers, she can feel his heartbeat. His eyes soften into something like sadness.

He gurgles. She feels his voice vibrate the screwdriver.

Emma?

She whispers back, not recognizing her own mortified voice. "Deek."

PART THREE

Do negative reviews bother me?

Absolutely not!

On Amazon and Goodreads I have my share of one-, two-, and three-star reviews, just like any established author. Criticism is all in the eye of beholder. And—this may be unpopular to say, but I'll say it: not everyone is smart enough to assess a book's worth.

Even Deacon Cowl—the author of one of my favorites, the bestselling true saga *Silent Screams*—has critics. Sometimes when I'm feeling discouraged, I go online and read his negative reviews. He's been called "tasteless," "exploitative," "callously disrespectful to the Stockyard Slayer's victims," and one of my favorite passages, courtesy of the *New York Times:* "For all its style, *Silent Screams* is laced with lurid details and no small amount of speculation into the mind of an unknowable man, ultimately written more like an unusually well-researched, mid-shelf commercial thriller than a true account of anything."

This helps me stay grounded.

Because not even the great Deacon Cowl is invincible.

—H. G. Kane, "How to Respond Gracefully to Criticism," 2019, hgkaneofficial.com

21

YOU'RE GOING TO KILL SOMEONE, SHAWN TELLS HER.

It's fine.

I'm serious, Em.

It would have been simpler to fly, but Salt Lake City's airport is swamped for the holiday. She didn't even want to go to this damn barbecue. She loves Shawn, but his family in Denver has always exhausted her.

Eyes on the road. Her husband's voice bristles. He points at her phone on her knee while she drives. *You're driving. Let me navigate.*

She's fine. She's always preferred to navigate herself, and right now, neither Emma's Waze nor Shawn's Apple Maps has the advantage anyway. Six hours on Interstate 80 becomes seven on Highway 40, then back again. Even the satellites are confused. The highway is blockaded with miles of cars stuffed with tents, coolers, and arguing kids. The heat wave is smothering, wildfire smoke from Yellowstone thickening the air.

Focus on the road.

She is.

There's an accident somewhere blocking the two right lanes. She's still cruising at seventy, but the traffic beside them is gridlocked. Metal, glass, and sideview mirrors hurtle past in strobes of reflected sunlight. She ignores the bleating horns, the gritty taste of campfire and exhaust, the migraine biting at her thoughts.

Her app chimes again. Stay the course? Or reroute to Highway 40?

Stay on the interstate, he says. *It's still fastest.*

It's not that Shawn's parents dislike Emma. But as an architect and a lawyer, respectively, living in a house that must be visible from space, they're also acutely aware that Emma majored in theoretical physics and teaches junior high math. They always ask her about work—the same immaterial questions about students and teaching methods, with their too-big smiles—but someday one of them will have one glass of perfectly aged wine too many and ask the true question: what's your *real* plan? Because this state salary can't be it. Surely their son didn't *just* marry a schoolteacher.

They like you, Shawn always tries to reassure her. *They just wish you'd talk more.*

She knows he's lying.

I wish you'd engage with my family.

She tries.

I wish you'd try harder.

She knows she should. But the selfish part of her dreads every holiday trip. It would be easier if his family were assholes, but they aren't. They just have painfully wonderful lives. Shawn's two brothers are bolder, brasher iterations of himself, too, and each always brings a more dazzling version of Emma on his arm. One year it was an actual actress with her own Netflix series. Whenever rich people find out you're a teacher, they sigh this same precious sigh, like you just told them your dog died.

And Shawn doesn't realize it, but she's not actually paying attention to her phone's map. It's her Outlook email app that she's secretly watching. Every time Siri's mechanical voice reroutes, it's an excuse to swipe to her email and check again.

Em, please stop looking at your phone.

Because if her coworker Crystal responds that she can't cover Emma's lesson plan next Friday (which she's eighty percent sure she can't), they'll have no choice but to shorten an exhausting six-day Denver visit with Shawn's family to a more survivable three. Her ace in the hole.

Emma swipes to refresh again.

There it is,

A new email from Crystal.

It begins with: Hey Emma—I think I can

Em—

Her husband's voice rises with panic.

When she looks up, an eighteen-wheeler has veered from the stopped lane directly into hers, the semitrailer's riveted tailgate oncoming at seventy.

"I'M SORRY."

Deek blinks. She's not sure if he can hear.

"Oh my God. I'm *so sorry.*"

She releases the screwdriver. It seems to hover there, impaled just below his throat. Her eyes blur with tears, locked with his, as Deacon Cowl takes a tottering step backward and bumps a wall. A framed photograph drops and breaks.

"Deek, I didn't know it was you—"

He slumps down the wall. She tries to hold him upright but loses balance and topples over with him, bruising her knees on hardwood. He claws blindly for the screwdriver, clasping his fingers around the handle—

"No." She fights him. "No, don't pull it out—"

Too late. A surge of fresh blood runs down Deek's half-zipped raincoat and Emma slams her palm against his throat. Warm liquid spurts between her fingers. She can feel the life leaking out of him, and *she* did this. Not Howard. There's no one else to blame.

This is my fault.

Like that hot day in July. Going seventy with her phone on her knee.

Oh God, I did this—

"Pressure. Keep pressure on it." She guides his hand to his collarbone. His fingers are weak. It's too dark to see the injury—did she slice his carotid? His windpipe? Can he even breathe?

The weight of it crashes down on her, crushing the air from her lungs. She's made an awful, irreversible mistake. Deek entered the house to *help* her.

This is manslaughter.

He's smaller than he looked in her telescope. Too small for his George Clooney head. He's a compact little man, almost leprechaun-like, dwarfed by his raincoat sleeves. Heartbreakingly frail. The brilliant mind who guessed her Hangman words with uncanny precision, who in a past life helped Texas police catch the Stockyard Slayer, now lies bleeding, dying, in her arms.

She tugs off her sweatshirt and presses it to his chest. Not good enough. She searches the drawers in a nearby desk. Pens. Scissors. Stamps. And rattling inside the uppermost drawer, the best thing she can find: a roll of clear mailing tape.

She grabs it.

"I'm sorry. This is going to hurt."

Deek unpeels his hands, giving Emma space to apply the tape in crackling spools. With bloody fingers, he points furiously across the living room. Over her shoulder, at the grandfather clock. He's struggling to speak, mouthing one syllable, syrupy-thick: *Run.*

Across the house, the basement door bangs open.

Howard is coming.

She ignores it all and bites off another loop of clear tape. Glossy plastic traps air bubbles against blood and skin. Deek is still pointing urgently, gasping.

Run.

Run.

Run, his fading eyes beg. *Leave me behind and run.*

She can't. She won't. And it's already too late anyway, because she hears combat boots enter the room behind her. Howard Grosvenor Kline is here.

It doesn't matter. Nothing matters.

Emma wishes to be underwater. Right now. In frigid darkness, her lungs bloating with seawater and her Osprey backpack gripping her shoulders with the weight of all her mistakes. She was always destined for this. Just like her mother, self-destruction is in her blood. Only Emma will drown in seawater instead of box wine.

She wishes it were simply *over* with, for this excruciating sensation to end, for the immense hurt to go away. She'd give anything for the hurt to go away.

She closes her eyes. "I'm sorry," she whispers. "I'm *so sorry.*"

To Deek.

To Shawn.

To everyone.

22

Up until this moment, Howard Grosvenor Kline had maintained exquisite control over the night's events. All vehicles were disabled. All means of communication were cut. All witnesses had been violently dispatched. His standoff with Emma Carpenter—a few unexpected developments notwithstanding—was perfectly contained on that isolated beach.

Until now.

Here's where *Murder Beach* escalates beyond the imagination of its creator; the turning point where the situation boiled over beyond even Howard's control.

At 10:08 P.M., two Strand Beach police officers arrived at Emma's address. Corporal Eric Grayson (a thirty-year veteran) confirmed arrival with dispatch while Officer Greg Hall (a new hire on his probationary period) exited the vehicle first and scanned the darkness. As they proceeded down the driveway, the officers likely passed within twenty yards of Jake Stanford's body concealed in the grass. The hard rainfall was a blessing; it had already washed away any noticeable blood from the gravel at their feet.

On approach, the officers noted nothing suspicious.

Corporal Grayson stepped up onto the porch and tried pressing the doorbell first—finding it intact but curiously nonfunctioning—so he rapped on the door with his knuckle.

"POLICE."

The voice echoes through the dark house.

Emma opens her mouth to scream, but a metal circle jams into the base of her skull and twists hard, forcing her down onto her stomach. She already knows exactly what it is. Clutching his taped injury, Deek watches in wide-eyed terror.

All three of them remain silent.

The second cop's voice, younger: "Emma? Is everything okay?"

Howard's gun barrel presses a painful ring into her skin, his finger perhaps a half ounce of trigger pull away from ending her life. The air pressurizes with rising sounds—the crash of storm swells, the hammer of the rain, the steady hiss of Emma's forgotten pan of water in the next room, now starting to boil.

The cops try again. "Emma?"

Deek raises a bloody finger to his lips: *Shh.*

She nods in the affirmative—slowly, with a gun to her head—but she knows the standoff is more complex than that. The threat is mutual and cuts both ways.

She can't speak—or Howard will shoot.

Howard can't shoot—or the police will hear.

No one is in control.

"Last warning," the older voice shouts.

The doorknob rattles—they're testing the lock—and then footsteps pace on the porch outside. With words trapped in her throat, she realizes the officers are taking up a position to kick the door in. Right now. They're coming.

Finally the killer speaks. He whispers behind her ear, tingling the hairs on her neck: "Emma, answer the door."

At first she thinks she's misheard him.

"Tell them . . ." He releases the gun from her skull, giving her room to stand up. She hopes he's resigning to turn himself in, that he'll write tonight's book from a prison cell and *Murder Beach* will be the first H. G. Kane tale in which the intended victims survive—

Then his voice hardens.

"I'll be listening to every word you say. You'll tell the cops that everything is fine here tonight, you're all alone, and you'll make them leave." Howard thumbs the pistol's hammer—a hungry metal *snick*—and jams the barrel into Deek's forehead.

The injured old man winces, gritting bloody teeth.

"Or I finish what you started."

23

SHE OPENS THE FRONT DOOR EXACTLY HALFWAY.

She leans against the doorframe in a way that she hopes looks casual. She tries not to overthink her words.

Hello? No.

Good evening? No.

What's the problem, officers? Hell, no.

They must have been seconds away from kicking the door in. Both officers back off, giving her space—one old, one young. The porch's roof is just narrow enough to bunch the men up uncomfortably close. The old one speaks: "Emma Carpenter, right?"

She nods.

"Is everything okay?"

No time to self-edit. Not now.

"Yeah." She hides her wet hands behind the doorframe. On her way through the kitchen, she'd hurriedly rinsed Deek's blood off, but she knows it's still visible under her fingernails.

"Any sign of that stranger?"

"Nope."

"Is there anyone else inside the house?"

"No." The headlights are blinding, spotlighting her in the

half-open doorway like she's onstage. The back of her neck still aches from Howard's gun barrel.

"You're sure you're alone?" Old Cop has a playful glint to his eyes. He looks inside, over her shoulder. "I thought I heard a male voice."

Shit, she thinks.

In the next room, she knows Howard Grosvenor Kline is listening to every word in sweaty-palmed silence with a gun to Deek's forehead. His finger tight on the trigger. His hostage slowly bleeding to death—oh *God,* she hopes her mailing tape holds.

She thinks fast. "The TV's on."

"I don't hear it."

"I muted it."

Jules's house doesn't have a television, but these cops can't know that. To fill the uncomfortable pause, she smiles.

In the kitchen, she hears bubbling. The water is at a full boil.

Finally, Old Cop glances to Young Cop. He sighs, clasps his radio, and murmurs something—police jargon, mixed with numbers—and then looks back to Emma. "Sorry to bother you so late. We're here for a wellness check."

Impossible. Deek tried to call 911, yes—but his phone was cut, too.

Right?

And . . . why did the old man run here to confront Howard unarmed, anyway? That was reckless. Near suicidal. It doesn't add up. He couldn't possibly have planned to confront his deranged fan with only words. One person has already died tonight.

Then she remembers the way Deek pointed across the room with a bloody finger. Gasping one desperate choked word as the killer approached, over and over, with a mouthful of blood and tears in his bulging eyes.

He wasn't saying *run.*

She's certain of this. A million percent. Because minutes earlier, while she hid flat against the wall with a screwdriver in her knuckles under strobes of wild color, she heard a hammer cocking. And she heard a dropped weapon hit hardwood the instant she attacked, a metal object sliding across the darkened floor toward the grandfather clock, exactly where he'd pointed so urgently.

Deacon Cowl came prepared, after all.

He was saying *gun*.

SHE'S BEEN SILENT FOR TOO LONG.

The cops are suspicious.

She tries not to think about the loaded firearm resting somewhere in the dark room alongside both killer and hostage. She needs to warn these cops of the danger, to get them on her side. Somehow. Without getting Deek murdered. Howard is listening to her words—but he can't see her lips. She'll need to choose her moment carefully.

To fill the silence she asks, "Did Deek call it in?"

"Deacon Cowl?" Old Cop glances north. "No. Wasn't him."

Young Cop squints into the rain, scanning the flatlands. "That's the true crime guy, right? Shooting off the fireworks earlier?"

Old Cop glances back to Emma. "You know him well?"

"We're friends. Kind of."

"Deek's an acquired taste. Him and I go way back."

She smiles politely. Trying to act like the poor man isn't actually one room away with a grievous wound to his neck and a gun to his head.

"A few pointers I've learned with him." Old Cop counts on his fingers. "Don't talk politics with him. If it's past three, don't let him drive. And don't get him started on the superfan who broke into his house a few years back."

Emma's fake smile inflates.

If only you knew.

She can hear the water bubbling furiously now. Overflowing.

Feigning calm, she glances toward Deek's house, at faraway windows warm with interior light. She can't read the old man's whiteboard without magnification, and thankfully neither can the officers. But inside the old man's crowded living room, she can just barely see the mantel above his fireplace. And a bare spot on the wall, where there used to be a mounted revolver.

This confirms it. He *did* bring his gun.

But an hour ago, Deek told her he didn't have bullets. Was he lying then? Or bluffing now? Uncertainty wriggles in her mind. She tries to navigate an unstable situation, to take it slow, one problem at a time.

So it wasn't Deek who called the police.

Then who?

She asks head-on: "Who requested the wellness check?"

The only person who knew she was in danger tonight didn't actually manage to call police. So who does that leave? She can't think of another soul. She's isolated herself on the Strand with Laika. She's perfectly alone, by choice.

Down the driveway, a car door shuts with a jolting clap. Emma peers around Young Cop's shoulder—he steps aside, turning—to reveal a new vehicle parked beside the patrol car. A black Lincoln. Slick and imperial.

"Speak of the devil," says Young Cop.

Old Cop points. "She did."

At the woman approaching the porch, shielding her face from the downpour. Even though they've never spoken in person, Emma recognizes the house's owner from the framed photographs.

Jules.

24

"EMMA." SHE HUSTLES UP THE STEPS. "IT'S SO NICE TO meet you in person. Finally."

Oh, for *fuck's sake*.

Emma smiles politely, trying not to wince, gripping the doorknob with her fingernails. Holding it exactly halfway open. Not a centimeter further.

Deek's coppery blood is under her nails. She hides her hand. She can do this.

"Sorry about all this." *All this* seems to mean the cops, whom Jules elbows through. She's short, stocky, with a silver Karen haircut and a fitted Burberry jacket that must cost more than Emma's car. She beams a bucktooth smile. "You weren't answering my calls or texts. I was in Ocean Shores this evening and I wanted to make sure you were okay up here."

"Sorry," Emma says. "The internet is down—"

"The yard's so dark." Jules frowns. "Why aren't my motion lights on?"

Christ, she can change topics quick.

It's enough to give Emma whiplash. She stutters, grasping for an answer, as both Old Cop and Young Cop study her with freshly piqued attention.

She can feel the situation slipping from her control.

She imagines Howard Grosvenor Kline crouched in the living room with his gun to Deek's forehead. Listening to every word spoken. She wonders—how keen is his hearing? He's hunted her with incredible precision tonight. But can he hear a whisper?

If I'm wrong, she knows, *Deek will die.*

Not just Deek.

Everyone might.

"Emma?" Jules is now staring.

And this woman is a wild card. Like the kids in Emma's classes that secretly terrified her—bubbly, rapid-fire, unpredictable. You can't prepare for them. You have to improvise to keep up. Jules is exactly the sort of personality that makes Emma's skin crawl, standing on the porch alongside two armed, increasingly suspicious cops.

She hears water sizzle in the kitchen. Uncontrolled and now boiling over, hissing off red-hot Nichrome coils.

Everything, boiling over.

"I turned off the motion lights," Emma lies. "The wind in the grass kept setting them off, and it was giving me a headache when I read—"

"Did your stun gun get here?"

New topic.

Jesus Christ, lady.

She tries to think—is it safer to lie and say she has the stun gun? Then Jules might ask to come inside and see it. Or to tell the truth, that she hasn't received it? And another seed of worry—the FedEx driver has been dead for over an hour now; his truck parked behind the garage. How long before his supervisor reports him missing?

"The stun gun I bought you," Jules repeats. "Remember?"

Emma mentally flips a coin. "I got it."

"Perfect. If Demon Face comes back, you blast him right in the nuts."

"Will do."

Jules glances to the cops. "You carry Tasers, right?"

Old Cop nods.

"Are you allowed to aim for the nuts?"

"Well, it's an electric current, so it doesn't really work like that." Old Cop scratches his mustache, clearly uncomfortable. "It disrupts your body's muscular control, so it doesn't matter exactly where the prongs make contact—"

"But the nuts are probably the most painful, right? Out of all the places on the body?"

Silence.

"I would . . . I'd guess so."

Young Cop agrees. "Probably."

Jules glances back to Emma. "Told you. The nuts." Then back to the cops. "I've been telling the city for years that the homeless population on the Strand is unacceptable. Southside, the beach is basically a tent city. Every winter, more stay—"

"Yeah." Old Cop is barely listening. "We're aware."

"And this hobo in a demon mask isn't new. My son was *terrified* of this weirdo last winter. Barking like a dog. Creeping around the grass, testing the locks on the house. And now this year he appears on my doorbell camera and scares the *shit* out of my house-sitter."

An unwelcome coldness slithers down Emma's spine. *Demon Face was here last year, long before I one-starred Howard's book.*

Meaning . . . *That wasn't Howard.*

She remembers Howard insisting he'd tried to save her life from someone *else*. Another entity. Maybe the greatest danger is still out there, watching from the tall grass? Her mind races;

lies and miscalculations and rodent poison and loaded guns and crude mailing-tape bandages over blisters of bloody air, fighting to hold a precarious seal.

It's dizzying.

"Keep your doors locked," Old Cop advises.

Emma exhales, hiding the shiver in her breath. No more waiting. She'll lower her voice and whisper that she's under duress, that there's a gunman in the living room with a hostage. The cops will fake their friendly goodbyes, leave the house, and radio for backup. Maybe—just maybe—they'll surprise Howard when they storm the house. If they're fast and lucky, they'll shoot him before he pulls the trigger and kills Deek—

"Emma?"

She's out of words again. The cops have noticed.

Jules, too. "Are you all right?"

It's right there. At the edge of her tongue. Just air. A whisper: *He's inside the house. He's about to kill Deek, right now.*

Say it.

On the porch to her left, Young Cop glances to the window and his brow furrows with concern. Emma's stomach drops—he's noticed the curtain stirring behind the glass, touched by a faint breeze that shouldn't exist.

He peers in.

Howard stood stone-still behind the curtain. On his way to more closely monitor Emma's conversation with police, he'd made an error. He'd slightly disturbed the hanging fabric.

Outside the window, Officer Hall stood inches away.

Howard could see the young man shadowed against floral curtain by headlights, and he knew exactly where to aim to deliver a fatal blow through the glass. But attacking would be a last resort. He needed to avoid triggering a firefight at all costs, because he knew these two Strand Beach officers standing on the porch were much more dangerous than Jake Stanford. They were armed. They were trained. Most important, they had radios.

In the trip-wire silence, Howard waited. The only thing keeping twenty-three-year-old Officer Greg Hall alive was a thin layer of fabric and glass.

And the words of Emma Carpenter.

Everything hinged on what she said next.

"I . . ."

Old Cop stares at her. "Is something wrong?"

She can feel Howard's eyes on her side. His finger on the trigger, a muscle twitch from firing. Young Cop has no idea.

All eyes on her.

Her plan is now impossible. She can't whisper to the officers with Howard standing *right here* on her left. Less than six feet away. He'll hear. He'll detect any gesture, any covert signal she tries to send, and he'll have no choice but to open fire.

"Emma?"

No words come. *Say something, damn it.*

It's all tipping out of her control. She can see the massacre now. Howard fires. The window shatters. Young Cop falls, clutching a hole in his chest. Old Cop raises his sidearm just before Howard's steel blade severs his hand at the wrist. And Jules, poor Jules, caught in the bloody cross fire—

"Emma." Old Cop leans close. "Is someone inside your house?"

She hears Howard take a small, surprised breath. She can sense his anxiety building alongside her own.

Still, words fail her. Like they always have.

Say something.

Old Cop slides his hand to his pistol and pops the holster button. She can see the silver hairs prickling on his forearm. His voice lowering: "Emma. If he's inside your house, you don't have to say anything. Just look at me and blink twice."

I can't.

"It's okay. Blink twice."

I wish I could.

They're eye to eye. A whisper of friction as his Glock slides from its holster. She senses motion to her left—Howard is preparing to shoot first—so she swallows and says something, *anything* to buy another second: "I'm . . . bad at talking to people."

Silence.

"I'm fine. I mean, I'm not fine, but everything is fine here tonight." She exhales through her teeth, ignoring the killer beside her. "I've always been this way, I think. I self-edit. I can't say what I mean to. People stress me out, even when they mean well."

Young Cop glances at her, away from the window.

Old Cop pauses, his pistol half-drawn.

"So . . . I hide. I push people away, and I push and I push until they give up. I act like my mother while she drank herself to death. I ignore phone calls. I only communicate online, through writing. I force people to engage with me through texts or emails or whiteboards. My next-door neighbor has been trying to meet me in person for weeks, for the sole purpose of being my friend. I'm *hard to know,* my husband used to say. I'm hard on the people who care about me. But starting now, I'm going to work on it."

She takes a breath.

"I never answered you." She faces Jules directly. "After the background check cleared, you asked me why a married twenty-something would drop her teaching contract in Utah and take a lonely house-sitting job all the way out here."

Jules nods.

No self-edits, she thinks. Like Shawn always said.

One.

Two.

Three.

"The truth is, I lost someone. Five months ago. And it was my fault. I was driving, and I looked down at my phone at the wrong second."

There it is.

It's out there.

"It wrecked me," she says. "I'm still processing it."

She feels naked, standing spotlighted in the doorway before three strangers. And an armed killer to her left.

Old Cop nods gently. "The beach can be a good place for that."

"Emma, I'm so sorry." Jules rests her palm on the doorframe, inches from Emma's fingernails stained with Deek's blood. "If you ever need to talk, I . . ." She manages a self-deprecating smile. "Well, I've been told that *I* like to talk. A lot. And I'd feel privileged to."

Emma nods. Maybe.

If she survives tonight, she'll do a lot of things differently. She'll stop hiding. She'll dump the rocks out of her Osprey backpack and she'll have that long-promised ginger tea with Deek—if he survives, too. Maybe, just maybe, she'll break out of her isolation, drive home with Laika to Salt Lake City, and try to reconcile with her past. The things she's done. All of it.

Maybe.

Because Howard Grosvenor Kline isn't an omniscient force,

and *Murder Beach* isn't penned by fate. Her decisions aren't written. There's no narrator. Just a sweaty, overweight man with a fetish for medieval swords. In a story, the author may very well be God.

But this isn't your story, Howard.

It feels like switching on the lights in a dark house. Retaking control, room by room.

You're in mine.

She nods politely as Old Cop recommends a local grief counselor and a raft of mental health resources, but she's not listening.

She's thinking about home, about late nights stargazing on that little roof with Shawn by her side. She's thinking about one particular night, after her obstetrician gave them the most heartbreaking assessment yet—that their chances of conceiving were likely to be less than one in a hundred—and Shawn had found her alone on that rooftop with teary red eyes and a lit cigarette in her hand. It hadn't yet touched her mouth. It was her first cigarette in over a year, ever since they'd started trying for a baby.

He'd crawled out the bedroom window and quietly scooted down to sit beside her at the roof's edge. He'd admitted that, in trying to cheer her up, he'd gone online and done something stupid. He'd named a star after her.

Emma's Star.

Somewhere in Messier 31, the Andromeda Galaxy. Her favorite.

She hadn't had the heart to tell her husband that those websites are mostly scams, that fifty bucks and a certificate doesn't mean the scientific community recognizes your vanity star. But the purity of the gesture overwhelmed her. She'd just sat there with her feet dangling over the driveway, fighting tears with her cigarette of defeat in her hand, afraid to let it touch her lips. For all the disappointment of that day, she remembers feeling so deeply grateful to have Shawn beside her, willing to buy her a star without doing even the most cursory research.

They'd fought infertility together.

But tonight Emma must fight Howard by herself.

With a final farewell the cops return to their car, the well-ness check more or less complete. In seconds, she'll be alone again. She senses motion in her periphery—Howard peels back the curtain with his finger to watch the officers leave. He's distracted.

This is her chance.

Jules is already turning away, too—but Emma places her hand atop hers on the doorframe. Pinning her fingers. Stopping her.

Holding eye contact, Emma mouths three words.

Howard.

Grosvenor.

Kline.

Like a dark incantation. All warmth vanishes from Jules's eyes. She glances back to the cops—her lips start to move, almost uttering her own death sentence—but she decides better.

Armed, Emma urgently adds. *Hostage.*

Jules nods once.

Message received.

It's an obvious nod—Jules would be a shitty secret agent—and Emma's nerves tighten with fear. She's certain Howard has turned his attention back to them, that he's noticed the plainly telegraphed signal just feet away. But nothing happens.

"Have a good night," Jules whispers with stiff cheer.

"You, too."

The older woman holds eye contact for a heartbeat longer. To confirm: *I'll tell them. Hang in there, Emma.*

Then Jules turns away and follows the two officers down the driveway without bothering to shield her face from the rain. She's gravely silent.

Emma holds the door in place while she watches the three depart. If Jules is smart, she'll wait until both vehicles have left the driveway before alerting the cops. Then they'll return with guns drawn. Right? Maybe they'll call in hostage negotiators? Or sharpshooters? Whatever it takes to end *Murder Beach* with an appropriately violent bang. Just not the bang Howard expects—

Old Cop stops with his car door half-open. "Wait."

Emma halts.

"There's . . . something you should know."

She waits.

Storm swells crash in the distance.

"My wife died last year." He forces a flinty smile. "For a time, I was in an awful place."

Her spine chills.

Another torrent of rain comes in, racing down the driveway and pattering over windswept grass. He raises his voice: "It wrecked me, too. I had bad thoughts when I was alone. I was afraid of myself. Like I imagine you might be. Anything to make the hurt go away. And my chaplain . . . he told me there are three T's. Time. Tears. Talking. They'll get you through it. Trust me. Trust them. Whatever it takes, keep going."

She nods. "I will."

Old Cop wince-smiles, as if that was hard to say. He makes a modest little hand-wave and climbs into his car with Young Cop. Farther back, Jules keeps walking to her Lincoln, still lost in her own private horror. The bomb's fuse is lit and burning.

It can't be stopped. Help is coming.

Time. Tears. Talking.

Emma exhales.

Whatever it takes, keep going.

Then, as both vehicles leave the driveway, red taillights fading away, Emma pushes the front door shut and turns to face her killer.

25

"IS DEEK ALIVE?"

She has to know.

Howard Grosvenor Kline says nothing as the noise of the two engines wanes in the distance. An uneasy stalemate hangs—for a few more moments, the cops are still close enough to hear a scream or a gunshot. With her dwindling time, she asks again: "Is he dead?"

Silence.

She dreads the answer. Why else would the gunman have left his hostage unguarded in the living room? In her soul, she knows there are two possible reasons: either Deek has fallen unconscious or Deek has bled to death.

And it's my fault.

The human Chucky doll's lips curl into a smile. The sound of it—of flesh wetly tightening—makes her stomach turn.

"I've always been a loner, too." The smile is wistful, vulnerable. "I'm . . . I know I'm not an alpha male. You won't find me in a sports bar leading a pack of betas and chasing females. I'm something else, a new archetype they recently discovered: a sigma male. Just as powerful and charismatic as an alpha, but solitary."

She watches the red taillights fade into sheets of rain. A silent countdown.

Going.

Going.

"Just like you, Emma, I don't have a pack. A sigma male is a true lone wolf."

The taillights are now gone.

Alone again. Emma's nerves fizz with adrenaline, but she glimpses motion on the gunman's cheek. Inching under his glasses, glistening through curly neckbeard.

A tear.

He's . . . *crying?*

He didn't cry.

Howard Grosvenor Kline rarely cried, even when he was a child. As the beach house sank back into darkness, he hefted his bloodied katana with a samurai's resolve. A massacre on the front porch was narrowly averted, but Emma's covert message to Jules hadn't gone unnoticed. He'd seen her lips move. He knew the police would soon return in force. At that moment powers beyond his control were now converging, and the slaughter that would make Strand Beach famous was now inevitable.

With bone-chilling calm, Howard explained his plans to her.

"I DIDN'T . . . I DIDN'T WANT TO," HE SOBS.

Emma can only watch in silence, an icy dread building within her. It's disorienting. This can't be right. The star of tonight's nightmare is melting down in front of her, his lips quivering, his skin flushed, rubbing his watery eyes.

What's happening?

What's really *happening here?*

He wipes his nose—a snotty huff—and lifts his sword. This close, Emma sees blood diluted sickly pink by rainwater, filling cracks in the steel. The sharp edge is damaged from tonight's hits, dulled against wood, glass, and bone.

"I didn't want to." His voice burbles. "I didn't *want* anyone else to die tonight."

He'd planned to take as many lives as possible that night.

The body of Jake Stanford, concealed in the tall grass with both hands severed and enough disfiguring slashes to the face to require post-mortem identification via dental records, would be only the first soul taken in the night's massacre—

"NO."

He punches the wall, leaving a splintered crater.

"No. Please." Red-faced, he grasps his temples and digs his fingernails into doughy skin, like he's arguing with a voice she can't hear. Emma takes a cautious step backward, toward the kitchen. He's changing before her eyes, mutating, a volatile chemical reaction.

"That fucking FedEx guy." Howard sniffles. "He just *showed up.*"

Emma remembers the hardening look in the delivery driver's eyes. The wet rock gripped in his knuckles, the blurred swing—

"He attacked *me.* And after his hand came off, I had to keep going. I had to. I couldn't stop. And . . . I wasn't ready for it. I thought I was. But it's different when they're alive. He looked so afraid while it happened, shaking his head, begging me to stop." His voice fractures, another choked sob. "While he . . . while he *came apart*."

She can still feel Howard's scream in her bones. A hundred decibels of shock, disgust, and guilt. In the new light she can see the blood on his clothes, cast across his leather trench coat and cargo pants. Even a droplet at the corner of his hairy lips, close enough to taste with his tongue if he wished to. But he doesn't.

The police are coming back, Emma knows. Any second.

I just have to survive until then.

But here, now, something is very wrong.

"I don't understand," she whispers. "You've . . . done this sixteen times."

He blinks.

"Your sixteen other books. *Murder Mountain. Murder Glacier. Murder Forest.* All those people you've killed for your books, in all those places—"

"They're fiction," he says.

Silence.

"Really?"

He nods.

She refuses to believe this. He's lying. He *has to be lying*—

"All of them?"

He nods again. "You . . . you assumed my books were real?"

Emma's mouth is paper-dry.

The entire world seems to quietly shift underfoot, a tectonic change. So . . . Prelaw and Psych's Appalachian nightmare never happened. The young women never existed. Neither did the seasoned, capable killer who hunted them. The blood and gore and high-heel lesbian romance read like masturbatory fantasy because it *was*. Howard himself is no serial killer. Even if he wishes to be, even if he writes himself as one.

He's something worse. A *wannabe*.

A seething, hateful kid with nitroglycerin in his veins. A school shooter prowling the halls of his high school with a military-style rifle he can just barely operate. Jealous and needful. Red-faced and sweaty. She can feel the warmth radiating off his skin, body heat trapped in a clammy leather exoskeleton. He takes a slow step toward her.

She steps backward but refuses to look away from his fogged glasses. Like staring down a rabid dog. If she looks away, he'll attack.

Keep him talking.

"What about . . ." She steadies her voice. "What about *Murder Beach*?"

Again he blinks. "What?"

"The book you're writing about me. About tonight. About murdering me—"

"There's no *Murder Beach*."

"You're lying."

"Why would I write and publish a book detailing a real murder I committed?" His nose pinches, as if offended. "And if I . . . if I did that sixteen times, over years and years, don't you think I'd have been caught by now? Is that really what you thought was happening tonight?"

She says nothing.

"Come on, Emma. A serial killer who writes books about the people he murders? That would just be stupid."

She can't believe any of this. This baby-faced figure is toying with her, manipulating her, feeding her falsehoods and studying her reactions. He's a storyteller, and all stories are built from lies. Who knows how many faces he wears?

"I didn't even kill Laura Birch," he whimpers. "Not technically."

She takes another step back.

No sudden movements.

He follows. Mirroring her, a python about to strike.

"I kept Laura's teeth and her earrings and the sword I used
to dismember her body behind a loose board in my bedroom
wall. Above my bed. It's still there. I suck on her teeth from
time to time and look at my Polaroids and try to pretend I did
it on purpose. But do you want to know the truth? What really
happened to Laura?"

His voice rings uncomfortably in the confined space.

"I *tied her knots too tight*. And she suffocated." He forces a jaun-
diced grin. "That's it. That's all I did. I'm basically innocent. I
needed her to stay in my basement. I hadn't even touched her yet.
But when I left for school, Laura tried to tip her chair and escape,
and the unlucky, one-in-a-million way Mom's stupid antique
chair landed must have constricted her airway. And she asphyxi-
ated on the floor while I was in class. She killed herself, basically."

Emma says nothing.

He's lying. All of it. She has no reason to believe a word he
says. She takes another slow step backward—into the living
room now—as he follows.

"Laura made it all my problem, you know?" He flashes a rancid smile. "It's like she got the last laugh. But I made it worthwhile for myself, too. You learn a lot about the female body
when you're cutting it up."

He hesitates, as if realizing he's said too much.

Emma thinks about Deek's revolver. Where it must have
landed in the dark room. She envisions herself finding it, turning around, and blowing Howard Grosvenor Kline's head off.
Pulling the trigger, making his insectoid brain bloom out on
the wall.

If she can only *get to it*.

"Being close to you was nice. While it lasted." His voice lowers and his opaque glasses level on her, a subtly alarming shift. He smiles and straightens his fedora. "I like . . . I like the way you made the house smell, Emma. I like the way you talked to your dog, as if she could talk back. I liked the way you'd sit and read for hours every day with your ginger tea and play whiteboard games with your neighbor. I liked your petite body. You were my kind of girl, you know? You were solitary, quiet. Smart. Introspective. Not at all like the other femoids. You reminded me of Laura in so many little ways."

Revulsion climbs her throat like a squirming mass of cold maggots. She feels a visceral tug in her stomach and wants to puke.

My kind of girl.

"Then you wrote that review." He sniffs. "And you broke my heart."

No. *Wrong.*

Impossible.

She one-starred Howard's shitty horror book *before* their lives entangled. Not *after*. There is no other possible explanation. She's staring at a hateful creature who poisons dogs and violates corpses, a mind untethered from time and space—

"But I . . . I still want to save you," he says with a woeful shrug. "Even after everything you've done to me. I guess nice guys really do finish last, huh?"

His teary eyes dance. It's subtle but chilling.

"You're trapped in your past, Emma. You love that dog too much. You have to learn to let go of things before they drown you. So here's my proposal: I'll spare your life if you come with me. Right now."

Silence.

He's holding out a latex-gloved hand. His gun is holstered,

his sword sheathed. As if all the night's blood and terror hasn't happened at all and he's just a gentleman offering her his hand at an old-timey ball. Then his palm opens and her skin crawls.

Braided rope.

"It's just for my safety," he clarifies. "We'll . . . we'll live on the road together. You and me. I have over a hundred and twenty thousand dollars in my bank account. We'll drive south, to Mexico maybe." His needy smile widens, his eyes running up and down her body. "I can . . . I can *save you,* Emma. I'm the only one who can save you from yourself. You understand that, right? You're broken and you can't recover from this grief alone. You're not strong enough. So come with me and be my girl."

Silence.

His *girl.* Something he's entitled to. Like Laura Birch's body parts in his basement, useful for as long as they last.

And this is all so *wrong.* It's another dizzying turn, an accelerating nightmare, but hope is within reach. Deek's dropped gun is somewhere in the dark behind her. If she turns and bolts for it now . . . *can I find it before Howard shoots me in the back?*

"Now or never, Emma." His voice sharpens. "What's your answer?"

BEFORE SHE CAN SPEAK, SHE HEARS A METALLIC *CLICK* BE-hind her.

Her blood freezes in her veins.

Slowly, she turns.

Across the living room, sixty-six-year-old Deacon Cowl—injured but alive—has clawed himself upright against the fireplace like a slouched corpse. Using the brickwork to support his aim, his revolver clasped in his bloody knuckles. It's here, all right, exactly as she called it, but he's recovered it first.

And it's aimed directly at *her.*

Emma's throat tightens.

In an instant, Deek has become a stranger again. The eyeball that made her skin prickle through his telescope; the canny mind that knew her name before she ever gave it. Now, in their sum, the coincidences are overwhelming: the fact that Deek knew Howard prior to all this, the fact that he intervened only when Emma's death appeared certain, the all-too-convenient fact that he kept a black *fedora* on his closet coat rack identical to Howard's. What are the odds, anyway? Two authors on the same beach?

No, she wants to whisper. *You were my only friend out here. Not you, too—*

With Howard at her back and a gun aimed at her chest, she's trapped. There's nowhere to run. Deek seems to know this, too.

The old man's eyes harden.

His finger curls around the trigger.

26

SHAWN'S VOICE RISES: *LOOK OUT*.

The semitruck has already veered into her lane. Glancing up from her phone, she sees it incoming at seventy. She stomps her brakes, all reflex, too late.

Look out. Look out—

Shawn's fingers tightening around her biceps, his hot breath in her ear. The riveted tailgate fills her entire windshield, a dusty silver shadow that swallows the July sun and darkens the interior around Emma as she twists the wheel right, a desperate final hope, swerving toward the highway's shoulder on locked tires—

Too late to avoid.

Impact.

A glancing blow to the vehicle's passenger side. A concussive metal bang. The world whiplashes left—her seat belt bites her shoulder, warm soda splashes into her lap, her phone clatters off the driver door—as both vehicles recoil from their metal kiss.

But it's not as violent as she feared. Not as bad.

Now skidding into silence. On the shoulder. Facing the wrong way. A swirl of gritty dust catches up and blows past. The acrid odor of scorched rubber, brake pads, straw, and cow shit. The semitrailer is still blocking the sunlight, but strobes of it flash through air vents as aggravated cattle snort and stomp inside.

Both vehicles—hers and the semitruck—have ended their encounter side by side but facing opposite directions like confused dance partners.

The collision was minor.

Practically a fender bender.

A cab door creaks open. A man's voice calls: *Are you okay?*

The world is gauzy, dreamlike. The cattle truck's shade is surprisingly cool. Loose straw flutters in the air. Emma tastes copper in her teeth and realizes she's bitten her tongue. And her phone—its Outlook email app still open—has landed neatly back in her lap. She sees her own face reflected on the screen, blood on her lips.

Crystal's email has loaded.

Hey Emma—I think I can handle that. Have fun in Denver! ☺

Six days, it is.

Minor accident or not, she has an awful feeling about these past few seconds. Somehow she knows already that her world has changed irreversibly, that a human life has exited the vehicle. Dread pulls at her stomach.

Then a hand touches her shoulder.

It's Shawn.

He's unhurt. Alive. His eyes are wide with adrenaline.

Holy shit, he gasps. *That was close.*

"EMMA," DEEK HISSES OVER HIS GUNSIGHTS. "GET *DOWN*."

She blinks.

Oh, *thank God.*

Then she dives to the floor. Behind her, Howard Grosvenor

Kline freezes at gunpoint. Now that Emma is out of the way, Deek has a clear shot on the killer.

"Surprise, Howard."

Emma scoots away, watching both men.

With his revolver aimed in blood-slick fingers, the old man tilts his head toward Emma—the bandage of mailing tape crinkles—and winks tiredly. "Still in this fight?"

"Yeah." She catches her breath. "Glad you're on my side."

More than you know.

Her nerves brace for a gunshot. She expects Deek to pull the trigger, but Howard's hands are now raised in surrender. It won't be self-defense. It'll be closer to an execution, and Deek seems to know this. He sighs, deeply conflicted. "Weapons on the floor."

The killer says nothing.

"Your sword first."

"It's not a sword. It's a *katana*—"

"I truly, deeply don't give a shit, Howard."

With his eyes locked on Deek's gun, Howard kneels and lowers his sword. It must be too precious to drop. The blade touches hardwood with a low, steely clatter.

"Now your gun," Deek instructs. "Pull it out slowly."

This, Emma knows, is the dangerous part.

She braces again as Howard slides his hand into his trench coat. Again Deek tenses, ready to fire. She holds her breath as that familiar semiautomatic pistol inches into view, muzzle down. Then with a glare, he drops it.

"Emma." Deek points. "Grab his gun and—"

She's way ahead of him. She's already snatching the firearm off the floor and now aims it at Howard's sweaty face. She stands and backs away, taking a two-handed shooting stance.

Deek smiles with approval. "You've done this before."

"Once or twice," Emma lies.

She doesn't dare let Howard know this is the first time she's ever held a gun. He watches them both, kneeling stone-still with two firearms now pointed at him. There's something unnerving to his stillness. He watched her sleep in her bedroom. He stalked her for days, a sentient shadow creeping room to room. Like a cold-blooded reptile conserving its energy, he moves only when he needs to.

The revolver trembles in Deek's grip.

Howard notices.

Please stay conscious, Emma thinks. He's lost a lot of blood.

"I signaled to Jules," she whispers. "By now she's told the cops. They'll be back here any minute. Any second."

Deek grits his teeth. "Smart."

Emma can't help but notice how conspicuously lightweight Howard's pistol feels in her hands, like it's plastic. She's afraid to study the weapon closer. She can't let Howard see her doubt. They have the advantage—but only barely.

"Howard, in case my answer wasn't already clear," she tells him, "that'll be a *hard pass* on the girlfriend proposition."

He says nothing.

But he looks down at the floor and blinks—once, twice, then rapidly—and she knows she's hurt him. Somewhere in his callow little brain, Howard must really believe his actions are understandable. All of them. Laura Birch's asphyxiation was a tragic accident. His butchery of that poor FedEx driver was self-defense. Even his planned murder of Emma came with a pre-installed excuse. She was on the verge of killing herself out here—so what was her life really worth? Evil works hard to rationalize itself.

Deek notices Howard's ungloved hand. "Did you smash his hand, too?"

She nods. "Sure did."

"With what?"

"A hammer."

"Nice." The old man pauses. "So why'd I get the fucking screwdriver?"

"Because you didn't announce yourself."

"I was entering a dark house to save you from a killer who could be hiding anywhere. Why the hell would I *announce myself*?" He lets out a breath and sags against brick, his gunsights wobbling, clearly light-headed. "You're welcome, by the way."

Howard spits on the floor, a startling wet glob. Jolted, Emma almost pulls the trigger. Something small clacks across hardwood, stopping by her foot and slowly spinning to stillness. It's a long earwig shape, gray and calcified.

A human tooth.

I suck on her teeth sometimes.

She swallows a nauseous shiver.

Licking his lips sloppily, Howard turns to Deek. "You should've stayed home and minded your business. You've just made the biggest mistake of your life."

"Honestly," Deek says, "this probably hasn't even cracked the top ten."

"That's fine. I've already decided how it ends for you." Howard's words are a soft monotone, like he knows something they don't. He nods across the room. "The police will find your body right there. Do you want to know how you'll die?"

"Not really, Howard."

"Disgraced samurai who have betrayed their kin can still regain honor in suicide. The ritual is called seppuku. First, you sit upright in the company of those you respect and trust to oversee your death. Then you plunge a blade into your own belly and slide it left to right to disembowel yourself. You won't scream or convulse. Your muscles will be on fire, your mind will race with adrenaline, but you'll remain stoic as your intestines slide out into your lap. Until finally—and this is the pre-Edo ritual, be-

cause I've always believed a simple decapitation is too painless—
you'll pull the dagger out of your stomach, hold its edge exactly
to your heart, and allow yourself to fall forward, ending your
life with honor."

Silence.

"Yeah, I'm not doing that."

"I know." Howard flashes a smile, warmly venomous. "I'll
do it for you."

Deek smiles back.

But he's only bluffing. Emma can see right through the old
man's defiance. He's afraid. Somehow, even disarmed and kneeling at gunpoint, Howard Grosvenor Kline controls the entire
room with a low, breathy monotone.

"Emma." Deek keeps his sights trained on the killer. "If
the police are coming back, you should go outside and wait for
them. Tell them we've got him. I'll keep Howard here and—"

"Bad idea."

"Please do it. It's not safe here."

Before Emma can respond, she hears a squeak from the other
side of the house. A door has just opened. A current of cold air
breathes through the structure and she can feel the temperature
change on her sweat-glazed skin.

Deek glances to her. "Wasn't the front door locked?"

She shakes her head. Not anymore.

"Then who the hell is *that*?"

The police, she hopes. Returning with guns drawn after
Jules passed on her message. But a SWAT team couldn't possibly
have gotten here this quickly. And regular cops have to identify
themselves, right?

Wet footsteps approach.

It's one person.

She thinks about Demon Face, the apparition that stood

outside the doorbell camera in a mouthless Halloween mask and dared her to open the door. The unknown man who prowled the Strand last year and terrorized the house's prior occupant.

And Howard's exact words: *He told me I had to kill you.*

And I stood up for you.

Emma glances back to Howard—dreading she'll see a wicked smile coalesce on his chubby face—but he's just as wide-eyed. He wasn't expecting this, either.

"Who is it?" Deek asks again.

The footsteps grow closer.

Through the kitchen.

And—finally—entering the room. Emma recognizes the individual immediately. The stout build. The Burberry jacket. The cropped gray hair.

Jules.

The woman halts, petrified to see the standoff in her own living room. And then her gaze lowers to the dark form of Howard, kneeling at gunpoint beside his bloodied sword. She shakes her head in slow, revelatory horror.

Emma whispers, "Where are the cops?"

Jules isn't listening. She's still shaking her head. With dry lips, she whispers, "*Howie?*"

Howard sulks. He doesn't dare look up at her.

"Mom."

27

"HOWIE, WHAT ARE YOU *DOING HERE*?"

He ignores his mother and stares at the floor.

"You're . . . oh my God, you're done. You're going to turn yourself in right now. Okay? Right now." Jules's voice quakes with grief. "But listen to me. This is important. Are you listening? The cops—they'll *shoot you* if they see your katana."

She kicks the sword out of his reach.

"Your knives. Your pellet guns, too. Anything that looks like a weapon. Just stay calm, and I'll call the police back here, and we'll turn you in safely and get this all sorted out. Okay?"

Anxiety stirs in Emma's gut.

She hasn't told the police yet.

"I'm . . . I'm so sorry." Jules turns to her. "I knew there was a trespasser. I knew my internet was down. But I didn't know it was *you*, Howie."

Until the police performed their wellness check.

Until the conversation on the porch.

Until Emma looked Jules in the eye and mouthed her son's name.

Howard understood his mother's horror.

It was perfectly justified.

Jules Phelps, née Kline, was faced with a soul-wrenching dilemma that night. In statements given thereafter, both Corporal Grayson and Officer Hall would recall her unusual behavior following Emma's wellness check. After swerving abruptly in front of their vehicle to get the officers' attention, Jules had exited her Lincoln and approached with one hand raised, wearing what Corporal Grayson would later describe as a "haunted and faraway look."

"I left something at my house," she told them. "I'm driving back."

Then, over her shoulder:

"I'll call you again if I need anything else."

"EMMA, I AM SO SORRY FOR ALL OF THIS. MY SON . . . HE'S A writer. He's always researching for his horror books. I promise, he's so gentle. He's so, so sweet. But he's also troubled. He has issues understanding personal boundaries—"

"No *shit*," Emma says.

"He house-sat here before you. But he moved out, months ago."

This washes over her.

It feels apocalyptic, nearly bringing her to her knees.

This is his house.

Howard Grosvenor Kline grew up here, on Strand Beach. The yard is his. The old toys in the basement are his. The teenager's bedroom, the strange and stuffy space with the fetid odor of adolescence, which Emma herself feared to enter. All Howard's. The samurai poster wasn't a coincidence. Tonight there are no coincidences.

He infiltrated the house so easily because he's kept a key. He knew to avoid every creaky floorboard because he's had *years* of practice. And as for how he found her address so quickly on the Strand? There was no black magic involved.

He's spent his adult life raging over negative online reviews, wishing he could strike back at his faceless critics. And now, for the first time ever, he's discovered a critic within his house. In his childhood home. Alone. Vulnerable. How could an ego as frail as Howard's resist revenge? *That's why my review was so special,* Emma realizes.

It wasn't my words at all.

It was me.

"Please," Jules pleads. "Both of you. Lower your guns."

"Nope," says Deek.

"He's surrendered. He's no danger."

He's still dangerous, Emma knows. He poisons dogs and sucks on human teeth. He's already slashed a man to pieces tonight.

And something Jules said to her son moments ago—*your knives, your pellet guns, too*—snags in Emma's mind. Without speaking, she aims the suspiciously light pistol out the window to the ocean (Deek notices: "Emma, what are you doing?") and pulls the trigger. It fires with a dry click. It's the same click she remembers from hours ago when Howard shot out the motion lights.

She sighs. "It's a pellet gun."

"*Obviously* it's a pellet gun," Jules says. "Howie has struggled with schizoaffective disorder his entire adult life. He can't legally own a firearm."

Of course.

Deek laughs. "Fuckin' *dork*."

She's glad Deek's antique revolver is real, at least. It's now the only threat keeping the killer on his knees. But still she worries: what if her neighbor didn't conveniently *find* his ammunition after all? What if Deek's weapon is unloaded—still—and once Howard realizes this, the fragile bluff will explode into violence?

Even kneeling, cradling broken fingers, Howard is the largest person in the room. The heaviest. The strongest. She's seen his katana sever human limbs and cleave an inch into solid plywood. Howard Grosvenor Kline won't be taken into police custody. Not tonight.

He has something else in play.

"By the way . . ."—Deek manages a woozy smile—"nice to see you again, Julie."

She refuses to look at him. "Go to hell."

"You couldn't have told the cops like Emma asked?"

"You caused this," Jules snarls. "All those years, my son idolized you—"

"Your kid broke into my fucking house. He stalked my daughters. I was so sick of his manuscripts. He kept leaving them at my door like flaming turds. All this gory slasher drivel. He kept begging to meet my agent, my editor, my publicist. And I lost my temper, yes. I said something I wish I could take back. I told your son that his garbage-juice, amateur attempts at writing would never succeed, because it wasn't coming from a real place. It was just gore and cruelty. Stuff he's cribbed from horror movies. It was *inauthentic.*"

So Howard didn't mail his endless manuscripts to Deek as a crazed superfan. He dropped them off by hand—a crazed superfan who lived *next door.*

Here.

"And . . ."—Deek hesitates—"and the day after I told him that, his classmate went missing."

Jules gasps.

Everyone understands. No one dares utter the name. And Emma knows it, too.

Laura Birch.

Strand Beach's decade-old unsolved disappearance.

Deek swallows. This next part must be difficult to say: "I *inspired him* to abduct that girl, I think. For research or practice or worse." He tightens his shaky aim. "And I'll carry that guilt forever. Whatever he did to Laura Birch ten years ago is partially my fault. And I could never prove it was Howard who took her, and I called in every favor I had with the police chief trying to, because I knew in my soul that he murdered that poor girl. And my drinking got out of control, and my marriage fell apart, and my daughters won't talk to me, and my publisher stopped buying my book proposals. So don't lecture me about guilt, Julie."

Emma gets it now.

She wants to squeeze the old man's shoulder. She knows what it's like to feel responsible for the unspeakable.

I'm sorry, Deek.

"My son . . . he has nothing to do with that," Jules hisses. "They cleared him."

"They never cleared him. They just didn't have enough evidence to—"

"He killed someone tonight," Emma interrupts. "In front of me."

Everyone falls silent.

The wind growls outside and the rain intensifies.

Jules blinks furiously, as if struck between the eyes. She looks between them, then down to her sulking son. "Is . . . is that true?"

He says nothing.

"Howie?"

No answer. The killer stares downward, his whiskered face betraying nothing.

"Howie, I'm your *mother*." Her voice cracks, then hardens. "Is it true?"

He wished his mother didn't have to witness this.

She wasn't even supposed to be in the same area code. Howard's carefully choreographed night had veered disastrously off course. It had been resisting his efforts from the beginning—first an unplanned FedEx delivery, then Emma's startling counterattack in the basement. And now, Howard found himself held at gunpoint by his intended victims in the very living room where he once opened his presents under the Christmas tree.

This living room is widely believed to be the site of the massacre.

But like much of Howard's rampage that night, the truth is more nuanced. Certainly the forensic photographs taken in this room are some of the grisliest. Jules didn't know it yet, but at that moment she was standing exactly where her body would be found—at the dining room's adjacent edge, at the foot of her own grandfather clock. Police would find her blue-faced and cold with smeared eyeliner, crestfallen horror drawn permanently across her features. And her death was arguably the most merciful of the night's tally.

Through the standoff, Howard remained focused on Emma.

Only Emma.

Smart, gutsy Emma Carpenter, who should've

died hours ago, who defied her planned fate and fought tooth and nail for a razor-thin advantage. She'd saved her dog. She'd saved her neighbor. She was even beginning to relax, rubbing her goose-bumped arms.

No one knew.

Howard waited patiently for his moment.

EMMA HAS A BAD FEELING.

About everything.

Even with tonight's killer cornered before his own heartbroken mother, the monster unmasked as a lonely, sweaty virgin with mental illness. The tragic *reality* of it. No demonic powers. No Michael Myers slow-walk with a sword. Just folly, grief, and despair.

And still the dread remains. Somehow Howard's story is already written on paper somewhere. *We're going to die.* She feels it in her soul. *Tonight.*

All of us.

Something else bothers her. Now that she's had a moment to think about it—what are the odds that she'd read a shitty book that just so happened to be written by a psychopath who grew up in this very house? Out of hundreds of thousands—no, *millions* of books in the world?

Another coincidence.

There's another dark layer to this. No one in this room is safe.

"Julie, listen to me." Deek lowers his voice. "We need to call the police back."

The woman wipes her eyes.

"Can you do that?"

She nods through tears. She fumbles into her purse for her phone.

"That won't work," Emma says. "He cut the internet."

Deek points. "Howard, empty your pockets."

Obediently the killer digs through his coat and sets items on the floor. Night vision binoculars. A black e-cigarette. Duct tape. Braided rope. With a heartsick flutter, Emma recognizes her own sterling silver locket from Shawn, the chain broken from the moment Howard tore it off her neck. She feels a stab of hatred for him. Then, atop it, he places a squashed rubber mask, pale and horned and mouthless.

Her stomach fills with ice. *Demon Face.*

Last item . . . a jingling key chain.

Deek points. "Give me those."

Sullenly he tosses them to the floor at Deek's feet.

"Emma." He kicks the keys to her. "Someone needs to drive downtown and get the police." He glares at Jules. "Again."

She studies the key chain. She recognizes a set of house keys similar to her own—these must open every lock in the house—and a Honda key, which she assumes must be for Howard's personal vehicle. Lastly a Ford key, smudged with blood.

The slain FedEx employee. A young man with a family, relationships, and dreams, carved to pieces on the rain-soaked driveway.

"Actually." Deek reconsiders and glances back to Jules. "You ride with Emma, too."

"I'm not leaving my son alone with you."

"It'll be ten minutes."

"I don't trust you. You'll shoot him."

"I promise, Julie—"

"You'll *shoot my Howie* and tell the cops he ran at you, that it was self-defense." Jules refuses to back down. "I'm staying. To be a witness."

Deek says nothing. His finger is on the trigger.

Emma can feel the nervous electricity in the room. She can't help but wonder—is Jules right? If left alone with "Howie," will the old man take a chance for revenge?

And . . . when the chips are down, whose side is Jules really on?

With a shiver, Emma realizes she's heard the name *Howie* before: the Amazon user HowieGK'sTopFan. Days ago. If nothing else, her guess was exactly right. That five-star review really *did* come from the author's own mother.

"Fine." After a pause, Deek huffs. "Stay here if you want to babysit me. But give Emma your keys, too. That big black loaf of shit you drive. If Howard attacks us and gets free, I don't want him to escape the Strand. This ends tonight. No one else dies."

Jules rolls her teary eyes.

"Just *do it*. Then tie your son up."

Emma finds herself impressed by how capably Deek has taken charge of a dangerous situation. Even with a serious wound. Deacon Cowl is certainly a man of many skills—and, it must be remembered, Howard won't be the first killer he's helped catch.

Reluctantly, Jules presses her key chain into Emma's hand.

Howard watches.

"Em, I've got this." Deek keeps his sights trained. "Take her car, drive until you have cell signal, and let's put this whole mess on a police report."

She closes a fist around the keys. "Can you last that long?"

"I'll be okay."

"You've lost a lot of blood."

The old man smiles weakly. "So drive fast."

She studies the revolver in Deek's blood-crusted hands, but it's too dark to see the cartridges in the cylinder. She wishes she could ask her injured neighbor up front: *Be honest with me. Do you really have bullets?* If this revolver is really just a bluff, she can't afford to let Howard figure it out. And she can't leave Deek unarmed. Not after he has saved her life tonight—and she has almost killed him in return.

She can't say it aloud without shattering the stalemate. But with the toe of her shoe, Emma pushes Howard's katana across the floor toward Deek, holding eye contact. *Just in case.*

He doesn't touch it.

He only nods with appreciation.

"I'm . . ." She's not sure how to say it, but it's going to burn a hole in her chest if she doesn't try: "I haven't always trusted you, Deek. I suspected you were working with Howard somehow. I had no idea. I'm sorry."

A heartbroken shadow falls over his face. "Why?"

"Something Howard said."

It hurts, but it's true. She's embarrassed to have distrusted the man who has saved her life twice tonight. "And . . . I'm sorry for what you've been through."

He smiles gently. "I'm sorry for your loss, too."

"I'll be okay." She touches his brittle shoulder. "When this is over, I'm taking you up on your offer."

"Ginger tea in person?"

"Deal."

She hopes to God that they get the chance. That the tense standoff and the improvised bandage around Deek's throat holds.

That *everything* holds.

"When this is over," Deek whispers, "I'll call my daughters. I swear it."

She nods.

All this time, she'd assumed Deacon Cowl's daughters were dead—he'd *lost them both*, in his own whiteboard words—but there are many forms of death, aren't there? It's possible to screw up in ways that transcend death, to kill yourself without killing yourself. As a fellow ghost on the Strand, Emma understands. And she empathizes, perhaps more than Deek knows.

She wishes she'd opened up to him sooner.

"Thanks, Deek. For everything."

As she turns away with Jules's keys, Howard whispers something after her. His voice is just a soft murmur, but it slides under her ribs like an ice pick. "You lied, Emma."

She stops.

What?

In the distance, a bolt of lightning strikes the ocean. The flash lights the room.

"You lied to the cops, at the door." Slowly Howard stands upright, glaring at her. "About why you're hiding on the Strand. About what you really did."

"Hey." Deek's aim follows him. "Don't move."

"Howie, *sit down,*" Jules begs.

But those eyes remain fixed on Emma, unblinking as he reaches his mountainous full height. Crowding the room. "You're not like Laura Birch," he whispers. "You're *worse.*"

"Howie, stop—"

"Leave her alone," Deek says. "Talk to me. Not her—"

"I know your secret." The human Chucky doll's lips curl into a hateful smile. "What you *really* did to your husband Shawn. You weren't honest with your little car accident story."

How does he know this?

Her heart squeezes. She takes a step back.

"Last warning," Deek shouts. "Howard, I will *shoot you*—"

Too late.

Howard lunges for her.

DEEK AIMS AT HOWARD'S CHEST AND PULLS THE TRIGGER—
but Jules grabs his wrist.

"*No!*"

The weapon fires into the ceiling.

EMMA RAISES HER ARMS, BUT HOWARD HAS ALREADY TACK- led her under a shower of glass—a lightbulb has exploded above—and she's slammed into the wall. Her skull cracks. Lurid colors pierce her vision as he snarls in her face: "You reviewed me? Fine. I can review you, too—"

His latex fingers grasp her windpipe and squeeze. She can't inhale. She thrashes, kicks, claws away his glasses, but he's pinned her.

"You're a fuckin' nobody, Emma Carpenter—" She's aware of Jules and Deek struggling for control of the gun somewhere to the right, scuffling and grunting, but Howard Grosvenor Kline is her entire world. His thick grip, his hot breath dripping spittle: "You should've just walked into the ocean and done it already. You're just a critic. You hide from the world. And you think you can judge *me*? You can't even recognize a good thing when it's right in front of you." His thumb twists painfully under her jawbone, crushing her lymph nodes. "You don't make things like I do. I'm a creator. What do you create? The only thing you've ever created in your entire life, you killed—"

She can't breathe.

Pressure rises in her brain. Her eyes are going to burst.

And she's going under. Falling, falling someplace black, a place beyond even Howard's reach, watching the stars fade below a roiling surface. Her weighted backpack gripping her shoulders, her sinuses aching, her lungs bloating with frigid seawater—

"*One star,*" he screams in her face. "What's it like to be reviewed, you cunt?"

An earsplitting gunshot.

The wall explodes by Emma's ear and gritty slivers cut her skin. Her eardrum rings as she processes what just happened—fighting Jules's grasp, Deek has squeezed off another shot at Howard. He missed. But it helped.

Howard's grip loosens.

Emma twists hard, shoving away, tries to run and falls dizzily into the laundry room. She rolls onto her back and kicks the door shut.

The room spins wildly, a sickening concussive blur. Her throat is sandpaper. She coughs and her nose bleeds, dime-sized droplets hitting the floor. The warble in her eardrum intensifies, an unearthly chorus of screams, a broken radio picking up back channels of hell.

"Emma," Deek shouts. *"Run."*

She claws herself upright against the dryer, but the dial breaks off. In the next room she hears struggling. Shoes squeaking. Fingernails digging into flesh. Then a trailing steel scrape—a sound that will haunt her nightmares, if she lives long enough—as Howard's katana lifts from the floor and Jules's muffled voice cries out: "Wait. Wait, Howie, please don't kill him—"

Deek's voice lowers—he sees it coming—and softens with acceptance.

"Emma," he says. "Tell my daughters I—"

A powerful strike cuts him off. She can *feel* it through the door—a sickening slap of split flesh and cracked bone. Jules screams again, a new and blood-curdling pitch, and Emma hopes

to God that the old man's death was painless. An instant decapitation, his last words to his estranged daughters still in his
bisected throat, forever unknown.

He's gone.

Her only friend is gone.

And under a crash of thunder, Emma knows: *Howard has the*
gun now.

"That was nothing, Deek. You deserve the real seppuku."
Howard pants, catching his hoarse breath. "And after all that, you
didn't even save her. She can't run. Just like *Murder Mountain,* just
like the same thing she one-starred me for. Can you believe it?
She's hiding in the laundry room, the one room without an exit."

His voice rises, a furious miserable laugh.

"Dumb bitch *trapped herself.*"

NO, I HAVEN'T.

Emma heaves her aching body onto the dryer, braces her
knees, and climbs up the laundry chute. She's always been mostly
sure she can fit her bony ass through it.

Mostly.

She hears the door rattle behind her. Howard is trying to get
in—but she's already tipped the washing machine to block the
door.

In the next room, a sobbing voice: "Please, Howie, *no more*—"

"It's okay, Mom." He releases the doorknob. "Everything is
okay."

Emma hoists herself upward inside the cramped space,
clenching Jules's key chain between her teeth. This passage leads
straight up to the second-floor bedroom. To Laika. She raises
both arms high and finds the upper floor with her fingertips.
There it is. Just a few feet up.

"Howie—"

"Mom. Hold still."

Their voices follow her up through damp, mothballed air. Stringy cobwebs stick in her hair and mouth. Spiders tickle her skin. The aluminum walls constrict on all sides and suddenly there's no space to bend her elbows and pull herself farther up. This isn't working; this was a mistake, she's *trapped* inside the house's clammy, smothering guts—

"Howie. I can't . . . I can't breathe—"

"Please, please stop crying." Howard's voice softens to a pained coo. "I'm sorry. None of this was supposed to happen. But you don't understand. I can't stop now. Just one more, and I'll be done forever. Okay? Just *one more.*"

Emma fights through it all and climbs.

For Deek.

Howard tied off the last loop on his mother's restraints, ending her struggle. Jules was now hog-tied with braided rope, her chin pressed into the hardwood, sobbing and snotty-nosed, begging her son to end the carnage.

He wouldn't.

Murder Beach would cost him his future, and Howard had to accept this. The night was a fire sale: everything must go. No regrets. No half measures. Save nothing for a sequel. As he stood up, he screamed Emma's name into the ceiling, a raw and primal roar that filled the house.

Outside, the storm was finally here. Rainy wind blasted through the broken window and swirled through dark rooms. The sky split with thunder.

Howard anticipated Emma's next move. He knew

his childhood home inside and out—every corner, every edge, every weak spot.

He stuffed the Smith & Wesson .38 Special into his pocket and raced to the staircase, his boots leaving sticky footprints of blood. A few steps up, he stopped. He pulled down a framed photograph—Jules and ten-year-old Howard smiling during happier times, holding dripping ice cream cones aboard the *Victoria Clipper*—then raised his katana, gripped the battle-wrapped handle, and thrust it directly into the wall.

IT PIERCES THE LAUNDRY CHUTE BESIDE EMMA'S FACE.

The steel edge slices her cheekbone, a long cut from her earlobe to her nostril. She screams, but there's no room to move. She's penned inside the cramped passage, one arm up, one elbow squished helplessly to her chest.

His voice through the wall, alarmingly close: "Fucking *bitch*."

Blood spreads warmly on her face. She gulps desperate breaths, the air stuffy and hot with carbon dioxide. But she's almost wriggled up onto the second floor. Her fingertips grip the edge and she can feel Laika's soft tongue on her knuckles, licking eagerly: *Mom. Keep climbing. You're almost there.*

His blade slides back out, raking her cheek a second time. Inch by grinding inch. She winces in pain, but keeps her teeth clenched, holding Jules's all-important key chain. She can't drop it. She won't.

She knows Howard is going to impale the wall again. He's found her. There's no space to escape. She squirms and forces her body upward, writhing snakelike, up, up, up, knowing she's exposing her chest and stomach now. No time for fear. She keeps going, through sticky spider webs, through the clammy darkness—

You're almost there, Mom. Almost.

On its way out, the killer's sword makes a strange, glassy pop—like a broken fluorescent light tube—then a steely clatter on the stairs. Fragments landing.

She hears Howard cry out in disbelief: "No."

Then horror. *"No."*

She keeps climb-crawling away from his voice. Using every muscle in her body. She knows exactly what just happened and it fills her with wicked glee. Stabbing the wall with a curved blade was a critical error, and in his rage, Howard has shattered his precious sword.

His voice howls after her, now childlike.

"No, no, *no!*"

30

EMMA HUGS HER RETRIEVER'S WHITE FACE. "I LOVE YOU."

I love you too, Mom.

Then she scrambles upright, races to the bedroom's sea-facing window, and opens it. A cold blast of salty air gusts inside. She punches out the bug screen.

Outside the barricaded bedroom door, she hears Howard's footsteps still climbing, his huffing breaths. Then six inches of jagged steel pierce the door—a remnant of his shattered katana, now as compact as a prison shiv. Mutilated to a hideous new form.

It stabs again.

Again.

Again.

He's breaking through. And Emma isn't sticking around.

"Fuck this *whole* house. We're leaving, Space Dog."

The second-floor window opens only a few inches. Too narrow. So Emma lifts the nightstand—letting Jules's lamp shatter on the floor—and carries it across the room, holds it legs outward, and rams them through the glass. Shards spray out into the night.

With a whoosh like a pressurized air lock, the full fury of

the storm races inside. The wind screams. She lifts Laika's sixty-pound body, hoists herself over the windowsill, and scoots outside onto the second-story roof. One leg at a time. Her shoes slip on wet shingle.

Laika squirms in her arms. *Not a fan of this, Mom*—

"It's okay."

The roof's incline is frighteningly steep. Rain explodes off shingle in a blinding spray. It pounds her shoulders like rocks. Her face stings where Howard's katana sliced her—she's not yet sure how bad it is.

On her first step outside, she nearly loses her balance—twelve feet down to barren flowerbeds full of hard-packed sand. If she breaks an ankle, she's as good as dead. But if she can circle the slippery rooftop and jump with Laika off the north side, Jules's overgrown hedges might break her fall.

Maybe.

She scrambles along the roof's edge, leaving the window behind, gripping Laika in a bear hug. The keys are still between her teeth. The animal is growing heavy in her arms, but she won't dare set Laika down. Forked lightning crosses the sky in a writhing crackle. She can feel the electricity in her bones.

Being atop a roof again gives her a startling pang of sadness.

She remembers the odds the obstetrician gave them that day: *a hundred to one*. She remembers crying until her throat hurt. She remembers sitting on the roof's edge in Salt Lake City with red eyes and a burning cigarette inches from her lips, certain she would never, *ever* be a mother, before Shawn crawled outside to join her and tell her he'd named a star after her. Because if the obstetrician said they couldn't create life, he'd create something for her.

Emma's Star is still out there somewhere.

Wherever it is, she can't see it now.

The sky is a black downpour. Rain cascades off the inclined roof in a dizzying current. Emma can't keep her paces straight. Her right foot twists off-balance and the gutter snaps away underfoot.

"Shit."

Laika thrashes again but Emma holds her tight. The broken gutter tumbles down to the flowerbeds below. She knees herself upright and keeps scooting along the slick roof, sideways now. The wind rips at her clothes.

Back in the bedroom, a splintering crash. The door is down. He's inside.

Racing to the window after her.

Emma reaches the roof's far edge. Twelve feet down, she sees the hedges. Not nearly as overgrown as she remembers. This is where she must jump. She lowers herself into a sitting position, her legs dangling over the overflowing gutter. A brittle creak. With Laika in her arms, she can't look down. She'll just have to take it on faith. All of it. Dizzying faith.

She kisses the top of Laika's head. "Trust me."

I absolutely do not.

She takes a breath. And jumps.

By the time Howard reached the broken window and aimed the Smith & Wesson out into the driving rain, Emma was already gone over the roof's edge. He heard snapping sticks as she landed somewhere in the hedges below with her retriever in her arms. He'd lost sight of her, but he was unbothered. He still had four shots.

He didn't know where she was, but he knew something better.

Where she would be.

He spun around, vaulted back through the cratered bedroom door, and raced down the stairs, taking bounding leaps down the steps. At the bottom he stepped over Jules's hog-tied body, ignoring her wailing sobs. On into the kitchen, and through the small window above the sink he glimpsed Emma running toward the driveway. He aimed and fired—the window exploded—but she was already out of view. A canine yip of terror pierced the night.

Too slow. He'd missed.

Three shots left.

His ears rang and the kitchen stank with scorched gunpowder. The Smith & Wesson's double-action trigger was difficult to control and didn't have the pixel precision of *Call of Duty*. Howard was legally barred from possessing a firearm and woefully inexperienced. He couldn't rely on his marksmanship. He needed to kill Emma up close.

This was fine.

He could do this.

FRIGHTENED BY THE GUNSHOT, LAIKA BOLTS. EMMA LUNGES to grasp at the retriever's collar—too slow—and rips off her bandanna instead. Laika disappears.

"Laika!" she screams into the storm. "Come back."

She stops at the driveway's edge, still holding the frayed *Don't Stop Retrievin'* bandanna Shawn bought so many years ago. She wipes rainwater from her eyes as another gust of razor wind snaps the tall grass.

"Laika. Recall."

She's running out of time. Howard is coming. His gunshot's echo fades into the distance as she shouts again: "*Recall.*"

Only wind, rain, and darkness. No sign of Laika at all. More than ever, she wishes her retriever had a voice, that it was ever anything more than her own lonely imagination.

Run, Mom, she would say.

I'll be okay.

I'll see you on the other side.

On his way to the front door, Howard heard Emma shout for her spooked dog. This was good. Anything to slow her down. He couldn't let her reach his mother's car in the driveway. If she reached the Lincoln, it was all over.

He sprinted through the foyer, thumbing the Smith & Wesson's hammer. In single-action, the trigger pull would be easier to control.

Outside, he heard a metal clap.

A car door shutting.

But this was fine, too. He'd already reached the front door and elbowed through it hard enough to crack the frame. Now descending the porch steps into the blinding rain, he hurried down the stone path toward his mother's Lincoln.

EMMA JAMS THE KEY INTO THE IGNITION.

Ignoring Howard's crunchy footsteps, she twists the key. Her fingers are slippery with rainwater. Her mind races—this is the part of the horror story where the car fails to start. Just like the truck in *Murder Mountain*. If this had been a shitty H. G. Kane novel, the engine would sputter and cough and die, and the enraged killer would storm to the driver's window and jam his revolver to her temple and blow her brains out because *the author is God—*

The engine starts.

A satisfying, visceral roar.

This is real life.

Howard approached his mother's 2019 Lincoln Town Car from the left, raised the revolver, and fired directly into the driver's window where Emma's head would be. Another blinding flash and tooth-rattling blast. Glass fell out of the window, revealing an empty driver's seat.

Emma wasn't there.

The car was empty.

EIGHTEEN MONTHS AGO, AS EMMA SAT WITH SHAWN ON THE roof of their Salt Lake City home with their legs hanging over the driveway, she brushed away drying tears and said something that surprised her husband.

"You know what? Forget the odds."

She tossed her cigarette to the pavement below.

"We'll keep trying."

His guard was down.

Rain was in his eyes.

He didn't see Emma coming up on his left, in-side Jake Stanford's FedEx Ford Transit snarling out from behind the garage with its headlights off. The van struck Howard at twenty miles per hour and bounced him over the hood. He pin-balled hard, kicking off a sideview mirror as the van raked doors with Jules's Lincoln in a grinding metal scrape, fiery sparks leaping into the night with dizzying streaks of color.

In another heartbeat, the vehicles separated and Howard hit the driveway with gravel in his teeth. He'd forgotten about the delivery van belonging to the man he'd murdered. Perhaps, somewhere, Jake Stanford got the last laugh after all.

And in the aftermath, Howard had dropped his gun. By the time he found it, Emma's red taillights were already fading into the darkness, too far away to shoot and still going, the heroine of tonight's story escaping into the night.

PART FOUR

All storytellers, fiction and nonfiction alike, have inspirations.

However, Deacon Cowl is so much more than that. I also consider him a personal mentor. Deacon (or Deek, as I call him) recognized my raw writing talent at an early age and throughout my life has worked tirelessly to help me sharpen my skills. He's confided his own secrets in me. He's invited me over to his house for dinner and a perfectly mixed Manhattan more times than I can count (and even when I wasn't old enough to drink!). He's let me test-fire the .38-caliber revolver presented to him by the Fort Worth police. He's read my horror stories voraciously—and he's always told me that with continued practice, I could be one of the all-timers.

That world-renowned Deacon Cowl was also my next-door neighbor is purely coincidental. Although, as far as coincidences go, perhaps it's divine? How else would you interpret it? Sometimes in the evening while I sip my favorite bourbon and lightly oil my katanas, I think back and examine the many twists and fortunes of my life. I wonder sometimes if it's all unfolded according to some grand plan.

Like I've been chosen, playing a part I don't yet understand.

Like it was all supposed to happen . . .

Exactly.

Like.

This.

—H. G. Kane, "Reflections on Fate," 2021, hgkaneofficial.com

31

It wasn't supposed to happen like this.

The heroine of H. G. Kane's magnum opus *Murder Beach* had broken the story and escaped her fate. Emma was supposed to be easy prey! An anxious, tormented wreck who barely ate and barely slept, waiting out a solitary existence on the Strand with nothing left to live for. She'd beaten the odds, all right. Truth really is stranger than fiction. Howard had been one-starred for far less "unbelievable" twists in his own books.

Just like real life.

As he'd always said. If only his keyboard critics could see this.

And he'd made peace with his own shortcomings, too. He wasn't the unstoppable villain he'd long envisioned. His prior fiction was fantasy by comparison, as silly and weightless as *Propeller Head*. In *Murder Glacier* the killer is a formidable marksman, landing a head shot on a moving target more than two hundred yards away.

But in the plain, inarguable reality of *Murder Beach,* he'd missed Emma at close quarters with a low-caliber .38 Special that his wet fingers could barely grasp.

It had to be coming to him now.

Just. Like. Real. Life.

He would embrace it.

Emma Carpenter deserved her victory. She'd earned her happy ending. Because *Murder Beach* wasn't an H. G. Kane horror story after all. It was a tale of redemption. Tenacity. Survival. A wounded woman at the edge of the world who in her darkest hour found something to fight for. It was unexpected and beautiful.

It was his masterpiece.

It's unknown exactly how long Howard Grosvenor Kline remained there, reeling and bruised, on the wet gravel of the driveway, nor what time he returned, limping and humiliated, to his childhood home. He was in no hurry. The police would be here soon.

He entered through the front door.

He shouted, "Mom."

His wool felt fedora was lost outside, but it didn't matter now. He peeled off his soaked coat and hurled it to the floor. He kicked off his boots.

"Mom, don't worry. She got away. I'm done."

On his way through the kitchen he passed Emma's pan of water on the stove, now cooled to room temperature. This faintly niggled him; it was a setup without a payoff. In fiction, if a character boils water for use as a weapon, something has to become of it. Maybe he'd find a way to embellish it. He was the narrator, after all.

Although surely he never imagined he'd write the night's saga in a prison cell. He'd planned to complete *Murder Beach* on the road in his Honda CR-V, whilst embarking on his long journey to confront other readers who'd one-starred his books on Amazon and Goodreads. He'd pinpointed addresses for four other prospective victims thus far, with the closest approximately twelve hours south near Sacramento. His exact plans were unclear—maybe he'd jimmy the locks at three A.M. and creep into bedrooms. Maybe he'd cut throats ear to ear while hushing screams with his latex gloves and gazing into the eyes of his former critics. Maybe he'd print their negative reviews, as he did to Emma, and read their hateful words aloud while they choked on their own blood. Whatever his exact designs, Howard was on the verge of a cross-country killing spree. Emma Carpenter, inhabiting his childhood home, was to be his first.

Instead, she became his last.

Howard knew there were worse fates for a writer than incarceration. There'd be a prison library (although he was secretly ashamed of his near-total disinterest in reading), plus supervised use of a computer lab. But sentencing and conviction would take many months. And what about the jails? Especially out here? He wanted to start writing this manuscript as soon as possible, while the sights and sounds and smells were still fresh in his mind. Maybe he would request a notepad and a pen from Strand Beach police. It could be a condition for his surrender. If he had to, he could hold Jules hostage—not as a real threat, of course. Howard loved his mother dearly. But the police didn't need to know that.

"It's all over, Mom. I'm sorry."

No answer.

He called again. "Mom?"

Just the roar of the storm. The crash of breakers on sand.

For the first time in minutes, his captive mother was silent in the next room. No more sobbing. No more begging for her son to end this reckless violence.

When he entered the living room, he discovered why.

Sixty-three-year-old Jules Phelps's cause of death would later be ruled by the medical examiner as positional asphyxia. In his haste to restrain the struggling and distraught woman, he'd tied her wrists and ankles and throat, twisting her body into a dislocating hog-tie. This, combined with Howard's sloppy knot-tying and Jules's heavyset build, constricted her airway to the point of suffocation. He couldn't possibly have intended this. Investigators would later find toothmarks in the hardwood where Jules had struggled to right herself and breathe. There were two profound ironies here, neither of which could have been lost on Howard.

The first: that Jules had died only moments ago. When he'd stepped over her body as he chased

Emma outside, she'd been suffocating. Begging her son for help. He'd ignored her.

And the second?

Positional asphyxia was also Laura Birch's cause of death. By his own admission he'd left her duct-taped to a heavy oak chair in his basement while he attended class. When he returned in the evening, he found her cold—the chair tipped, Laura's airway shut.

His high school crush.

His mother.

And an innocent FedEx employee.

All three of these lives were taken in accident, by Howard's own incompetence. For all his cruelty, he was a tragically inept serial killer. And amid all this collateral damage, the lone woman who escaped the dark night of horrors was the one life he'd intended to take.

He didn't cry.

He didn't scream.

He didn't move his mother's body. He didn't need to. Jules had no pulse and her face was a rotten purple, her pupils dilated. There was nothing else to do.

Howard had so many things to process now. The humiliation of losing control of his own story. The ache of being body-slammed by a car. The shock of shattering his most prized katana. Now, chief of all: the heartbreak of killing his own mother, knowing it was this very book that cost her life.

Slowly, like ink spreading in water, his feelings toward Emma were darkening.

She was his heroine, yes.

But in the end, wasn't *Murder Beach* still a horror story? On the altar of his creation, Howard had sacrificed his own mother. He'd sacrificed the rest of his life, his freedom. He would never play *Call of Duty: Warzone* again. He would never buy another katana or eat another crispy cod and chips platter with two calamari appetizers. This was it. From here on out, his future was bland cafeteria food and supervised activities.

Meanwhile, what had Emma sacrificed?

She'd escaped the massacre cleanly. Too cleanly. Stories are unsatisfying without consequence. Save for a snarl of ripped hair and a gash on her cheek, Emma was unharmed and unmarked. By Howard's logic, she needed to lose something meaningful, too.

That was when he saw her English cream golden retriever.

The animal stood at the room's edge and eyed him, still skittish from the Smith & Wesson's report. But as the storm calmed, she'd returned to the only structure she knew. The creaky old house that sheltered her and Emma alike for three months.

Howard whispered, "Laika?"

The retriever shied away.

He crept after her. "Laika? Here."

In the kitchen he tried aiming his Smith & Wesson at her head, but he couldn't trust his own marksmanship. If his bullet only grazed Laika's skull and she bolted away again, he'd never catch her. This was his only chance. He tried grasping for her collar, but she flinched away.

"Laika?" He tried to sound friendly. "I won't hurt you."

The retriever eyed him suspiciously.

Howard concealed the pistol in his pocket, just in case her animal brain recognized it. Finally, after more episodes of frustrating touch-and-go, more coaxing and shy backward glances, he cornered the dog near the front door, and a few paces closer, he could touch her rain-soaked fur. He patted her head. She was still deeply uncertain.

"You're a gorgeous dog. Yes, you are."

He'd always hated dogs. Every last one of his mother's Chihuahuas.

He scratched the bridge of Laika's snout right between her eyes, in her natural blind spot, and she seemed to like that. Then those black eyes looked up at him, as if recognizing his true intent. She stiffened and tried to tug away, but it was already too late—he hooked his thumb under her collar. He'd do it up close. No bullets.

His voice lowered.

"Emma loves you, doesn't she?"

Laika struggled, her nails scratching tile.

"You're all she has left."

Whining, twisting away—

"That's why I have to do this." With his unhurt hand, he raised what remained of his beloved katana, a malformed six-inch shard of steel, to Laika's throat.

32

"DON'T *FUCKING TOUCH* MY DOG."

Emma jams electric prongs into Howard Grosvenor Kline's eye socket and gives him forty thousand volts to the face. Under the stun gun's popcorn crackle, she can hear the electricity pulsate in the author's scream: shrill, earsplitting, girlish.

Escape wasn't the plan.

She didn't choose the dead man's vehicle to surprise Howard (although hitting him with a goddamn car was her favorite part of the night thus far). She chose it because of the undelivered parcel inside. And once she'd driven a safe distance away, torn the box open, and inserted the battery, she drove back with Jules's stun gun in hand.

For Space Dog.

Laika backs away now, frightened but unhurt.

It's not quite the testicles, as Jules once recommended, but the face still seems plenty painful. Emma keeps her finger on the stun gun's trigger, sending more and more and *more* sizzling voltage into Howard's cheek, his mouth, his throat. She smells burnt neckbeard. His eyes bulge inches from hers. He's rigidly taut, every muscle and tendon clenched granite-hard under his skin. His blade clatters to the floor.

This is for Deek, she thinks. *And the delivery driver.*
And Laura Birch.
And everyone else you've ever—
The gunshot surprises her.

A thousand-pound sledgehammer strikes her thigh. The blast rattles her teeth, the flash blinds her, but most of all she feels a strange heaviness, as if her leg has instantly turned to stone. And spreading liquid heat. She's never been shot before. This is what it's like, apparently.

The electric chitter ceases.

Her stun gun hits the floor.

Howard screams with furious, red-faced power as Emma backpedals, hobbling to catch herself against the kitchen stove. Blood runs down her leg and pools underfoot. Devastating blows exchanged, predator and prey make eye contact.

Raising his gun, he grins.

"I got you."

He got her.

It's so tragic—and frustrating, to many readers—that even with thousands of volts seizing his nervous system, Howard Grosvenor Kline still managed to wrench the gun from his coat and shoot Emma at close range. Maybe it was his adrenaline, or the natural insulation of his heavyset physique. No nonlethal solution is a hundred percent effective, and there are numerous documented cases of suspects overpowering their arresting officers with electrode barbs still hanging from their flesh.

Now Howard aimed his Smith & Wesson to finish her.

One cartridge left.

Emma was cornered in the kitchen, wide-eyed and rapidly losing blood. She grasped for the stovetop behind her. She was reaching blindly for the pan she remembered boiling water in hours ago, to splash her killer with a gallon and a half of scalding liquid.

It was clever but futile. He knew the water was already cooled to room temperature, completely harmless to—

EMMA SWINGS THE ENTIRE GODDAMN PAN DIRECTLY INTO Howard's face. The water may be cold, but the pan itself is reinforced aluminum. She feels the man's nose break with a bludgeoning crunch. He screams in pain.

Attack. Hide. Repeat.

But she staggers only six feet farther—just out of the kitchen—before her body fails her and she crashes down hard to her stomach.

So she crawls.

Down the hallway.

The walls seem to spiral around her. Her leg is dead weight now, so she drags it. Everything below her right hip throbs with bone-deep pain. Blood fills her jeans, soaking the fabric to her skin and leaving a smeared trail on the floor—and behind her she hears a tinny *click*. She knows the sound.

She pushes open the nearest door and rolls inside before he can fire. She kicks the door shut. Then she locks it.

She scoots away from the door until her backbone hits a bedpost. A flimsy bedroom lock won't stop Howard. She's trapped in here, grievously injured and losing blood fast. She can't run. She has no weapons, nothing to fight back with.

She's in the teenager's room.

No. *Howard's* room.

A fitting place to die. The bedroom that's always unsettled her. The dense funk of body odor, the persistent and indescribable *sickness* that lived here. Time slows and smears, and in her peripheral vision Emma sees the mattress sag. Someone is sitting beside her.

She's glad he's here.

She shuts her eyes and smiles. "Hey, Shawn."

Get up, Em.

"I can't."

You can still do this. Get up.

"I'm sorry. I can't."

Yes, you can.

She shakes her head dizzily, fading fast.

Don't give up.

"I'm sorry, Shawn. I'm out of weapons."

Please, Em, get up. He's grabbing her shoulders now, shaking her, but still she refuses to look at him. *You're so close. Trust me, okay? You've gotten this far. You've been so strong for other people tonight. Now, be strong for* you.

And then, Em, I'll meet you there.

Those words always give her a chill.

I'll meet you there.

Her eyes tear up when she remembers twenty-one-year-old Shawn's surprised, genuine smile before the ambulance door swung shut. Two transfers. Nine hours in three waiting rooms. When they discharged him, she remembers buying a giant pack of Sour Patch Kids candies because she had to buy him *something* from the dingy little hospital café but didn't know what food he liked. Or even his last name.

I'll meet you there.

And every time she's stepped out into the lapping Pacific tide, she's made this same heartsick wish. She'd give anything to go back in time with her husband, to before everything changed. But it's impossible. She's always known it, and now it's time to face it.

I'll meet you—

"No," she says. "You won't."

Silence.

"I love you, Shawn. So much. You were my soulmate and I miss you more than I can say." She fights the shiver in her voice. "But you're not real. You're just my imagination. I'm not really talking to you. I never was."

She opens her eyes. Blinking away tears as the empty bedroom sharpens into clarity around her. The itchy carpet. The dusty computer. The fetid air.

On the mattress beside her, no one.

She's alone.

"It's only me," she whispers. "It's always been me."

That strength, too, was always hers.

And . . .

I'm not unarmed.

She rolls over, grips the bedpost with bloody knuckles, and pulls herself woozily upright onto the mattress—staring now into feudal Japan. Bamboo glows blue with moonlight. A stoic samurai warrior sharpens his katana.

Behind her the locked doorknob twists and jangles—Howard is at the door now—as she remembers his own admission, that he kept the sword he used to dismember his classmate's body behind a loose board.

In his bedroom wall.

Above his bed.

SHE RIPS THE POSTER DOWN WITH HER FINGERNAILS. THE samurai tears away to reveal bare wall. The loose board is hidden from the eye, but she finds the gap with her fingertips. She peels it away, revealing a deep orifice inside the wall, and all the secrets spill out onto her, the house's dark entrails released.

A lock of blond hair.

Dusty eyeglasses.

A clear pillbox rattling with bones and teeth.

And photographs. Dozens of Polaroids of unspeakable horrors, slapping to Howard's mattress around her. She won't dare look at them. Reaching deeper inside, she finds what she's looking for: a small sword. Wrapped in milky plastic, brown with flaked rust—probably Laura Birch's decade-old blood—but still sharp.

With a splintering crash, Howard kicks down the bedroom door. She whirls to face her killer with her new blade up in defense—but he calmly raises his gun. Emma's heart plunges. There's six feet between them, and no way she can cross the room on her bad leg before he fatally shoots her. Sword or no sword, he's still won. She knows it. So does he.

He aims at her face.

She braces.

She can't quite process what happens next—from the hallway, a racing white blur latches onto Howard's forearm. He grunts in pain. It's not a particularly powerful bite, because Laika is only a golden retriever acting on protective instinct.

But it buys Emma a moment.

By the time the man has wrestled his hand free of Laika's fangs, Emma has staggered across the bedroom and plunged the blade into his chest.

To the hilt.

"Howard," Emma says to his fading eyes, "your book *really* sucked."

33

EMMA RECOVERS HOWARD'S PHONE FROM HIS POCKET—
damp with blood—and then she crawls down the hallway to
collapse against an armchair overlooking the shattered windows,
the vast beach, and the snarling waves beyond. The storm is
passing now to reveal miraculous glimpses of pristine sky. Messier 31 peeks through, just for her.

Laika sits beside her, still panting.

"You're a good dog."

Yes, I am.

Emma kisses her furry head. "The best dog."

That's me.

"Thanks for saving my life."

You too, Mom.

She supposes they're about even.

With smearing thoughts, she raises Howard's phone—
connected to Jules's wireless network, with full signal—and tries
to guess his passcode a few times before remembering that emergency calls bypass the home screen. Duh.

She dials 911, leaving a bloody thumbprint on each key. The
line is silent for an anxious moment. A puff of static.

Then, at last . . .

Strand Beach Police Department

Incident No. 001373-12C-2023
11:58 PST

Operator: 911. What's your emergency?

Caller: Send police to 937 Wave Drive, please.

Operator: Okay, ma'am. Tell me what happened?

Caller: I . . . uh, it's hard to explain. Just send police. And an ambulance.

Operator: Okay. Can you please try?

Caller: A . . . total *psychopath* attacked me tonight with a ninja sword. Lots of people are dead. Jules Phelps. Deacon Cowl. I'm the only survivor, I think. And I've been shot, too. I'm losing blood.

Operator: Are you in a safe place? Where's the attacker now?

Caller: I killed him.

Operator: You killed him?

Caller: Yes.

Operator: You're . . . you're sure he's dead?

Caller: Pretty damn sure.

Operator: Okay. Stay calm. Units are on the way right now, and I'll talk you through some first aid. Can you tell me where you've been shot?

 . . . Ma'am?

 . . . Ma'am, are you still there?

EMMA FREEZES. SHE'S HEARD SOMETHING.

The dispatcher repeats: "Ma'am?"

At her side, Laika's ears perk. She heard it, too. And again, there it is—shuffling, bodily motion. It's coming from the bedroom.

He's still alive. Somehow.

Please, God, no.

It's impossible. She's certain she stabbed Howard in the heart. But still, the inexplicable sound moves closer. Down the hallway. Over disjointed footsteps, a wet and wheezing gurgle.

"Ma'am? Are you still there?"

No, she thinks. *I killed him—*

She waits as the choked sound comes closer. Closer. Until, clawing itself upright, the shadow of Howard Grosvenor Kline rounds the corner with Emma's blade still jutting from his chest. His pale face swivels drunkenly to her. Hit by a car, electrocuted, impaled, still somehow animated with a few more minutes of hateful and impossible life; a ghastly creature with butter vape on his breath and greasy fingers.

In a story, the author is Go—

Emma raises the gun and shoots him in the face.

His head whiplashes, leaving a chunky spatter on the wall behind him, and he goes down hard with a rattling crash. She'd searched Howard's pockets minutes ago, and she took special care to recover the downed killer's phone *and* his gun. In H. G. Kane's *Murder Mountain,* Prelaw forgets that and it gets her killed. But not Emma.

Emma Carpenter isn't a fucking moron.

She sets the revolver down. Then she leans back into the armchair and rests her eyes.

Strand Beach Police Department (cont'd)

Incident No. 001373-12C-2023

Operator: Ma'am? Was that . . . was that a gunshot?

Caller: Yeah. *Now* I'm sure.

34

EMMA WAKES UP AT HOLY FAMILY REGIONAL HOSPITAL WITH needles hooked under her skin and a plastic tube in her throat. A nurse explains in an irritating schoolteacher voice that the .38-caliber bullet ricocheted off her femur and exited just above her knee, barely missing her femoral artery. She'd lost two pints of blood by the time paramedics arrived.

"Cool," she slurs.

She spends three nights in intensive care, then a week in a recovery room overlooking downtown Seaview, a bricked-up and boarded-over fishing town that has nothing on Strand Beach—except, apparently, a hospital. Through the window's farthest corner, she can see a row of dirty warehouses and a sliver of gray Pacific Ocean.

"You did good, Emma."

She didn't hear Old Cop enter her room. He's stopped by a few times this week to give updates on the investigation. He stands now by her bedside looking at her with gentle eyes, almost grandfatherly. She feels genuinely awful for never bothering to know his name. "Not just good," he adds. "Incredible. Most people wouldn't fight that hard."

"A dog person would."

He smirks. "Maybe."

They found Howard Grosvenor Kline's body on the living room floor with a wakizashi sword in his chest and a .38-caliber bullet through his forehead. One of the responding officers was heard exclaiming: *Holy Jesus.*

I'm never, ever breaking into this chick's house.

Howard was, by all accounts, a loser. Coworkers and neighbors described him as a shy and socially awkward young man with a penchant for gaming (his Portland apartment contained more than seventy Xbox game discs but fewer than a dozen books). Over sixteen horror novels self-published under the pen name H. G. Kane, he'd tallied a few fans and countless digital scuffles with reviewers like Emma.

In Howard's world, any and all criticism was an attack—so whenever he was hit by a negative review, he sought a way to hit back harder. He falsely flagged Amazon and Goodreads accounts for inappropriate content. He pursued detractors across social media. He spread rumors of racism and pedophilia. He threatened pets. He weaponized Yelp to review-bomb private businesses he believed associated with his enemies, with varying accuracy, until lawyers were mustered in 2019 and his social media accounts were permanently disabled. In daylight hours, Howard was a software engineer for a respected financial planning firm in Seattle. He worked remotely, balancing a lonely but handsomely paid career with the even-lonelier rigors of writing and releasing two to three novels a year. He'd spent his winters house-sitting his childhood home on the Strand for his mother and moved out only this most recent spring.

In the fall, Emma moved in.

And when she read and panned his latest novel, Howard was thrilled to finally discover a keyboard critic within striking distance. He'd cast her as the unwitting star of his new masterpiece *Murder Beach,* both as an act of revenge and as a desperate lunge for fame. As a denizen of the internet, he understood the dark celebrity that can accompany violence. If Jeffrey Dahmer had written a book, wouldn't it surely have been a bestseller?

That's the official conclusion.

But to Emma, something still doesn't fit. The one-dimensional Howard they've reconstructed and the Howard she battled that night seem to be different men. Police saw a calculating, numbers-savvy sociopath aiming to turn his first (intentional) murder into his literary magnum opus. But Emma saw a wounded soul, tormented and volatile and grappling with his own unrequited romantic feelings for his mother's house-sitter, hot in all the ways they believed him cold. And the most puzzling loose end: his own words.

There's no Murder Beach, he'd said.

Why would he lie about this? He had told the truth about his prior novels, and even about Laura Birch's tragic death caused by his own error.

Last, and most disturbing: *He told me I had to kill you.*

To refute this, police point to the autopsy's toxicology report, which found no trace of antipsychotic medication in Howard's body. After missing several days, if not weeks, of his prescribed paliperidone, he was almost certainly suffering hallucinations and delusions. Mystery solved, right? Even Demon Face was a creation of Howard's, they reasoned, a firsthand tale he'd fabricated months ago and then staged with Jules's doorbell camera in a clever attempt at a red herring for police. He likely planned to kill a local transient, plant the rubber mask and some evidence, and frame the dead guy for Emma's murder.

On paper, it all fits together.

But Emma can't shake the gnawing suspicion that investigators have missed something. A nagging unease as persistent as a hangnail. Her hard-fought victory feels tenuous. Somewhere, she imagines a narrator struggling to reassemble the story of

Murder Beach with mismatched pieces. Somehow, she feels, she's still got her enemy—her true enemy, whoever and whatever he is—briefly within reach. On this island *somewhere*.

If she leaves now, if she drives home to Salt Lake City with Laika, she will only give him time to regroup and attack in a week or a month or a year. She'll be vulnerable.

"You need to stop dwelling on things that have already happened and move forward," Old Cop tells her the day of her discharge. "You've earned this. Every minute of it. You fought for your life back, and you won."

Eric Grayson, she corrects herself. Not Old Cop.

The man has a name.

"*Live,* Emma. And don't look back. If you do, you're letting Howard win."

Post-recovery, Emma Carpenter fell into a deep depression.

She refused to speak to media outlets, even as the massacre brought the sleepy town of Strand Beach to national prominence. The author turned serial killer gripped the news cycle for weeks, and in an ironic turn, several of his e-books rode the ensuing attention to online bestseller lists before vendors deleted them. Eventually the source files themselves were cracked, and to this day H. G. Kane's PDF files circulate the dark web like snuff tapes—Howard's cynical worldview at least partially vindicated. He came within reach of the fame he so coveted, if only posthumously.

His victims' names faded from public memory.

As it always goes.

And still, Emma withdrew from her contacts on the Strand. Her statements to police grew increasingly vague and terse. She dwelled on conspiracy theories—that Howard had a secret accomplice on that terrible night, or even that he was being manipulated by an unseen hand. She'd recovered from Howard's gunshot, but her true wounds were deeper, more difficult to see. The battle she fought had altered her in some way, deep, silent, invisible, and unfelt to everyone but Emma.

Such is the reality of trauma.

Disturbingly, Emma refused to contact her friends and family back in Salt Lake City. Their calls, texts, and emails went unanswered. Despite the urging of nurses, doctors, and her assigned mental health counselor, she remained isolated. She refused to eat. Her negative habits intensified into free fall. Days after Holy Family Regional Hospital discharged her, she made a worrying decision: to return alone to the Kline house. The site where it happened, where four lives violently ended.

In her mind, she had nowhere else to go.

She reentered the long driveway under a winter sky darkened with rain clouds. Swells crashed ashore and the wind rippled the grassy dunes. The first thunderclap rumbled, herald to the coming storm.

SUNSHINE BREAKS THROUGH THE FOG AS SHE RETURNS, A rare sight in January. The sky opens up, hard and clear and a perfect blue. Emma feels the sun's warmth on her face through the windshield as she parks in the gravel driveway. She glances to the back seat.

"Excited to be back?"

Laika chuffs. *Hell, yes.*

"Even though you almost died here?"

It's still the beach, Mom.

I love the beach.

"Fair enough." She glances up at the beach house and feels a strange tangle of emotions. Sadness and elation are so deeply entwined, she can't separate them.

The Kline house has taken a beating. Three windows are boarded up and tarped. Walls have been sawed open to extract stray bullets. Sections of flooring have been gutted by forensic and cleanup teams. But Emma suspects the lingering unease will fade, and maybe the spirit of Laura Birch can finally move on. Her teeth and earrings are no longer sealed inside the walls, her family has closure, and her killer is dead.

Emma leaves her crutches in her car and walks down to the beach unassisted. The sandy footpath is hard on her still-healing muscles, but pain can be progress.

By the ocean's edge, she tosses a Frisbee and watches seven-year-old Laika bolt and duck and spin in whirls of white fur and kicked-up sand, all fangs and flapping ears, moving in ways she hasn't since she was a frenetic puppy on the carpet of Emma and Shawn's first apartment together. It's like going back in time. She thinks about her husband's shy Schmendrick smile, the chemical odor of model paint, late nights of stargazing on the roof lying under a blanket and giggling until her cheeks ached, all the moments she's now permitted herself to revisit and enjoy.

She realizes—*I'm laughing.*

I'm actually happy.

She was deeply unhappy.

This grief would follow her like a shadow. The life she took in that tragic car accident months ago continued to haunt her. As hard as they tried, no one who knew Emma could possibly understand the depth or immensity of her private pain or know that she'd already made her final preparations to end her life on the Strand.

She would never leave.

"WE'RE LEAVING TOMORROW," SHE TELLS LAIKA. "ENJOY the beach while you can."

She's learned, after a lifetime, to ignore the negative thoughts inside her head. Like Shawn's imagined voice, like Laika's, like everything else, it's all self-generated.

That's the trick.

It's never easy. But it is surprisingly simple.

She's in control of her life. There's no narrator. And she's more than the worst thing she's ever done. It's all her, the good and the bad alike, because we can't pick and choose the pieces of who we are. And together all those pieces brought her this far. They made her strong enough to defeat Howard Grosvenor Kline.

"Almost forgot." She ties something around Laika's neck. "There you go, Space Dog."

Laika races off with renewed exuberance, a blur of fabric at her collar.

Don't Stop Retrievin'.

Back at the Kline house, as Emma packs her belongings for tomorrow's long drive home to Utah, she comes at last to her green Osprey backpack. This worn pack has seen the Grand Canyon, the lava tubes of Mount Saint Helens, the first time she made love to Shawn. It's a part of herself, one of her very favorite parts, and she's reclaiming it. Outside, she unzips the back, turns it upside down, and dumps out the stones. Every last one. It gives her a joyful sensation, like she's carried these heavy rocks for months and is finally free of their load.

BEFORE SHE LEAVES, SHE TAKES UP A FRIEND'S LONG- standing offer.

"Sorry I stabbed you with a screwdriver."

He shrugs. "It could've been worse."

She pours him a mug of ginger tea and they sit at the dining table in mellow silence, watching the setting sun fade behind bloodshot waves.

"I never said thank you," he adds. "For saving my life."

"I thought Howard killed you." Emma shrugs. "I came back to save my dog."

He laughs.

Ultimately Deek had survived the attack with a cracked skull and a severe concussion, courtesy of the blunt handle of Howard's katana. Police theorize Howard had meant only to deliver a merciful knockout blow to his longtime idol—although the resulting brain swelling still nearly killed him anyway.

Emma hates to say goodbye. Her things are packed in her trunk and tomorrow she'll leave the Strand forever. But as surely as they've both survived Howard's rampage, she senses it's now time for each of them to face their respective demons.

Deek seems to sense this, too. He sighs, pulling in a long breath. He hasn't touched his tea. "I'm . . . I'm going to call my daughters tomorrow."

"Good for you."

"I've . . ." He watches the waves break beneath the setting sun. "I've been a shitty father."

"You never told me their names."

"Annie and Alexis."

"How old?"

"Twins. Twenty-two now." He blinks, as if hearing it aloud for the first time. "My ex-wife . . . she took them to Boston after it became clear I'd never clean up. Annie is in a nursing school up there. Alexis does something with animals. And I'll be honest, Emma. I dumped my bottles down the sink, you know, tried to come at it with a clear trajectory, and I still have no idea what I'll say to them. I'm terrified of tomorrow."

"Anticipation is worse than reality," Emma says.

He looks at her.

"Something my husband used to say," she adds.

"Not always."

"Almost always." She smiles without showing her teeth. "Don't self-edit. Don't second-guess. You can polish words on paper all you want. But not speech. Talking has a special, in-the-moment honesty. The flaws make it real."

"That's why I'm a writer."

Emma finishes her tea and watches the tide. "Fuckin' *writers,* man."

He laugh-snorts. "We're the worst."

"I never said congratulations. For your book deal."

He shrugs modestly.

"Think it'll be big?"

"My publisher does. They already bought it."

"Even though you haven't written it yet?"

"I'm almost done with the first draft, which is basically the manuscript's bones. Howard's past, Howard's actions as he stalked you, the night of the attack. All woven together. But there's going to be lots more research. Transcripts. Statements. Drier stuff my friends downtown will gradually release. And you, if you don't mind." He looks at her directly. "Emma, I'd . . . be honored to interview you in the coming months. Every detail you can remember. If you're comfortable, of course."

"I am." She smiles. "I'm done hiding from the past."

More than you know.

Deek leans down and scratches Laika's ears. "His name was Shawn?"

"Yeah."

"He sounds like a good man."

She nods.

"I wish . . ." Deek sighs. "I wish I could meet him."

It's time to face the truth, Emma knows. No more denial. Mortals like Howard Grosvenor Kline can be shot in the face. But some things can't be so neatly vanquished. Only reckoned with.

As if on cue, her phone rings on the tabletop between them. A jagged, teeth-grating buzz. She flinches, only slightly.

Deek notices. "Emma?"

She sets down her empty mug. She glances to her phone, expecting a local area code—the police again, requesting their zillionth statement—but her heart squeezes when she recognizes the caller's number. It's not from Washington at all.

"Emma? Are you okay?"

Her stomach tightens into a ball. Her throat dries up. Because she's seen these digits many, many times before.

It's Shawn's number.

35

Howard made several errors on the night of his attack.

He failed to anticipate his mother's Amazon delivery and police wellness check. He fell for Emma's ambush in the basement, where his katana was too cumbersome to swing and she rewarded his arrogance with two broken fingers. And most fundamentally, he misunderstood the true nature of Emma's past. While studying the woman in her bedroom during the nights prior, he'd overheard her whispering her husband's name in her sleep. He'd observed that she still wore a wedding ring. And he reasoned, logically enough, that her husband, Shawn, was dead, perhaps in the gruesome car accident that left Emma guilt-addled and broken.

But that wasn't true.

In fact, Shawn Carpenter was very much alive. Back in Salt Lake City.

Emma and Shawn were still married, albeit estranged. They hadn't spoken in months. At the time, Shawn didn't even know his wife was in Washington.

That July, after an unknown but presumably heated argument, Emma had packed a bugout bag, taken Laika, and vanished. She severed every social thread from her life in Utah. She left her job and emptied her bank account. She ditched her iPhone. She'd always been a solitary and fiercely intelligent woman, and she dropped off the grid with slick tradecraft. She retreated into her books and made herself unreachable, unfindable.

And to be candid: I agonized over whether to include this detail. It's heart-wrenching. It's unspeakable. It's also, frankly, no one's business. But it is integral to understanding the depth of Emma's pain. I don't want readers to judge her.

Emma and Shawn had an infant daughter.

Her name was Shelby.

She was four months old.

And on July second, Emma and Shawn were driving to see family in Denver. Shawn was in the passenger seat; Shelby's car seat was in the back. When Emma took her eyes off the highway to look at her phone, for just a moment, an eighteen-wheeler changed lanes in front of her. Her reaction time was delayed. At seventy, Emma hit her brakes and lost control.

Even still, the collision was miraculously minor. She'd slowed significantly by the moment of impact. No airbags were deployed. The total damage to Emma's vehicle was a single cracked headlight cover and a crunched front panel; technically a fender bender. The semitrailer, too, was almost entirely undamaged.

Emma was unhurt.

Shawn was unhurt.

In the back seat, Shelby died instantly.

It's well documented that infants face the greatest risk of death in automobile accidents, but this particular tragedy has been described as "one in a million." It can only be inconceivably cruel misfortune that Shelby's tiny head would be turned exactly so, that the car seat would be positioned exactly so, that the glancing collision would send a kinetic jolt to travel exactly so through the vehicle in such a way as to surgically fracture the still-developing bones inside her neck.

And as a math teacher, Emma had to understand—acutely—that every element of this intricate physical equation was directly responsible for the outcome. Change one integer, and Shelby would have survived. The position of the sun in the sky. The weight of the gasoline in the tank. The tread on the tires. The fine layer of gritty dust on the pavement.

Emma's decision to look away from the road, to check her phone.

Just *exactly* so.

DEEK RAISES A GUN TO EMMA'S CHEST. "DON'T ANSWER your phone."

She stops with her hand outstretched. On the tabletop between them, the phone continues to ring on silent, vibrating harshly against wood.

Her mouth is suddenly dry.

Buzz.

"I'm sorry," Deek whispers.

Buzz.

"I wish . . ." His voice cracks. "I wish there was another way."

Icy fear climbs Emma's throat. She recognizes the gun in his hand—it's the same silver Smith & Wesson .38 Special she killed Howard with, the weapon that almost took her life. It should still be bagged up in police custody. How is it here?

Buzz.

She sets her palm down flat. Six inches from her phone.

"If you touch your phone," the old man whispers without blinking, "I will shoot you. I swear on my daughters' lives, Emma."

Buzz.

She takes a breath and says it. "Howard was supposed to kill me, wasn't he?"

Deek says nothing.

Buzz.

"That's why you just conveniently *found* your bullets that night."

And why the old man waited so long before intervening to "help." Only after the katana-wielding killer had cornered Emma in the basement and her death appeared certain—

Buzz.

"I wish this didn't have to happen." He takes a long breath. "Please believe me, Emma. I'd sell my soul for it. I've always enjoyed our conversations."

"I considered you a friend," she whispers.

"I still am."

"I *trusted* you."

"No. You didn't." He winces. "That's the problem."

She doesn't understand.

"Three words," he says. "You said them that night. Don't you remember?"

She . . . can't.

"That's why I'm here." He rubs his eyes with knobby fingers. "I'm not going to prison, Emma, and I'm not living the rest of my life in paranoia. We could have gone our separate ways, you and me, as survivors, if not for three *fucking* words."

She remembers now.

When Deek captured Howard at gunpoint and Emma was about to leave with Jules's keys, she'd confessed that she hadn't always trusted him: *I suspected you were working with Howard somehow.* She remembers the mournful shadow that fell over the old man's eyes, the deep seismic shift she couldn't comprehend, as she uttered those last three words.

Something Howard said.

Now a loose end.

Her own death sentence.

"You were right. All along." He smiles grimly, keeping his gun trained on her. "You should've stuck with your gut."

"That's the thing," she says. "I did."

He blinks.

He wasn't expecting that.

Between them, the phone has stopped vibrating—Shawn's call has gone to voicemail. Emma's heart flutters, and she knows she's close to the end. She's so close. She hardens and compartmentalizes everything she's feeling, because she has one more thing to do. One final, crucial thing.

Say it, Em. Don't you dare self-edit.

"Deek, I have a question for you."

Silence.

He's listening.

"Out of all the millions of e-books available to download in the entire world, I just *happened* to read *Murder Mountain*. And the author just *happened* to grow up in this very house. What are the odds, right?"

He watches her.

"That's a mind-blowing coincidence. Utterly insane. Distracting, even. I'd one-star a thriller for such a believability gap. And don't get me wrong—it's perfectly possible. People get struck by lightning and win the lottery multiple times over. And after what happened to my daughter, I know all too well how random and improbable and shitty life can be. And the police are fine with it. They love you. You're a local celebrity, so you even got your fancy little gun back early. They turned over every stone and told me not to overthink things, that I was letting Howard win. But it's still a *coincidence.*"

Deek says nothing.

"Coincidences are fine in real life. But in fiction, they're bad writing."

His eyes narrow.

"Until I realized it wasn't a coincidence at all." She lowers her voice. "Because I didn't read *Murder Mountain* by chance, did I?"

Still, he says nothing.

"Don't you remember?" She leans forward, her voice a scratchy whisper. "You recommended Howard's shitty book to me."

In the distance the breakers pound ashore, thousands of tons of crashing seawater. In. Then out.

In. Then out.

Finally Deacon Cowl shrugs. He's not used to being confronted, but he's adapting, leaning forward to match her stance with his finger on the trigger. The remorse was just an act and it fades now, replaced by a reptilian cunning. He flashes a wrinkly smile, revealing yellow teeth, and she smells whiskey and coffee.

"Then how come I still got the drop on you, Emma?"

She smiles back. "You didn't."

With her left hand still concealed under the table—where it's been this entire time—she presses the stun gun's prongs into the old man's nuts and unleashes forty thousand volts.

36

DEEK TWISTS AND THRASHES, VEINY EYES BULGING, LURCH-
ing off his chair and splashing an arc of hot ginger tea against the
wall. He utters a strange and strangled noise through his teeth.
His mug shatters on the floor beside him.

Emma stands, twirling the stun gun in her hand. "I'm starting to love this thing."

Thanks, Jules.

Maybe she'd been right, and the testicles really are the worst
possible place to receive forty thousand volts. Seen firsthand,
it sure doesn't look fun. Howard may have fought through the
paralyzing shock, but this frail old man has already crumpled to
the floor. Emma doesn't care if his nuts have exploded like popcorn, but she hopes she hasn't caused him cardiac damage. She
needs Deacon Cowl alive.

Laika watches wide-eyed. *Holy shit, Mom.*

Wasn't expecting that.

Emma circles the table and picks up Deek's gun. He writhes
painfully, grasping at her ankle—

"Nope." She stomps his hand.

He cries out.

"You thought I was in your trap? Motherfucker, *you were in mine*." Her mouth is dry, her words coming almost as fast as her thoughts: "Your career was dead. You helped the cops catch an evil man in Texas, but that was two decades ago and your family dumped you, you're an alcoholic, and you haven't sold a book to your publisher since. Your words."

Deek groans on the floor.

"But what if a killer attacked your neighbor? And what if you heroically intervened to shoot him? That's your comeback bestseller right there. And not just any killer. There are thousands of murders a year and yours needs to stand out, like the Stockyard Slayer did. Good thing you know Howard Grosvenor Kline, wannabe writer with a history of home invasions, who's finally snapped after years of ridicule and is confronting his latest keyboard critic. That's a fresh premise. Hell, I'd read that book. And you've known Howard for years, watching him grow up—how volatile he is, his insecurities, his triggers. You've got firsthand backstory. Deacon Cowl, you were *born* to cover this true crime story. The only problem: the true crime hadn't happened yet."

He whimpers.

She aims the revolver at his face.

"You encouraged Howard to murder me, right? For research? To improve his shitty horror fiction by trying the real thing, just like how you accidentally sent him after Laura Birch. But this time, you manipulated him on purpose. Because you'd kill him afterward."

She studies his eyes for a reaction. Fear. Shame. Guilt.

Anything.

"You *served* me to Howard. A grieving, suicidal woman living alone inside his own childhood home without witnesses, cell signal, or weapons. The perfect victim."

Instead, I kicked his ass.

"While you'd secretly cast yourself as the heroic neighbor, showing up to betray Howard with a bullet to the face."

And instead, I stabbed you with a screwdriver.

There's something viscerally gratifying to being underestimated, to shattering the diabolical plans laid around her. Surviving her scripted death, killing the would-be villain, wounding the would-be hero. Emma can't be controlled. She's a goddamn wrecking ball.

All her paranoia. Vindicated.

"And after Howard surrendered, you couldn't shoot him in front of witnesses, as much as you wanted to. It had to be self-defense. That's why you insisted Jules and I leave together."

He says nothing.

It's like she's finally won a game of Hangman with the ingenious old bastard. She's outguessed him. She's defeated his magnified gaze, his penetrating observations. Still, she must acknowledge and give credit where credit is due.

"You were smart to come after me." She hefts the revolver in one hand, Jules's stun gun in the other. "Just not smart enough."

Wincing, he pulls himself into a sitting position on the floor.

"Maybe this is how you felt ten years ago, when Laura Birch disappeared?" She tries to see it that way. "The police didn't believe me about Howard's words, no matter how much I begged them to investigate you closer. They called me paranoid. They said I was *letting Howard win*. But I think they'll believe me now."

She points across the room, at the audio recorder tucked on the bookshelf. Silently listening, logging every damning word.

"Want to say hi?"

He looks sullenly to the floor.

"Trust me, Deek, I wish we could go our separate ways, too. But I'd be looking over my shoulder for the rest of my life, just like you, and putting Shawn's life in danger. I couldn't risk you coming for us both." She pushes him over with her foot. "Now lie down."

She tucks the pistol into her waistband and presses the stun gun prongs into his neck. With her free hand she searches his raincoat pockets, finding his leather wallet. His keys.

"Won't be needing these."

Then, zip ties. Duct tape.

"For me? You shouldn't have."

Blue surgical gloves.

She whistles. "Scary."

In the old man's deepest pocket, she finds a small glass bottle. A tincture? The fine print on the label is difficult to read. It takes a moment; her eyes can't focus. Among many chemical names, she recognizes one.

Propofol.

Deek's very first Hangman word, months ago. It's all come full circle.

"That's how, huh?" Emma shakes the tiny bottle. "You came here to *poison* me. With the Stockyard Slayer's formula."

Finally, Deek speaks. His voice is a dry croak.

"I already did."

37

THE WORLD SEEMS TO WOBBLE UNDERFOOT. HER MOUTH IS paper-dry. She sets the bottle on the table's edge but misses.

Deek watches.

She tries to think of something else to say, to rebuke him, because she knows it's impossible. She would have felt the prick of a syringe. She hasn't even allowed him *close* enough to touch her. For twenty minutes, she's carefully coaxed the dangerous man into her trap while the audio recorder listened. She's been watching his hands, studying his breathing. Holding her concealed stun gun under the table an inch from his crotch, the twin silver fangs ready to bite.

But she can't deny the sluggish, woozy terror that now washes over her. It feels like being suddenly and uncomfortably drunk.

I was watching you the entire time, she wants to snarl.

How did you do that?

Her voice comes out weak. Childish, almost petulant: "I don't believe you."

Deek says nothing.

"I said, I don't believe you."

He smirks.

"Say something."

He doesn't have to.

Only now does he crawl to his feet like a heap of old bones assembling itself, all elbows and knees and cracking joints. Near his throat, she sees the Frankenstein stitches and pink scar tissue where her screwdriver missed his carotid artery by less than a centimeter. He watches her as he rises, just dispassionately *watching,* a cool and unsympathetic intelligence. She's felt those eyes on her through her windows. On the beach. He knows every detail of her life. He knows about Shawn. About Shelby. Her isolation. Her self-destruction. Her escape into books, her secret daily cigarettes, her nine-hundred calorie diet, her ginger tea—

My tea, she realizes with a jolt of slithering fear.

He poisoned my ginger tea.

She spent almost two weeks at Holy Family. Deek could have entered the Kline house at any night and dosed her tea bags or her bottled water or even her creamer and sugar. Exactly how he did it doesn't matter.

She glances down at her mug.

Empty. She finished it minutes ago.

"I'm sorry," the old man says. "It won't hurt."

He's barely over five feet tall, but she feels smaller. He seems to grow as she shrinks, as she feels her thoughts slip backward. Her heart is slowing. Her muscles are turning heavy, mushy, starting to tingle.

Those cold eyes watch her fade.

I take no pleasure in writing this final chapter. The story should be over. The monster is dead. But ultimately, and tragically, Emma Carpenter still lost her life. Not to Howard Grosvenor Kline's bloody attack on that now-infamous night.

Two weeks afterward.

Shortly after her discharge from Holy Family.

It's heartbreaking that this remarkable young woman could fight Howard so tenaciously, and even survive a close-range gunshot, only to succumb to her own demons just weeks later. Emma improvised and adapted. She used the layout of the killer's own childhood home against him. Even while making her hard-earned escape in a stolen vehicle, with the safe city lights of Strand Beach just miles down the road, Emma chose to pull over, rip a stun gun from its packaging, and walk back into danger to save her beloved golden retriever.

And maybe that's it.

She fought for her dog's life. She fought for the life of a FedEx employee whose name she didn't know, and the two responding Strand Beach officers at the door. Not least of all, she fought to save my life, too, as I lay bleeding and unconscious on the living room floor. There's no telling what grisly mockery of samurai seppuku Howard might have planned to force upon me. And I truly believe, hand over heart, that I'm alive today to write this book because of Emma's actions that night. I wish I could thank her.

But when there was no one left to save, and she was left to her own devices on the foggy loneliness of the Strand, it finally happened on January twelfth.

Emma Carpenter took her own life.

SHE JAMS HER FINGERS DOWN HER THROAT. HER GAG RE-flex is alarmingly delayed—but finally she wretches, her eyes watering, and spits up a milky brown fluid. Tea, creamer, stomach acid.

"Doesn't matter," Deek says. "It's already in your nervous system."

She coughs and spits.

"Emma. Stop fighting it—"

She shakes her head, her throat raw. Her stomach is empty. She's purged what she can. But unlike Laika's poison pellets, she's already absorbed the fatal dose, because liquids enter the bloodstream much faster than solids.

"It's too late."

She ignores him. The house is tilting. She nearly doubles over.

"Sit down. It's almost done." She feels his bony hand on her shoulder. That deranged anesthesiologist in Texas may have done unthinkable things to his paralyzed victims, but Deacon Cowl is a gentler soul. "You should know, you were wrong about Howard—"

She pulls away. Refusing to look at him.

"He couldn't stomach the idea of taking an innocent life. But I'd found him the perfect compromise: a woman on the verge of taking her *own* life. You were dead anyway, and your life would either go to waste, or it wouldn't."

It gives her a sickening chill. The coldness of what he says, how he says it.

"He'd been watching you for weeks. Long before you read his shitty little book. Living in his SUV parked up by the seawall, coming and going freely in the big house. I think he even slept in his old bedroom a few nights. Did you ever feel haunted? Did Laika behave strangely? It probably stank of Howard, like a phantom roommate."

The bedroom. The fetid odors of butter vape juice and sweat. The toilet that seemed to flush autonomously. All of it.

"And he was developing a crush on you. Like Laura Birch all over again."

Scritch-scratch.

Even fading, it gives Emma a revulsive shiver.

"He just liked living around you, I think. Close quarters with a female. I think that's why he resented your dog so much: he was jealous of the attention you gave her. And even though you were getting closer to drowning yourself every day, Howard couldn't bring himself to finish you off. He wasn't truly a monster, as much as he liked to write about them. He was just a lonely, envious kid with no social skills, wishing for fame, wishing for validation, maybe most of all wishing for a girlfriend."

She feels something new. A stab of sympathy, crystalline in its power.

"And finally, he told me he'd changed his mind, that he wouldn't kill you after all. That left me with a problem. I needed him to *hate* you. Somehow."

She can sense the muscles in his face moving beside her ear.

A wrinkly smile.

"So I stirred things up. I recommended you read his newest dumpster fire, *Murder Mountain.* Just to get you talking about it."

Her online conversation with Howard is still thudding in her memory. The betrayal in his words. What had made her criticism sting so acutely, a perfect stranger among millions? Now she knows it's because she wasn't a stranger at all. Howard was watching her, perhaps even from the next room. Close enough to identify the species of bird that hit her window and inject its name into their conversation as a subtle, spooky hint.

I won't ask you again.

Good.

"You had no idea your killer was about to pack up and leave town," Deek whispers. "Until you typed up your own death sentence on Amazon."

In a way, Emma's fate was inevitable.

She'd isolated herself on the Strand. She'd fled her job, her husband, and her life. The beach can be a site of spiritual renewal—it's why I moved to Strand Beach myself, after the success of *Silent Screams* blessed me with the means to escape the bustle of Dallas. The chance for my twin daughters to grow up in an idyllic coastal town, for my wife to find her own second act, and for me to focus on bettering myself. But the sad truth is, Emma was not here to recover.

She was here to disappear.

And every day brought her closer to the moment she'd vanish under those rolling gray waves. She'd started this grim trajectory months prior to Howard's attack. Her death occurred neither because of him nor despite him. I only wish I could have spoken to her first.

I wish this, so badly.

Just a simple conversation. Or one more whiteboard game of Hangman. Or that face-to-face meeting for ginger tea (she loved ginger tea) that we'd always promised each other. It's hard not to become emotional as I write this. I'm a solitary man with deep-running flaws. I've never formed friendships easily, and neither did Emma, but I would give anything to speak to this extraordinary woman one last time.

My dear friend, to whom I owe my life.

Emma, if you could speak to me, what would you say?

"FUCK YOU."

She presses the stun gun into Deek's chest to deliver another nerve-frying blast—but he rips it away. His other hand grasps her biceps with surprising strength, pinning her. She feels her own desperation rising, an animal panic. She needs to get away.

"Stop," he whispers. "This is hard for me, too."

She clenches her other hand into a fist and swings—a drunken roundhouse that glances off his shoulder. He barely reacts.

Get away.

She fights his grip, dropping, hitting her kneecaps on hardwood. She tries to hit Deek again but misses entirely. Her arm feels like it's made of wet bread.

"Emma. Please stop."

Get away.

She twists free.

"Emma—"

She's on the floor, bruising her elbows, kicking away from his grasp like a clumsy sea creature on land. She rolls onto her back. In her hands is an object she's pulled from her waistband. Something she's certain the old man has forgotten about.

His gun.

Now aimed at his forehead.

She sees surprise flash over Deek's face. Just a blink. Then that icy judgment is back. Even staring down a gun barrel, the old man's voice barely wavers. "You're still dead."

"Yeah." Emma manages to grin, her cheeks turning to rubber, her tongue thick and alien inside her own mouth, as she pulls the trigger.

"But you first."

_____

THE HAMMER STRIKES.

A hollow *click*.

"This isn't a murder," Deek says. "It's a suicide."

Disbelieving horror washes over her. She keeps pulling the trigger anyway, dry-firing into his face as the cylinder turns— *click, click, click*—and he wrests the gun away. She can barely hold it. Her fingers are alarmingly weak.

"I'm so sorry, Emma."

He studies his revolver in the lamplight, as if checking it for scratches. Then he tucks it back in his raincoat, satisfied that the unloaded weapon has served its purpose. *A deterrent,* she realizes drowsily. *In case I struggled while the drugs kicked in—*

"Just let it happen. I'll wait with you."

Shut up, she wants to say. But she can't speak.

"And I won't hurt Laika." He scratches the retriever's ears. "She's a lovely girl. Named after history's first dog cosmonaut in 1957, right? It's a good name."

Of course he knows the exact year.

"I'll handle everything." The old man leans in close. "Okay? In a few days, after they rule your death a suicide, I'll drive Laika out to Salt Lake City. I'll find Shawn. And I'll tell your husband, in person, that you were a hero. That you saved my life. I *promise* I won't hurt either of them. I understand why you can't trust me, but I give you my word. As your friend."

The thought of the evil little leprechaun sitting in their dining room, consoling her husband, turns her stomach.

"You wanted to die, Emma. It's why you're here."

No.

"Honestly, if I killed my baby, I would, too."

No, no, no—

The house lists like a sinking ship and Emma grips the floor to hold on. Outside the waves are deafening through the tarp, a roaring chorus filling her mind. The raw power of the sea. Time seems to clot. She tries to scream, but her lungs are jelly.

"The working title is *Murder Beach*." Deek lifts her audio recorder from the shelf and inspects it. "It's an on-the-nose title, but Howard's stupid novels are viral now, and my publisher wants to align clearly with that. Honestly, I'm just happy to be working again."

Pocketing her recorder, he flashes a sad smile.

"More than you know."

He seems to teleport around the room.

Blinking dizzily, Emma struggles to follow the human shadow. First . . . he's staring down at her as he slips on his blue surgical gloves: "In my book, I'm trying to write Howard to be scarier. More evil, cold, calculating, something like Michael Myers with a katana. Any extra flourishes I can get away with that won't . . . you know, contradict your statements to the police."

Then . . . he's rearranging glassware on the table. "I have to."

Now . . . he's mopping up spilled tea with paper towels. "You know as well as I do that the real Howard was a fucking *dork*. He couldn't take a leak without catching his dick in his zipper."

He's staging the scene, she knows.

Suicide by overdose.

"That's the big secret," he grunts as he cleans. "In real life, most murderers are boring as hell. Sit down and interview one through prison glass, and after five minutes, I challenge you to give a shit about anything they have to say. They're never smart, either. They're the lowest and least of us, perverts or sociopaths or bedwetters who can't control their feelings. True monsters, like the Stockyard Slayer? One in a hundred million."

Knives, she remembers thickly.

The knife rack.

Behind her.

She heaves her body over and reaches up toward the kitchen counter. Her outstretched hand feels like it's a mile from her face. She paws at the knife rack until it crashes to the floor. Blades skitter across tile.

Across the room, Deek glances up and frowns. He's teleported to her laptop now. "Come on, Emma. You know I'll just clean it up."

With numb fingers, she grabs the closest knife. She raises it toward the old man in a shaky grip, blade out. If he touches her, she'll slice him open. But he doesn't need to touch her, and he knows it. He needs only to wait for her to die.

He glances back down to the laptop. Typing with blue surgical gloves.

A suicide note.

"Don't worry," he says. "I'll make it respectful."

Deacon Cowl has thought of everything. She may have tilted the story off course when she killed the villain and survived the night, but the author has a cruel and ingenious mind. Howard always liked to say something about that.

A stupid saying.

She can't remember it.

And she doesn't want to waste valuable brainpower on it. Because there's one last thing she can do. She brings the knife's serrated edge to her forearm and cuts. Her skin splits open and her blood seeps out, dark and tarry. To her horror, she can't even feel it.

She carves one letter at a time. While Deek types a fake message across the room, she's writing a genuine one of her own. Outrunning her own fading consciousness, her letters clumsy and childish—but she knows the medical examiner will find it.

Their long-distance friendship has always been about handwritten messages, right? Here's one more for the road.

DEEK KILLED ME

She lets the knife drop and collapses onto her back.

Have fun, she thinks to Deek, who is now meticulously wiping the tabletop for fingerprints. *You'll go through all that work, and you'll still get caught.*

She's falling into her own skull now. It's a disturbing sensation, entirely different from falling asleep. She can feel the cells in her brain fading, withering, turning into little blue raisins. Before darkness wins, one last realization. A pierce of heartache, all the way to her soul.

Shawn's voicemail.

She'll never hear it.

T—Mobile ID 20775392

1/12/24 8:02:15 PST
Voicemail

Hey, Em. It's me. I . . . (INAUDIBLE) so I got your new number from the police. They said you're all the way out in Washington, and that some bad things happened the other week. They won't tell me over the phone. I just . . . I hope to God you're okay. I miss you. Wherever you are. Please call me or text me or something. I love you so much. Bye.

Wait.

There's, uh . . . there's one more thing I have to say. I've said it before, I know, but I'm saying it again. I'm sitting on the roof right now, where we used to watch the stars, and I just . . . I have a bad feeling tonight. I'm worried you're in an especially bad place right now, and maybe you need to hear this before you do something drastic.

Listen to me. What happened to our daughter is *not your fault*.

I love you so much, Em.

Please, come home.

38

SHE'S IN A CAR.

The hum of a motor. The creak of suspension.

She's riding down a black coastline, someplace cold and damp and far from home. No headlights. The driver must be navigating by moonlight. Pinpricked stars, sand, and whitecaps race outside. She's stuffed in the back seat. The seat belt holds her upright.

A man sits beside her.

It's Howard.

Her chest hitches with terror, but he's only a fellow passenger. He's buckled in, too. His neck twists to face her—a knuckle-popping crack of bone—and on his breath she smells vape juice, Mtn Dew, and a new earthy odor. Decay.

She braces for more hate, for vitriol. *You can't create, Emma. The only thing you've ever created in your entire life, you killed.*

It never comes.

In his lap, Howard holds gleaming handfuls of steel. The shards of his katana. He looks down at his broken toy, then up at her with milky eyes. "I'm sorry," he says.

She can't speak. Her mouth is too dry.

They're not alone. In the seat row behind them, Emma recognizes Jules Phelps sitting silently with her face buried in her hands. And a man whose name she can't remember. His eyes and nose are slashed away. His wrists are glistening stumps.

Emma shuts her eyes.

The Jeep keeps cruising up the dark beach.

The visage of Howard leans in closer to her, his bones creaking, now uncomfortably close with his neckbeard tickling her cheek. "You didn't get the full dose. You threw some of it up." He glances forward, to the driver. Then he whispers in her ear: "You can still make it, Emma. If you *want* it badly enough."

She ignores him. She's had enough of Howard. She's in a car full of slumped corpses riding to eternity, and of course the only person she wants to see isn't here. Shawn is a thousand miles away.

She calls to the driver with a creaky voice. "Hey."

Deek glances up into the rearview mirror.

"Can you please add something to that suicide note?" she asks, fighting the drowsy slur in her words. "A message to Shawn. I . . . I disappeared when he needed me most. After Shelby died, I didn't know how to grieve. I just shut it out. I was afraid to feel it, with him, and that's no excuse. I need Shawn to know . . ."

She chokes. Even though her face is numb, she feels tears coming.

"I just need him to know I'm *sorry*."

Silence. The suspension jostles over a sandy rise.

Deek nods.

He glances forward at the dark horizon and then back at her in the rearview. "No," he says finally. "I like what I wrote better."

THERE IT IS.

Her green Osprey backpack rests in the center of the rocky

path. She can see that it's stuffed again, bulging with sixty or seventy pounds of rocks. Deacon Cowl, in his thoroughness, has packed it heavier than she ever did.

Maybe his version really *is* better.

She's vaguely aware of his wrinkly hands on her body, lifting her out of his Jeep, dumping her onto packed gravel. They're a hundred yards out onto the boulder seawall at the island's northernmost tip—as far as he can safely drive his rig—and the sky is cloudless, a vast and starry void. She can see galaxies. She remembers pointing out constellations to Shawn, boozy and giggling together on their roof. *That, right there, that big cluster, is Cygnus. The Swan.*

That's Serpens.

And Sagittarius.

Now Deek is guiding the weighted backpack over her shoulders—first the right strap, then the left—and pulling the buckles tight. She's too weak to resist. Her muscles feel like slush. She can't even hold up her head. Deek slips off her sneakers, one at a time, and sets them neatly atop a boulder beside her phone and wedding ring. A nice touch.

"Almost forgot."

Beside it, he places Emma's silver locket, opened to reveal the face of Shelby Lynne Carpenter, red-cheeked and yawning, less than six hours old.

"I lied about calling my daughters tomorrow." Deek sighs. "I'm sorry, but there's no point. I broke their mother's cheekbone when they were fourteen. I don't even remember hitting her. Or why I did it. I just remember frantically apologizing, trying to drive her to the emergency room, but I was too drunk to notice Alexis had hidden my keys. Then Annie locked me outside. Like an animal. I sat in the driveway and cried while the ambulance came. It was the worst low of my life, the biggest mistake I've ever made, and a single phone call a decade later won't change it. They'll never, ever forgive me, and I've made my peace with that." He looks down at her. "I know you'll understa—"

He stops.

Then he frowns. Roughly he lifts Emma's forearm and thumbs away the drying blood to reveal her carved letters. The message etched in her flesh.

She croaks: "Surprise, asshole."

He studies it.

Then he lets her wrist drop. "Doesn't matter. You'll be fish food."

She feels another stab of hatred for this man, dulled by anesthetic. She understands now that the carefully mixed cocktail isn't intended to kill by overdose. It's only to paralyze her, to render her helpless and unable to free herself from the weighted backpack when she's underwater. A new take on the Stockyard Slayer. Deacon Cowl studies serial killers for a living, after all.

By the time her remains wash ashore—in weeks or months or maybe never—they'll be unrecognizable. She'll become the clay-faced specter she used to imagine in mirrors; her eyes and mouth gone, her flesh soggy gray. Her carved message will be gone. All traces of the chemicals in her system will be gone, too. He's planned everything.

The canny and precise mind that dismantled her at Hangman, that knew Emma's name long before she ever gave it to him.

He sits her upright now. Eye to eye in starlight.

"I'm finishing my first draft tonight." He kisses her forehead. She barely feels his papery lips and focuses on the sky above.

Orion.

Taurus.

Mensa.

"I wish it ended differently for you."

She's too drugged to feel panic or fear. She's past it anyway. All that remains is a dense sadness that fills her chest like wet cement, heartbreak for what she's leaving behind.

And that. See that group of stars? That's my favorite, the Androm-eda Galax—

She's not sure how exactly the old man drops her over the jetty's edge. Maybe he shoved her. Maybe he dumped her like garbage. She only knows she's suddenly weightless, cold air whistling in her ears. Then she hits a barnacle-encrusted boul-der. Then another, and she rag-dolls sideways, a sprawling tum-ble, and then an ice-cold blackness rushes in from all sides and she realizes she's now underwater.

Already.

It happened so fast.

She didn't even have time to take a full breath. And she's sink-ing. The weighted backpack twists her faceup and she watches the watery stars fade as she's dragged deeper, deeper into dark-ness. Her fingers are numb, sluggish in frigid seawater. She tugs the backpack's straps but they're fastened impossibly tight. Her fingernails bend. And she's running out of oxygen.

She now understands: her recurring nightmare of drowning in the ocean was real. It was always real. Everything *else* was the dream. In a sickening way, she's just finally woken up, in the cold, dark place she was always destined for.

Even without air in her lungs, she wants to scream at the un-fairness of it. She's fought so hard. So fucking hard.

She struggles, flails, kicks.

No difference. She's still sinking.

But still . . . pulling, *pulling,* she unclasps one backpack strap. It snaps open—*yes!*—and she twists her left shoulder out.

Halfway free—but not really. Her right shoulder is the problem; the plastic buckle is bunched up under her armpit.

Unreachable. Too dark to see. She's far below the surface now, somewhere in the graveyard of the Pacific, the starlight waning, the backpack dragging her deeper still.

She tries. She can't.

She's fading.

Above, the stars are now gone. Even they will die someday.

Her mouth and sinuses are full of salt water, but somehow she tastes the acrid odor of rubber smoke. Burnt brake pads. The black water opens up and white-hot sunlight stings her eyes. She remembers thrashing to her right, holding a protective hand to the lip of Shelby's car seat in the back seat as they skidded, just a split-second instinct, and she's fully aware that this tiny reflex added one more integer to the terrible equation.

Her phone lands faceup. Her Outlook app open.

Her seat belt constricts her throat.

In the surreal silence after impact, Shawn grabs her shoulder. "Holy shit. That was close."

And he's right. It looked like a fatal collision but became only a glancing hit. Barely a fender bender. And now Emma expects to hear Shelby amid the disorientation, rudely jolted from her nap, starting to cry—but she hears nothing from the back seat. Nothing at all.

The air seems to thin.

"Shelby?"

Her words are thick with coppery blood. It doesn't matter how minor the collision was—there's no such thing as *minor* when you have an infant on board.

Please, God.

All that matters is Shelby.

Please—

She twists out of her seat belt, a heartbeat faster than her husband, and swings the door open into sweltering July heat, and the driver of the semitruck is already climbing out of his cab and asking if they're all right, and she ignores him, skidding on shaky feet and grabbing the back door handle, tugging it open—

Please-please-please—

She unbuckles the car seat, grabs Shelby's frail body, so light and so terribly limp, and lifts her upright and out of the car, falling to the gravel shoulder and holding her daughter, knowing what she's always known, that inertia and gravity and kinetic force and her own selfish desire to avoid Shawn's family have aligned *exactly so*—

Shelby's eyes are open.

She's alive.

Emma realizes this as she lands hard on her tailbone. She can't believe it. Shelby's eyes are the clearest blue, pupils searching and locking onto hers, full of life and curiosity. It's impossible. It's not how it happened. But it's real.

She presses her daughter to her chest.

"I'm here."

She breathes through a swirl of fine hair. Blond, just like Shawn's. She hasn't smelled that sweet, soapy dandruff scent for months. She was so certain she'd never smell it again. She feels the tiny body stir again in her embrace with grasping fingers, in that special way that's both heartrendingly weak and alarmingly strong, and Emma stares up at the hard blue sky and lets out a strange, choked gasp. It explodes out of her, five months of compressed agony, all gone in an instant as Shelby touches her face with soft, developing fingers.

"I'm here." Emma knows it's impossible. She doesn't care. Somewhere far away, in a cold dark vault, her fingernails remain clenched around the final plastic backpack strap, which is holding someone else underwater.

Shelby is alive.

Shelby is okay.

Everything is okay.

"I'm here, baby."

In her final moments, I hope she found peace.

There's one solace we can all take in Emma Carpenter's memory—the knowledge that wherever she is now, she isn't hurting anymore. My heart breaks so utterly for her, because in the immensity of her silent and unceasing pain, suicide truly appeared to be the only way out. As a parent myself, I can't fathom what it must have been like to lose an infant daughter in such a way. Such guilt must be seismic, earth-shattering. Emma coped with the unthinkable the only way she knew how—by leaving her husband, isolating herself in a controlled environment, and attempting to process it one small bite at a time. Like eating a mountain. Sometimes it's simply not possible alone.

This account of Howard Grosvenor Kline would be remiss without including the brave woman who stopped him—and her own tragic fate in the weeks that followed. In this way, it's as much Emma's story as it is Howard's. To me, she wasn't just an extraordinary young woman who fought to save the lives of strangers and her golden retriever alike.

She was also my friend.

I hope she knew how much I admired her. I'll

always remember our long-distance games of Hangman, played via telescope over many lazy afternoons on the Strand. She always beat me! She
guessed my words with supernatural intuition,
every time. To this day, I don't know how she
did it. And our countless whiteboard conversations, discussing books we'd read, movies we'd
loved. She was so sharp. Incisive. Opinionated.
She may have been a quiet woman, reluctant to
speak, but when she put her thoughts into writing? Watch out. Sometimes to this day, while
I brew my morning coffee, I still look out my
window at the Kline house and half expect to
see a whiteboard message in Emma's handwriting.
I wish.

God, I'd kill for a chance to speak to her
again.

Just one more time.

I would tell her this: What happened to your
daughter was not your fault.

But—and this is hard to say—perhaps I do understand her pain. Because the truth is, a part
of me will always blame myself for what happened
to Emma. Yes, I'll always feel personally responsible for her death. I'm sure I did everything
I reasonably could as her neighbor and friend—
and we'd saved each other's lives multiple times
that night—but still I wish I could have helped
her more. If only I'd known.

If only.

They say the greatest battles we fight are in-
ternal. And it's true. During the Strand Beach

massacre she won every external battle with Howard Grosvenor Kline—his blade and bullets alike—but on that near-freezing January night two weeks afterward, under a clear and starry sky, Emma Carpenter lost her greatest battle within herself.

THE END

ACKNOWLEDGMENTS

All books take a village, and *Murder Beach* is no exception.

First, my eternal gratitude to the fine men and women of the Strand Beach Police Department for their cooperation, assistance, and friendship over many years. To the administrative team: I can't thank you enough for your help. To my old friend and fellow whiskey connoisseur, district attorney Ted Wilcox: thank you for privileged access to this many-layered and constantly evolving investigation. To veteran Corporal Eric Grayson: you are a fine lawman, a true friend, and I'll always treasure my memories of evening barbecues with you and your wife, the indominable Star Grayson (may she rest in peace). My work as a journalist has often placed me adjacent to law enforcement, where I've witnessed and appreciated the danger they face every day. They are truly the finest among us. Thank you, again, to all officers of all jurisdictions, for your tireless work in keeping us safe from creatures like Howard.

I should reemphasize here that I feel no vindication or satisfaction in being proven correct on the circumstances of Laura Birch's 2011 death—only renewed and profound grief for her and her family. I never personally met her, but I do recall seeing both Howard and Laura together for after-school study, and even at a distance I know I witnessed a dynamic young woman, bright with promise. In the aftermath of the December massacre, the community's heart has broken for Laura Birch all over again.

A great big thank-you to my editors Sara Paulson and Haley Bradford, and to my legal and publicity teams as we embark on the adventure of whipping this draft into shape. And to my new agent Lauren Michaelson, for signing me in record time as we inked this major deal.

They say a writer never chooses the book—the book chooses you. As a sixty-six-year-old divorced hermit who (until recently) thought himself retired, I can't help but agree. I never expected to pen a follow-up to *Silent Screams* in my twilight years, nor could I have imagined that this time, I would bear witness to the atrocities firsthand. I'd always known my neighbor to be a troubled individual, but no one could have anticipated such hidden depths. Sometimes the blackest evil isn't prowling out there in the woods of campfire myth. Sometimes it's next door. Sometimes it's lived there for years.

Mind your neighbors, dear readers.

You never know.

Fifteen percent of this title's proceeds will go to the families of Howard Kline's victims. Ten percent more to the Dallas-based victims advocacy group The Way Forward. A final fifteen percent—as well as the first installment of my own advance—

will go to various suicide prevention and aware- ness groups nationwide in Emma's name. I hope she'd approve.

And finally, with a compassionate heart, this book is dedicated to the memory of those who lost their lives by the hand of Howard Grosve- nor Kline. To Jules Phelps, Jake Stanford, and Laura Birch. And, lastly, my dear friend Emma Carpenter.

Your pain is over.

You can rest now.

Strand Beach Police Department

Incident No.: 000197-1C-2024
9:05 PST

Front Desk: Strand Beach Police.

Caller: Hi. Good morning. This is the nonemergency line, right?

Front Desk: Yes, sir.

Caller: My name is Deacon Cowl and I'm . . . well, I'm worried about my neighbor.

Front Desk: What happened?

Caller: I walked over to see her last night, but she didn't answer her door. And it's morning now, past nine, and I still haven't seen her lights turn on. Can I please request a wellness check?

Front Desk: Maybe she's out of town?

Caller: I just have a . . . gut feeling. Something is wrong.

Front Desk: We can do a wellness check for you, sir. What's her address?

Caller: 937 Wave Drive.

Front Desk: Okay. And what time did you knock on her door last night?

Caller: About eight or nine. I wanted to catch up with her now that we were both out of the hospital. Plus I had some paperwork I needed her to sign.

Front Desk: Paperwork?

Caller: Yes. I'm Deacon Cowl. Local author. I've been retired for some time, but I'm

covering the Howard Kline murders for my
next book. And this woman is a hero. I'll
hopefully be interviewing her extensively—

Front Desk: When did you see her last?

Caller: That's why I'm worried. I . . . I
know she's been struggling with depression.
Even before the attack. She was grieving
the death of her infant daughter. I
remember how I used to see her take these
daily walks out on the beach. And I'd
notice she'd stand ankle-deep or waist-deep,
sometimes deeper, like she was thinking
about going farther, and when I asked
her about it, she was always so evasive,
embarrassed. I'm worried she might be
struggling with . . . (INAUDIBLE)

Front Desk: Struggling with what?

Caller: You know. Suicidal thoughts.
And the other day, I saw her out in her
backyard with this green backpack. She was
collecting heavy rocks from her garden, it
looked like. And stuffing them in it.

Front Desk: You're saying you think she
might have drowned herself?

Caller: I'm afraid of that. Yes. I'm just
so worried Emma has gone and done something
terrible. She's so smart. So tough. So
brave. But I know she's always wrestled
with her own inner—

Front Desk: Wait. Her name is Emma?

Caller: Yeah.

Front Desk: Emma Carpenter?

Caller: Yes. Why?

Front Desk: She's here.

Caller: What?

Front Desk: She's at our station. Right
now. She walked in just a few minutes ago—

Caller: She's alive?

Front Desk: Yes.

Caller: You're . . . you're sure?

Front Desk: Just buzzed her in, right before you called. She just came through the front lobby door—no shoes, no wallet, no phone—and asked to speak to an officer.

Caller: No.

Front Desk: We're still learning what happened to her last night, but yes, sir, I can confirm your neighbor Emma Carpenter is alive and safe with us downtown right now. You must be so relieved.

. . . Sir, are you still there?

. . . Sir?

CALL DISCONNECTS

39

WHEN SHE GIVES HER STATEMENT TO POLICE, RED-EYED and hungover with her bare feet raw and cut from walking eleven miles to downtown Strand Beach, she's deliberately vague about what she can remember in the moments after Deacon Cowl threw her off the rocky seawall. She'd been drugged, concussed, and near unconscious, with a weighted backpack pinning her far beneath the waves. Memory loss is to be expected.

But the truth is, Emma remembers holding her daughter close in bright July sunlight.

"I love you so much."

She remembers every detail. The tears clouding her eyes, the way Shelby's tiny fingers grasped curls of Emma's hair, so strong and weak and confident and curious.

"Dad and I both do," she said. "You're our little miracle girl. You helped us beat the odds. You should know how much we miss you. I can't even put it into words, baby. You're my heart. My whole heart. And someday I'll see you again, Shelby. I promise. Someday I'll be with you forever. But . . ."

Kissing her daughter's scalp, she'd lowered her voice.

Just a whisper.

"But *not yet*."

As the backpack's second and final strap unbuckled between Emma's fingertips. A plastic snap under her armpit. Like handcuffs releasing, a powerful force unchained.

She felt her body race upward.

Not yet.

And then exploding to the surface under galaxies of pristine stars, the clearest and most beautiful night sky she's ever seen, Caelum and Taurus and Andromeda and even the ruby-red cosmic dust of the Orion Nebula before the current took hold and carried her ashore.

Goodbye, my heart.

EPILOGUE

AN ARCH PASSES OVERHEAD LIKE THE NECK OF A CONCRETE dinosaur.

W_LCOME TO STRAND BEACH

Emma has always felt an odd mix of emotions while driving home from long trips, a sort of happy melancholy. Home calls warmly, but the days spent here are gone. When you return, you'll be older. Maybe you won't return at all.

As she crosses the thin concrete bridge, the Strand shrinks in her rearview mirror, transitioning from a place to an idea. She doesn't look back. She rolls down a window so Laika can slide her face outside and enjoy the rush of drizzly air, her tongue wildly flapping, the buoyant glee of *going fast*. It's not quite orbit, but it'll do.

We're going fast, Mom.

"Yes. We are."

The road is long. Winding up hills cloaked in dripping evergreens, around brackish estuaries and sandy mudflats. The land rises. The trees thicken. The sea mist thins away and the world seems to sharpen.

We're going so fast.

On the highway, miles tick by and Laika rests on crossed paws in the back seat. With a power nap planned at midnight, Emma estimates she'll reach Salt Lake City by dawn. Somewhere around Port Swanson or Port Hanson or maybe Tortland (the rainy little towns all blur together), she sees deer at the road's edge. A whitetail doe and a tiny spotted fawn climbing the grassy berm together.

The fawn timidly follows her mother on still-new legs—but glances back at Emma.

As if recognizing her.

Then both brown shapes whip on past, and by the time Emma glances to her rearview mirror, they're gone.

THREE THOUSAND FEET ABOVE SEA LEVEL AT A MOUNTAIN pass in the Cascades, she's finally gathered the courage to call her husband. She stands outside the visitor center at the parking lot's edge, watching the sunset turn the snowcaps orange.

On the fourth ring, he answers.

"Emma?"

She's still not ready for it. The sound of his voice squeezes her heart.

"Are you there?"

She tries to speak, but her lungs are empty.

"Emma? Are you okay?"

"Yeah. I am." She swallows, gripping her phone, steadying her voice. "Some things happened. I'll explain later. Just know that I'm okay, and Space Dog is okay, too."

Silence.

He says, "You don't sound okay."

"For the first time in months, I think I am." She looks back at her Corolla, at Laika's white face in the window. "And I'm coming home."

Her husband sighs.

An unsteady, crackling breath. An emotion she can't read.

She repeats, "I'm coming home."

Her mantra, whispered a thousand times to the racing highway. *I'm coming home.* Is she asking him? Is she telling him? Does she even have a home to come back to? Maybe her things are boxed up in a storage unit. Maybe they've been given away. Maybe Shawn and his family have already mourned her, too, and said their goodbyes to Shelby and Emma alike and moved on. Maybe she's only her own ghost and she's already too late. She doesn't know. She can't know. And there's more to say, so much more, but it's all clotted up painfully inside her chest. She's trying to form the words.

Say it.

She can't.

"Emma? Are you still there?"

Say it.

No self-edits.

"Emma, I don't understand what you're—"

"I'm sorry." It comes out like a slashed vein: "I'm so, so sorry, Shawn, for what I put you through. And I understand why you're angry. You should be. We were supposed to be a team. I took a vow on that. We should have grieved together and supported each other, and instead of doing that, I got in my car and ran away and forced you to suffer our daughter's death alone. I made everything so much harder for you. For us both. And you don't have to forgive me. That's your right. I hurt you."

She stops for a breath.

He sniffs. A crackle of static.

"Shawn, I *abandoned* you when you needed me."

He says nothing.

Dusky light falls over the visitor center. She's alone here. She checks her phone's screen—yes, the call is still connected. The call timer still ticking seconds.

Emma feels it again, the inexorable downward tug. The enormity of things unspoken, unspeakable. Maybe this was a mistake. The sun is dimming behind the nearest peak, the mountain pass shadowed into a cold lake of darkness. Still, her husband says nothing.

She pats her purse on instinct, wishing for a cigarette. Before leaving Strand Beach, she'd smoked the last one in her squashed pack, also vowed to be her last one *ever,* with Old Cop on a boardwalk bench overlooking the waves.

Fuckin' writers, man. She'd taken a long drag. *Maybe they're all nuts.*

Old Cop—no, his name is Eric—had laughed until he coughed. What else can you do? And then he'd softened and touched her shoulder.

Remember, Emma. Time. Tears. And talking.

She'd nodded.

That day, she'd also visited Jake Stanford's parents. On their front porch she told them that their son's last delivery that night, the parcel that cost him his life, was an item that helped save Emma's. She felt they deserved to know that.

Last of all, on her way out, she stopped at Strand Beach's secondhand bookstore and purchased a yellowed paperback of *Silent Screams.* On the back cover, a black-and-white Deek, two decades younger and clearly at the apex of his life, nods knowingly with a hand raised to the brim of his fedora. A gesture she's seen before.

M'lady.

Howard studied his idol, all right.

The face still gives her a chill. The silver hair. The square jaw. The piercing eyes. This face will always exist in history—

even if police found the man himself dead in his recliner with his bowels released and his honorary revolver still in his mouth. On his whiteboard, a fully drawn stick figure hung on a noose.

Emma's forearm still itches as it heals. The scar, however subtle, will remain on her skin forever: DEEK KILLED ME. Like a tattoo, a reminder of what she almost lost.

Almost.

She shivers in the mountain air and checks her phone screen again—it's been more than a minute now. Her husband still hasn't spoken. She can hear his distant breaths, a faint rhythm to the static. "Shawn?"

Aching silence.

She dreads the answer.

When it finally comes, his voice is barely audible over the hum of the highway: "Emma . . . where are you?"

She reads a sign. "Glacier Ridge."

"The ski resort?"

"No. A visitor center."

Silence again.

Her chest tightens.

"Okay," he says. "It looks like the exact midpoint between that visitor center and our house is . . . uh, some little town called Brighton. It's in Idaho. Five hours and fourteen minutes from me. Five hours and eleven minutes from you. I'm getting in my truck, right now . . ."—in the background, she hears a door shut—"and I'll meet you halfway. Okay? I'm sorry, but I can't wait until tomorrow. I just can't, Emma. Your call is the best thing to happen to me in I can't remember how long, and I need to see you and Space Dog as soon as possible. Today. To-night. In five hours and fourteen minutes."

Tears cloud Emma's eyes and she laughs with a shiver. She slides into a crouch against the building's brick wall.

He pauses. "Is that . . . is that okay?"

"Yes." She nods hard, wiping her eyes. "Yes, yes, yes—"

"I love you so much."

"I love you, too."

"Brighton," Shawn promises. "I'll meet you there."

ACKNOWLEDGMENTS

Thank you to everyone who made this book possible.

To Jaclyn and to my parents, thank you for your critically important early reads and your ongoing support and patience as I often sat in a tranced, zombie-like silence, trying to solve problems in my head. This was a fun novel to write—how often do you get to write a false acknowledgments page for your story's *villain*?—but it was also a challenging puzzle that I couldn't have managed alone.

A huge thank-you to my agent, David Hale Smith, and to Naomi Eisenbeiss at Inkwell Management for guiding this project from idea to completion, and to my manager, Chad Snopek, for a hugely valuable early draft read.

My endless gratitude to editor Jennifer Brehl at William Morrow for helping sculpt this story (particularly its third act) and giving me all the right feedback at every step. And many thanks to the entire team at William Morrow and HarperCollins, including Nate Lanman and Danielle Bartlett, and to copy editor Nancy Inglis for bringing this book to readers in its best possible shape.

And a shout-out to the real Laika, the golden retriever who sat faithfully by my side while much of this novel was written, along with our Chihuahua Clementine.

Last, a thank-you to my readers for your support and enthusiasm. I realize that, given this acknowledgment is in a novel about an evil author terrorizing a reader, that may sound like a threat, but I *promise* it's not! Thank you all for reading. I'm so lucky to be able to do this.